THE
ELEMENTAL
UNION

Nikkole
thank you so much!
I hope you enjoy.
Shanna M. Busage

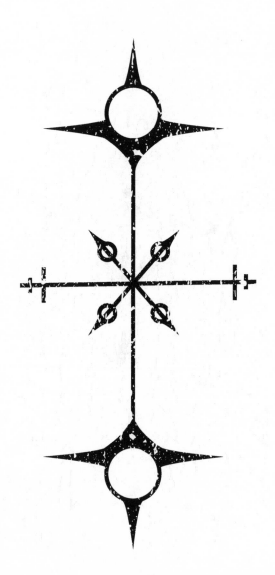

BOOK ONE
DEVIAN

Printed in the United States of America

First Printing, 2018

ISBN 978-1-7323575-0-1

ACKNOWLEDGMENTS

Without these individuals Sterling and Brom would still be collecting dust in the recesses of my mind.

To my editor, Trisha, you have been wonderful. Without your guidance and experience I would still be writing "towards."

To Brian and Christopher, two of the best illustrators anyone could ask for. You brought my world to life with your extraordinary talent.

To Marta, my dear, you are a beast and the cover you created is second to none.

To Terry and Lamar, thank you for always asking me how my book was going. Your gentle nudging kept me on track.

To Geniene, thank you for your super grammar skills. I still owe you lunch.

To Mom and Dad, you are my rocks. Without your love, help, and guidance in life I would be a puddle of goo. I love you so much.

To my wonderful daughter. Thank you for putting up with my what-do-you-think-about-this questions.

To Max, thank you for buying my first one hundred books.

kai'

Pan'dale

Th

Meanrik village

Fende'Lima

Dorre

Jatori Gates

Fal'Traqer

Griviner Inn

Fol'Barbner

The Midori Forest

Var'Khundi

Fan'Gorn

Dal'Rymp

Vari

Sandori Forest

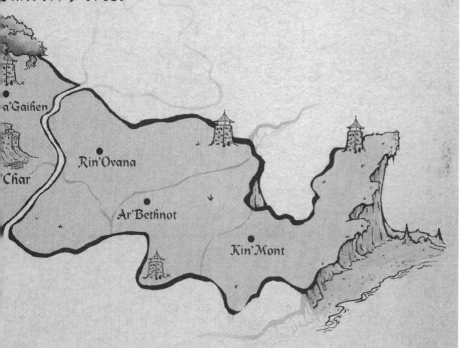

a'Gaihen

Char

Rin'Ovana

Ar'Bethnot

Kin'Mont

NERI

LEYEN

MORRA

orphanage
shee

new
alden

THE SARNO
FOREST

EBEVIA

aken

hemrac

sionaad

MORVEAN

DUENIN

flint

THE
SANDORI
FOREST

LAKE
ALAIN

an dale

dagaihen

rin'ovana

VARI

Sela'Char

DU'GALD

koenida bay

FIN'VARRAR

TABLE
OF CONTENTS

Dan'Yin, 14th Ignis 1000.

> *To my beloved Khort. I write this to you knowing that by the time you read it I will have passed through the Veil and returned to Fin'Varrar.*
>
> *Do not be saddened my love. I have lived a long life and my time is coming to and end. For 264 years I have walked upon the hills and valleys of Fin'Varrar. I have seen the majesty of the Midori and felt the warmth of the Kai'Vari sun and her people. I have seen wars ravage the land and peace make it whole. I have seen close friends grow old before my eyes. For the long life I have lived, you are and will always be my one true love, my soul. I remember the day we first met. You were a young 24-year-old warrior with much to prove. I was mesmerized by the power that emanated from you and your overwhelming presence. I admit, I fell in love at first sight.*
>
> *I was determined at that moment that you would be mine and I would marry you, but you were so stubborn. Ignoring my advances and spouting off how you had given your life to Orla. But I was persistent and victorious. It still makes me smile when I think of our wedding day. Your family welcomed me with open arms despite my Devian eyes. I was so accustomed to the side glances and glares from others, but the Rin'Ovanas welcomed me. The cheresha blossoms were in bloom, it was raining pink petals with a sweet aroma. In all my life I have never been as happy as that day. Now seven years later, we are about to welcome our child.*
>
> *As the end of my gravidity draws near, I have felt the essence of Devi in this child. It is known among the Devians that a child will draw*

on the mother's powers, but the mother will regain her abilities after the birth. However, the power that our child draws from me is far too great. My abilities are waning and will be gone by the time our child arrives. With our child's birth, I will pass, but I do not want you to be sad. This should be a joyous time. Our child will need your love and your guidance in the future, as will Brom, for he will be a fine Veillen.

It's been four years since Brom and Moira lost their parents and are still reeling from their grief. I worry over Brom, he suffered greatly as the object of Norden's rage. He is still very protective of his sister and will need time to overcome his trauma. With you as his teacher, he will grow to be a great Veillen with many victories. I smile as I recall the serious look on his face as he vowed to protect our little one. He will truly be a great man with your tutelage. Moira is such a sweet child, she will grow into a beautiful young woman. There will be no end to the suitors that will come calling for her hand. The Pan'Dale heir will be a great choice as a husband for Moira. He has great potential and their family is one that garners great respect. Hemi will help you with the children, he has great influence on Brom and will teach him patience and control.

As of late, I grow tired easily and must retire to my bed, but I must impart my final words to you, my love. There is a great power that lingers on the edges of my vision. I feel it's presence in my dreams, waiting for the day our child is born. I fear what this eidolon wants with our child, is it a Velkuva or some other dark specter? I cannot see him, but his presence is overwhelming. Guard our child, be vigilant, and train her well.

My love, do not mourn my passing for we shall reunite in Empyrean.

All my love,
Sylvie

PROLOGUE

Dan'Yin, 25th Ignis, 1000

Hemi knew something was wrong. The smell of putrid flesh hit him square in the chest before he could reach the row of small houses that sat isolated from the rest of Sela'Char. These confinement rooms were reserved for the women of Kai'Vari who were with child and close to giving birth. Khort and Sylvie had come here just yesterday when Sylvie's pain had become unbearable. They were both so happy, Khort beaming from ear to ear knowing he would welcome his first child into the world. They were expecting a son. The Sabolan midwife had sensed the presence of a Velkuva in the unborn child. Khort was excited about having a son, but his excitement was shadowed by the fact that his son would be a warrior like himself, a Veillen that would fight against the demons that plagued Kai'Vari.

Hemi, being a slave, was forbidden in the birthing house so he had waited in his chambers at the main castle of Sela'Char. He'd received scathing glances from the castle guards, as a native Dueninian he was unwelcome in the Kai'Varian capital. Even more of a mark against him was the fact that Khort Rin'Ovana, Veillen

High Guardsman and close friend to the King, treated Hemi more as a friend than as a slave.

The overwhelming smell caused his nostrils to burn and his eyes to water. There was only one thing that could cause such a stench, a graekull. Khort had spent his life protecting Kai'Vari from the demons of Abaddon. Hemi had heard of the most recent battle near Sela'Char, but he hadn't thought the graekull had made it this far east and into the city. It was true though, when the wailing warning sounds of the Veillen Manuk horns had reached Sela'Char, the Veillen warriors stationed at the capital had barely enough time to rally before the first demons attacked the outlying villages. Hemi supposed it was possible one or more graekull could have slipped through the Veillen lines.

Knowing that protecting Khort and Sylvie was more important than the midwives' rules, Hemi had rushed from the castle and made his way toward the tiny confinement rooms. As he neared, he saw the row of isolated houses still stood in defiance of the battle that had quickly moved in and still raged around them. Now running with his sword in his hand, Hemi's boot heels thudded softly on the wood planks as he approached the birthing house. The smell overwhelmed him and he had to force the bile back down.

Hemi's heart stopped and then started racing when he noticed the splintered wood scattered across the walkway. He hurried his steps until he stood in front of what used to be the door to the house. What remained was a gaping hole. The door lay in broken pieces with deep claw marks marring the planks. The cottage was dark inside, the candles long extinguished by what must have been the tremendous force that knocked down the solid door.

Hemi listened for a moment, then stepped over the broken pieces, nearly stumbling on the body of the midwife that lay in a heap, blood pooling under her lifeless body. His heart was in his throat as his eyes adjusted to the dim lighting. "No," The word was an anguished whisper on his lips that were dry from the cool spring air. "No, no," he repeated, as if the denial would undo the scene that lay before him.

PROLOGUE

His vision was drawn to the hideous, putrid graekull that stood frozen in death above Khort, whose sword had pierced the demon's skull from forehead to crown. Despite having killed the graekull, Khort was pinned to the wall, beneath the beast. Moving closer, Hemi could see its claws had sliced through Khort's flesh, rending him to his very heart. In the bed lay Sylvie, her lifeless eyes staring off into the distance, her hand outstretched toward some unknown treasure. His eyes followed hers, attempting to see what her outstretched hand was trying to grasp.

A sudden whimper startled Hemi, causing him to jump. It was then he realized what Sylvie was so desperately trying to reach. Hemi hurried across the room and carefully removed the splintered planks of the door to find Sylvie's newborn child lying asleep in the center of a charred circle. Smoke was still rising from the ring that was burnt into the floor.

A girl! Hemi couldn't help but smile down at the babe, despite the death of her parents that were only steps away. He wondered what Khort had felt when presented with a daughter instead of the son he was expecting.

The babe whimpered again, her bottom lip turned under in a pout. Before she could start to cry Hemi swaddled her in a blanket and lifted her into his arms. Carefully he carried the babe to Sylvie and knelt beside the bed. He could feel the tears start to build behind his eyes. He took deep breaths but could not contain the sob that escaped.

"*Why?* Why did you make me leave?" he asked through the tears. "I could have protected you both." He could have protected them, he knew how dangerous the graekull were. Khort had trained him to fight the demons even though he was not as powerful as the Veillen warriors. "Damn it!" Hemi swore, wiping away the tears that dampened his cheeks.

He took a deep breath and steeled himself, "Syl, your daughter, she is beautiful just as you always will be." He caressed her cheek pushing the dark hair out of the way and gently closed her eyelids over her haunting silver eyes.

"Hem-"

Hemi jumped at his name and looked up to find Khort staring down at him from where the graekull had pinned him against the wall, his feet dangling. "Khort!" Hemi jumped up to help Khort, but the man slowly shook his head.

"No," Khort managed to breathe the words, "no time. You," his words were just whispers past his lips as he struggled to form them, "mus- ta- her away." He took a deep breath then spoke his last words, "Take Sterling awa- from here t- safe place. Hid- her. Tak- key to Fen- Lima."

"What key?" Hemi stood to search for a key.

"Necklace," Khort managed, before his body went limp as his life force finally surrendered. Hemi watched as a blue light slowly formed beneath Khort's skin where the graekull's claws cut deep into his flesh. The light grew, forming a small ball that slowly rose until it left Khort's body and hovered above his head. The ball of light dispersed in the air in a blink. Hemi had seen this before. It was the Veillen's essence passing through the Veil to Empyrean.

"Take her where?" Hemi knew Khort would not answer as he searched for a necklace. He noticed a glint of gold around Sylvie's neck and he brushed her hair out of the way. The chain hung around her neck and at the end was a cylindrical gray stone that seemed to hold an unearthly glow. Gently, he pulled the chain over her head and tucked it safely into his pocket.

Khort wanted Hemi to take his daughter and hide her. From whom or from what was he supposed to hide her? Hemi would never get the answers he needed, but he trusted Khort with his life and would in turn give his life to Khort and now, Khort's daughter. He glanced down at the babe who was staring up at him with a slight smile on her tiny lips. Her cheeks were rosy, her sparse hair a soft chestnut like her mothers, and her eyes... her eyes reflected his image in their pure silver depths. "Sterling," Hemi said softly to the babe, "I'm your Uncle Hemi."

I

NIGHTMARE

Sarno Forest – Northern Duenin
Twenty-One Years Later
Dan'Kell, 23rd Ignis, 1021

Thunder vibrated the ground with ominous rumbles. Sterling narrowed her eyes against the wind blowing through the storm-ravaged land. The sky was a roiling cauldron, filled with dark and angry clouds turning and tumbling on top of themselves. From her vantage point, Sterling could see across the long valley. Waves of grey sheets of rain slowly marched through the countryside, seeming to eat away at the very earth. The heavy drops pelted the ground where the land sloped and dipped. The water was already beginning to rise in the small streams that slithered across the valley's green skin.

Another silver fork of light streaked down from the seething cauldron. Sterling watched helplessly from her patch of dry ground as the lightning struck the tree that had stood sentinel in the center of the valley. The ancient tree bark was peeled in an instant, leaving behind only a charred remnant of its once great self. The rocks that had protected and supported the tree for ages were now blackened and shattered bits of debris that no longer offered resistance to the storm's anger.

The rains were coming down from the snowcapped mountains that were framed on the not too distant horizon. The fierce storm was carrying the ice and snow from the mountain's peak

The steep walls of the valley rose to surround her. The oddly familiar isolation of this place was overwhelming. Sterling felt so alone and helpless in the lowlands, which seemed to be transforming into a desolate prison.

Heading quickly toward her, the storm was now threatening to overtake her small patch of dry ground. The wind tore at her hair, fiercely driving the freezing rain as it irritatingly hit her face. A sliver of ice struck her cheek. Surprised, she put her hand up to the small bloody cut.

Suddenly, Sterling felt the odd sensation that a presence was with her... watching her. She scanned the surrounding area but could see no one. An intense pricking arose on the back of her neck that felt like a thousand pins were being driven into her skin. She rubbed the spot but received no relief. "Who's there?" she asked lightly, her words all but defeated by the storm's fury as they were quickly carried away on the wind.

Turning in a circle, she became aware of her current predicament. The storm had surrounded her. There was no avenue for escape; the paths, the roads, and even the small game trails leading from this prison were disappearing one by one beneath the rising waters. A sense of panic and genuine fear began to bleed deep into her being. Her skin prickled with it. Without warning the prickling intensified until she thought she would pass out from the pain. And from the ethereal void of her mind came a voice. Booming... commanding. The words seemed to vibrate through her, sending waves of nausea to the pit of her stomach, "*Othail ghee Elementals!*" And as quickly as the words were spoken the pain and nausea were gone.

Sterling watched in helpless terror as the storm clouds seemed to draw closer. The sky lit up and bolts of lightning shot from the storm striking the ground near where she stood. She jumped back, but before her feet could hit the ground a second bolt shot from the rolling clouds and struck Sterling, throwing her into the rising waters of a nearby stream. Pain coursed through her body, and unable to move she began to sink beneath the murky surface. She tried to scream but had no breath to speak.

Sterling jolted awake, gasping for breath. It took her a moment to realize that she was still in her own bed, safe in the tiny cottage she shared with her uncle. Sweat drenched her nightshirt. Her skin was clammy, and her heart raced with an unsteady beat. The dream had started as the same dream that she'd had since she could remember. Oddly, this time it was different. In the past, the lightning had only struck the ground around her, but this time the lethal bolts had hit her, sending her to drown in the murky flood waters.

Sterling shuddered as an unusual feeling of dread washed over her. She contemplated the significance of the change in her dream. Despite having slept all night, she was exhausted from the effects of the nightmare. She tried forcing herself to get some added rest, and she leaned back and covered her head with the threadbare blanket. She closed her eyes and tried to go back to sleep, but it never came. Her mind was too full of the dread that surrounded her. The sound of twittering birds in the predawn light kept her company in her dark cocoon. A yawn forced stale oxygen into her burning lungs. She tried once again to relax her body, but no matter how hard she tried she could not go back to sleep. The fear of having the dream again and hearing those unfamiliar words, *Othail gee Elementals*, was in the back of her mind. Ever since the dreams had started plaguing her nights she'd heard those same words repeated, but their meaning still eluded her. Sterling threw the covers off and stood, allowing fresh air to finally reach her lungs.

Sterling moved the curtain back from the window and found the sun struggling to push the night's darkness aside. There was still some time before the sun was full up. She poured fresh water into the basin and splashed the frigid liquid into her face. She followed the same routine every morning, the water refreshing the body and readying the muscles for work. This morning the water seemed much colder than usual. The iciness of her dream came back to her thoughts momentarily. She pushed it aside as she scrubbed the last dredges of sleep from her eyes and felt much better for it. Continuing her normal routine, she pulled on the leather pants that her uncle hated. He thought them unfit for a girl, but she'd protested the dreaded skirts that the women in Shee wore, claiming they were too cumbersome.

She wore a chemise under the cotton shirt and then a leather vest. The specially made vest laced on the sides and had a sewn hood. She pulled the hood over her head, concealing her eyes from possible onlookers. Satisfied she was complete, Sterling made her way quietly down the hall so as not to wake her uncle.

In the small kitchen, she raided the larder and found dried meat and a hunk of stale bread, perfect for an early morning breakfast. She put the hunk of bread between her teeth, so she could grab a lambskin of ale. Her boots were held under her right arm, the meat in one hand, and the lambskin in the other. It took her three attempts to open the door. When she did finally get it open, it banged against the cottage wall making an awful racket. She paused motionless for just a moment to make sure she had not woken her uncle. When no sounds emitted from his room she hooked the door with her bare foot and pulled it shut. She turned to make her way across the yard and nearly walked into a leather clad wall. She was so startled she dropped everything she had gathered, even the bread that she had held clenched between her teeth.

"Whoa, careful lass."

"Damn, my breakfast is ruined," Sterling replied with a mixture of surprise and dismay.

"Watch that tongue, girl." She now knew why the old man didn't wake when she was clanging around the kitchen like a bull in a glass house. His imposing frame stood there frowning gently down at her. Though he did not abide curses from women, he held no reservations from his own, and so she had picked up on his bad habit.

"What are you doing up so early?" Sterling asked in lieu of apologizing.

Her uncle hefted two chickens over his shoulder, grunting out a simple, "I wanted to get a jump on the chores." Sterling knew he was lying and he knew she knew. She followed his hand as he massaged the withering muscle of his thigh. Her eyes jumped back up to stare into his.

"It's getting worse, isn't it?" she asked tentatively.

He avoided her question by asking his own. "What are you doing up so early? You're usually snoring like a soldier this time of the morning."

"I do not snore," she protested. "I guess I just wanted to get a jump on the chores," she threw his evasive comment back at him. They both knew the other was lying and they both knew the reason why. They'd played this game many times in the past.

"Well, get to them then. I've collected the eggs, so you can milk the cows." She suddenly glared up at Hemi. He knew she hated milking the cows. She wound up with more milk on her clothes than she did in the bucket. "After that, I need you to collect some pheasants for tonight's supper. Mother Anwell's requested them for her guests this evening," he continued to order, completely ignoring her icy stare.

"Let me just get my boots on," Sterling mumbled as her teeth ripped off a small mouthful of beef.

"Ale, meat, and bread are no breakfast for a young lady." Hemi groused, shaking his head.

She handed the fare up to him, so she could pull her boots on. "What difference does it make? It's all going to the same place."

"I should have sent you off to school like Mother Anwell had suggested," he grumbled back at her. Sighing, he set the chickens down and moved to the cottage door. Holding the door open, he threw his head into the kitchen. "Get back in there and I'll fix you a proper breakfast." Sterling didn't argue with him. Hemi's breakfasts were filling and lasted until lunch. She leapt up, still hopping on one foot as she squeezed into her boot, following him into the small kitchen.

"You know it would have been a waste of time if you'd sent me off to that silly finishing school," Sterling said as she sat at the small table and watched as he pulled out the fixings for breakfast.

"You had the dream again." It wasn't a question.

"Yeah," Sterling's dread came back the second she acknowledged her uncle's statement. She didn't go into detail, after all she'd told this story more times than both cared to remember. She could see the worry in his eyes when she told him of the lightning. The smell of bacon slowly curling over itself on the iron cast stove caused Sterling's stomach to growl. "What's taking so long?" she protested.

"Keep your drawers on," he said lightly as he went about pulling off the biscuits, eggs, and small bowl of spiced gravy.

The plate of steaming food delighted Sterling. Her cold breakfast paled in comparison to Hemi's. He sat across from her. "Aren't you going to eat?" she asked around a mouth full of egg.

"I ate when I woke."

"You probably had the same thing I was going to eat." His silence told her she guessed right. "Here, have some," she said as she took a portion of the breakfast and piled it on a clean plate, "besides you gave me too much." Sterling made quick work of the food and wiped her mouth with the napkin Hemi handed her, instead of wiping her sleeve across her mouth.

"You eat like a soldier," he lightly teased.

"I've had a great teacher," she shot back, letting out a very unladylike belch followed by a coy smile. "Now I'm off to my chores."

"Sterling," Hemi stopped her, "there's no need for you to hide yourself behind that hood."

"I know." She avoided his eyes, not wanting to see the concern in them.

"Don't forget to feed the horses," Hemi shot at her as she raced across the yard. She waved that she heard him and entered the musty barn.

The smell of hay filled her nostrils when Sterling threw the barn doors open. She loved the barn and its aromas, a comfort to her since she had sheltered herself among the stacks of hay as a child. When visitors had come to the orphanage she'd hidden away, afraid they would look upon her in disdain. So often she had been teased about her appearance. Her olive skin and odd colored eyes had led people to call her any number of names. She had taken to wearing a hood whenever she left the house to avoid the hateful words. The girls at the orphanage were no less cruel. A few had befriended her, but when they were adopted she would be alone once again. Sterling remembered on one occasion she'd grown tired of the mean girls and had punched one of them in the nose. She had her backside tanned by Hemi's belt and it was then she'd sown the hood onto her vest, so no one could see her shame. Hemi had claimed she'd inherited her eyes from her Devian mother. It was a gift that she would gladly give back to the woman she had never known. When asked, Hemi had skirted the topic of her mother saying only she was a Devian and shared the same silver eyes as Sterling. When she pestered him for more details he'd change the subject. She didn't really know what it meant to be a Devian, other than having silver eyes and to be hunted by the Severon.

Sterling had also found refuge among the bales of hay when one of the violent storms bombarded the land with its wrath. She'd been afraid of lightning for as long as she could remember. She would hide in the haystacks hoping to mute out the rumble of the thunder and the flashes that tore open the skies. Her fear had only intensified when the nightmares had started. She rarely left the safety of the cottage when the skies filled with ominous dark clouds. Mother Anwell had prayed over her many times as she lay huddled and shaking from the fear. Over the years her fears had waned, but she still was not comfortable being outside during a storm.

She shook away the daydream as the low mooing of the cows reminded her why she was here in the first place. She lit the lantern that hung outside the stalls. The small flame illuminated the black and white body of her nemesis, Barda. The cow's head swung around lazily to see who was disturbing her meal. Sterling didn't think cows could glare, but she swore that this one had a hatred for her that was unnatural in the otherwise docile creatures. Sterling placed an empty bucket under the cow and sat down on the low stool. Cautiously, she started to draw milk. The sound of the thick liquid rhythmically hitting the bottom of the bucket filled the cavernous barn.

The only other sounds were those of the birds that fluttered from beam to beam in the high places of the curved ceiling and the sound of Barda forever chewing. Sterling's mind began to drift, to relax. Without warning, Barda shifted her weight toward Sterling, causing the stream of milk to miss the bucket and soak Sterling's boot. She cursed and pushed the back flank away as she sighed, "I don't know what you have against me, you old heifer." Sterling continued to milk, only this time she kept her shoulder pressed into Barda's side, so she would not try the stunt again.

Sterling felt proud of herself, the bucket was three quarters of the way full and she was still relatively dry. Perhaps she'd get out of milking the cow without having to change her clothes before finishing her other chores. It seemed, however, that her overconfidence was her downfall. Barda shifted away from Sterling and with all her weight pushing into the cow's side there was nothing to stop Sterling from falling face first into the bucket of milk. With a sputter, and more than a few choice bits of language, Sterling managed to stand, wiping the thick liquid away from her eyes and mouth as it seeped slowly down her shirt. "Y-You…" Sterling was so angry she picked up the empty bucket and threw it across the room where it hit the wall with a loud clang. Needles began to tingle at the base of her skull as she sputtered, "*I'm going to kill you!*" The only response was the light, almost taunting 'moo' that rolled out from Barda's throat. Like a challenger accepting a duel.

Hemi was outside feeding the pigs when he heard the bucket hit the wall followed by the loud stream of curses that would have turned a hardened soldier red with embarrassment. Sterling came bolting out of the barn. The door was two times her size, but her anger gave her the strength of three men. He watched as she marched across the yard. The hood had fallen back, and her hair was dripping with milk, shirt plastered to her skin. He swore he could see steam rising as she marched across the yard looking like a drowned rat. And even though there would be no milk for tonight's supper, he couldn't help but laugh at the sight of the poor girl.

His laughing caught her attention and she stopped midway from the barn to the house. She glared at him and pointed a finger back at the barn, "You think that's funny, do ya? I'm going to *kill* that cow and serve *her* for dinner!" Her words made Hemi laugh all the harder. With a look that could stop a man just by its power alone, Sterling finally threw her hands up in resignation and continued back to the cottage to change clothes. He knew she hated milking the cow, but he thought it good for her to have a challenger that wouldn't back down. She was used to people being intimidated by the fierce anger that showed in her eyes when she felt threatened. Hemi knew it would take her a while to wash the milk off and redress so he was surprised when the cottage door slammed open a minute later. Sterling emerged with a cleaver clutched in her tight fist.

"Sterling? What are you doing?" He yelled the question as he started on a course to intercept her.

She did not take her eyes off the barn, "I told you. I'm going to kill that demon cow and serve her for dinner." She was much faster than him and she knew it. Yet even though he could only limp his way across the yard, he was still surprisingly agile. He managed to catch up with her just as she was about to enter the darkness of the barn. "Easy, easy girl, give me that blade." Despite the limp, he was still heavy with experience and muscle that belied a different life he had led. He could pry the dagger from her clenched fist as easy as a man would be to split a piece of warm bread apart.

"*I hate that cow!*" she spat at Barda.

"Cool your temper girl. Killing her is not going to solve anything. You need to figure out a way to solve this problem with your head, not a damn knife. You can't kill everything that makes you mad. Now clean this mess up and go change your clothes, we have deliveries to make in Shee."

She glared up at him with those silver eyes. The anger that he saw in their steel depths was frightening. He'd seen and felt that anger once before and the results were nearly fatal. He knew if he backed down the anger would overtake her, and he'd have a hell of a time getting her back. In as quiet and commanding a voice that he could muster, he stared at her and calmly said, "Mind what I say lass." He didn't back down and he could see the anger slowly dissipate. Her shoulders slumped when she realized she couldn't kill Barda.

"Fine, but don't be surprised when one day you find her missing and a nice juicy steak on your dinner plate." As she marched off toward the cottage his hand went to the withered muscle of his right leg.

Yes, he knew all too well what her anger could do. But he was thankful that she herself was unaware of what she'd done so many years ago.

He'd promised Khort he'd protect Sterling and so far, he'd succeeded. This quiet, isolated orphanage had been the perfect place to raise her. With Mother Anwell's assistance he'd raised Sterling in a land that was hostile toward those of her kind, but this far north the citizens were more concerned with surviving the winters than the color of one's eyes.

It had not been easy raising Khort's daughter... she was the image of her father. She had strength beyond what was normal and a temper that could raze the flesh with a mere look. What he had not expected were the girl's blackouts and fainting. It had frightened him the first time it'd happened. It had been during one of those episodes that she'd attacked him with the relentless goal of killing him. He'd managed to get her under control and thankfully she had quickly returned to her normal self. Sterling was unaware of her actions when she blacked out and he'd sworn Mother Anwell to secrecy.

Hemi left the barn and started toward the main house and his thoughts turned to telling Sterling of her parents. She would be turning twenty-one soon and it was time she knew the truth of her heritage, the truth that he was not her uncle. It was time she went home.

2

THE HUNTER

The cicadas were singing again.

Commander Remus Engram noted as he and his men made the long journey along the Riuukan Pass toward the highlands of Northern Duenin. How he hated Northern Duenin. The weather was unpredictable – snowing one moment and violent storms the next. He never understood how the peasants survived up here in the foothills of the Izanami Mountains. They were uneducated farmers and merchants that lacked any sense to move away from this harsh environment. *Maybe it makes them think they're hardy and stout folk to survive in the ice and snow,* he mused. But to him, it only made him cold. And he detested the cold.

Thankfully, once his mission was over he could return to Sionaad. To warmer and more inviting climes. But, more importantly, to his family. And for a time, before his liege called him once more to tarry forth his will, he would enjoy the dry clear nights with his wife, as he listened to the cicadas' melody before they disappeared once more.

But his mind must be in the now and present, for the mission at hand. The Orom had sent him on this trek to the far north after hearing rumors of a Devian seen in the trade city of Shee. As any man, he was curious. Why hadn't the Orom sent one of the lesser ranked soldiers? This task was beneath his position. In fact, it was far too showy. A smaller unit would draw less attention and draw far less comments that would tip off their potential target. It made him wonder, but never question. If the Orom demanded him to march a small army, then that is what he would do. Regardless of whether it made sense, logically or tactically.

By mid-day he and his men had made their way to the city. In this drab and lifeless looking hamlet with its drab and lifeless looking people. Immediately, he began asking the various merchants whose booths lined the streets if they'd seen anyone with silver eyes around the city. Most had shaken their heads, but a few had pointed toward the pub at the end of the street. *Typical*, Engram sighed. "Not a coin to spare for taxes, but they always manage to drown their woes in ale." Engram sneered slightly and pushed open the door into the Scarlet Bull.

The pub was crowded with merchants and farmers filling the many tables and booths throughout the main hall. The room was also filled with smoke and the smell of stale ale and sweat. It was enough to make a lesser man sick. And, judging by the looks of more than a few of his recruit's faces, it looked like they were about to be.

"Spread out," he ordered the men that had accompanied him from Sionaad. The raucous laughter and chatter went quiet as his men took up position throughout the room. He scanned the commons examining the occupants – weathered and cold worn farmers and merchants stared back at him. It was no secret the Northerners detested the Severon. Even though the cleansing of foreign blood had taken place over fifty years ago, many Northerners still remembered the war the Orom had waged against those who had invited the Na'Durians and Leyenese into their homes. Even if the King would not push out the vile foreigners, the Orom would.

The dining room returned to its normal bustle as he turned from the room and approached the bar. The barkeep appeared nervous, avoiding eye contact. "Ale for you, milord?"

Ignoring the man's question Engram said, "A Devian has been seen in this area."

The barkeep tensed at the statement. "Haven't seen one." His eyes darted past Engram's shoulder and then quickly back.

Engram turned to where the barkeep's eyes had shifted and scanned the area. His eyes stopped on a girl in the back of the pub. A hood was pulled low over her face. She was sitting next to an older man in a darkened booth. They were in deep conversation, oblivious to the happenings of the pub. He moved away from the bar toward the booth, side stepping a waitress and drunken patrons along the way. He was almost on them when he noticed the pendant resting between her breasts. He sucked in a breath when he realized what she wore around her neck. Could it be what they had been searching for? Could a Shard have been hiding like this in plain sight? The Orom would be very pleased with him if he returned to Sionaad with a Shard of Abaddon. Engram continued toward the girl but paused again when she looked up and the hint of silver glimmered beneath the woolen hood. *She was a Devian?* Could his luck truly be this great?

He silently motioned for his men to be ready. They could not let this gem escape. He put his hand on the hilt of his sword and continued toward the back of the dining room. They were unaware of him; things could not be any more perfect. With this prize, the Orom would truly give him praise and a promotion. He'd been scouring the country for these damn Shards and here sat *not only a Shard but a Devian!* He couldn't help the smile of triumph that crossed his lips.

He slowly began to unsheathe his sword and took another step toward the back of the dining room. Ten more steps and he could leave this awful place. He had his sword out of the sheath when suddenly two drunken patrons started yelling. An overfed lout shoved the other drunkard into Engram throwing him off balance and into one of his men. Engram's sword was knocked from his grip and skittered across the rough planks.

"Commander!"

He shoved the two drunkards off him and angrily took back his sword from his subordinate. He turned back to the booth, but the girl along with the man had vanished. "Damn it! Spread out and find them! Find that girl!"

Engram sheathed his sword and stepped outside into the bright sun. There was no sight of them among the bustle of Shee. Were they tipped off? They hadn't shown any indication that they'd seen him and the other Severon, but perhaps they had and escaped right at the last possible moment when he'd been distracted by the two drunkards. He turned back to the dining room and found two men passed out in the back corner opposite where the girl and man had been. "Wake up!" When neither responded, Engram kicked the smaller of the two men, "I said wake up!"

"Hey! What did you kick me for?" The man rubbed his face and looked up at Engram, his face went deathly white when he realized it was a Severon Commander standing over him. "Oh, begging your pardon, milord," he said as he stood and brushed off the dirt from his filthy trousers.

Engram stepped closer to the man and whispered in his ear. "Pay attention to what I have to say, I will not ask twice. There was a woman sitting at that booth," Engram pointed to the booth just across from where he stood, "she had silver eyes. What do you know about her?"

"You lookin' for Sterling?" There was a puzzled look on the man's face, "Yeah she shows up here with her uncle on occasion. They deliver vegetables and such to sell here in Shee, but that's all I know. I swear."

Engram was losing patience with this backwoods farmer, "Where is their stall?"

The drunkard slurred and tried to cower even more, "As far I know they don't have one. They deliver to the pubs in and around Shee."

Engram pushed the man into the wall and drew his dagger. Pressing the blade into the man's tanned neck he snarled a threat. "You know more than you are saying. Tell me what I want to know."

The drunkard was on the verge of tears. "I-I don't know any-anything else, milord. I sw-swear," he stammered and blubbered out. The man had broken out in a sweat and his face was red with fear. He was grasping at straws, trying to deflect Engram's anger. With a quick gasp, inspiration finally struck him. "The-the barkeep might know more! They-they deliver here as well."

"Commander." Engram released the man and turned. Scout Phayo had returned from tracking. "We lost them in the crowd Commander. We followed them all the way to the market place and they just disappeared."

Phayo was his best tracker, probably the best in all the Northern Arm. Interesting, in how they had managed to lose him so completely and so… fast. Fleeting thoughts made their way through his mind. *Had they seen him?* Did this squabble hide their trail? From the best tracker in his unit? No, even though the girl had looked up she never actually glanced his way. One last thought found focus in his mind. The Shard around her neck. *Damn it.* He had to find that girl. She was too important to his career. He pushed the farmer away and turned his back to Phayo. He had to think. The farmer had said they delivered vegetables to the pubs around Shee, including this one.

A snarl touched his lips as he looked at the barkeep. He would have the information one way or the other. "Get the horses ready. We'll know where they are soon enough," he said to Phayo as he started toward the bar.

"Commander!" Engram paused when Kerl, one of his other trackers came to a halt beside him. "We heard back from our informant. A merchant has been found smuggling girls out of Duenin and into Leyene. His last known whereabouts were on the merchant road that connects Shee and New Alden." Engram nodded and dismissed Kerl.

Engram slid quietly into a seat directly in front of the bartender. Slipping a hand down at his side he drew forth his dagger and laid it gently on the bar top in front of him. Resting his elbows on the counter, he gestured to the barkeep. "Tell me what I want to know, and maybe I'll leave you with just enough fingers to wipe yourself with…"

3

LOST IN THE SARNO

Dan'Yin, 25th Ignis, 1021

She was lost. How could she get lost on this day of all days? Hemi was going to kill her if he found out how far she'd ventured from the orphanage. He'd sent her out this morning to hunt rabbit for tonight's meal, a birthday celebration for her twenty-first. But when she couldn't find any rabbits in the surrounding forest she'd traveled further south than normal. Now in this unfamiliar area of the large Sarno forest she was completely turned around. Where was that path she'd taken into the forest? She remembered a tree that was split in a fork at the end of the trail, but now she couldn't find the only land mark she recognized.

"Damn it. Hemi is going to kill me," she said as she ducked under a branch and scanned the forest. She knew she was headed north by the location of the sun in the sky, but how far had she traveled away from the path? She continued north knowing eventually she would reach the Merchant Road that connected Shee and New Alden. Sterling paused when a distant rumble of thunder vibrated the silent air of the forest. "Great, just what I need." The urgency she felt at finding her way out of the southern Sarno increased with the threat of an oncoming storm.

The timber began to thin, and she eventually stepped out of the solitude of the forest and onto the hard packed and rut filled Merchant Road. A signpost pointed west toward New Alden. She heaved a sigh; she had traveled farther west than she had first thought. But the sight of the Merchant Road was a welcome relief. If she hurried she'd make it back to the orphanage before Hemi started missing her and hopefully before the storm got any closer. She glanced to the south and the high clouds of the weather front that rose threateningly to the heavens. Lightning flashed through the clouds as if warning Sterling it was coming for her. She started walking east toward the smaller road that would lead north toward the orphanage and safety.

The Merchant Road was a busy thoroughfare that allowed for safe travel between Shee and New Alden. As she made her way down the deeply rutted road she was passed by merchants and travelers on their way to and from Shee. It was a major commerce center for Duenin due to its location near the border with Leyen. Leyen was within a day's journey so merchants and farmers from their northern neighbor brought their goods to Shee.

She was cautious when one of the caravans passed by for it wasn't uncommon for corrupt merchants to kidnap young Dueninian maidens for the purpose of slavery. They'd sell them off to the Menazarin, the rich nobility of Na'Dur where they would live out their lives as captives in their master's harems. It was good that Hemi had taught her how to wield a knife and how to protect herself. She felt safe enough as she made her way toward home, but it would not hurt to be cautious.

Thunder rolled in the distance, masking the sound of a wagon laden with knickknacks as it rattled to a stop beside her. It was a

Leyenese merchant's wagon. They traveled the countryside selling their wares hoping to entice unsuspecting suckers into buying useless baubles they didn't need. Sterling continued to walk as the wagon kept pace with her. She glanced sideways and found all manner of wares dangling from hooks and ropes, from cooking utensils to toys for children, and brightly colored scarves to attract the young ladies of Duenin.

"Give you a ride, *vishca*?" The driver asked as he kept measure with Sterling's pace.

Vishca was an endearment in Leyen. Hemi had made sure she could speak several languages, especially those of countries that were not always friendly to Duenin. He taught her to always know her enemies and that included their language. Sterling gave a sideways glance at the man driving the wagon and gave a cautious, "No thank you." Ignoring her he continued to ride alongside of Sterling. She did not look at him, but kept him in her peripheral vision, keeping her body ready in case she needed to run.

"Come *vishca*, I have plenty room for you. Where you like go?" He patted the empty place beside him.

"I'm fine. Thank you," she said again.

"I insist, let Motego give you ride. You go to Shee? Come, I take you." His tone had risen as if the excitement of her riding beside him was almost too much.

She could feel her temper rising. She finally lifted her head and looked at the man, "I said I was fine, now please leave me alone."

She cursed silently when she saw his face light up at her silver eyes. *Now I've done it*, she thought as she continued to walk along the uneven road. She wished Motego would get the hint and leave her be.

"Very well, *vishca*." He nodded and jerked the reins veering the horses in front of Sterling, blocking her way. "Now, you come with Motego. Menazarin pay extra for silver-eyed girl." His face split into a sinister grin. Sterling was startled when Motego jumped to the ground and landed just a foot in front of where she stood.

No sooner had the dust settled around his feet then the flap of the covered wagon flew open and another man jumped to the ground eliminating her chance for escape. Sterling dropped the bag of rabbits she'd been carrying and backed away while pulling the knife sheathed at her back.

Motego laughed, then lunged for Sterling, but she quickly jumped back, avoiding his grasp. He was a grisly old man and when he smiled Sterling could see the gap where two front teeth should have been. Deep lines creased his forehead and the lines around his mouth cut deep into his cheeks. Skin weathered by the sun hid dark brown eyes beneath sagging eyelids. What hair he had left had gone pure white, a testament to his age or the time spent in the sun? He was a smallish man, not much taller than Sterling's slight frame. But where Motego was small his companion was his exact opposite. Tall and built like a bull, but despite his size he had a pudgy face almost akin to a baby. There was no malice in this man's eyes like there was in Motego's. Despite Motego's sinister appearance, Sterling was more concerned with the large man than she was with Motego.

"Such a pretty *vishca*, don't you think Franto? Such pretty eyes."

Sterling was angry at herself for not having worn her hood. She was never without it, but today she thought there no need.

Franto giggled and covered his mouth as if hiding the childish smile, "Pretty. Franto want pretty." Sterling eased away from the childish giant, trying to put as much distance as she could between her and his club-like arms. She held her knife in a loose grip as she took another step off the road toward the safety of the forest. Sterling jumped when Franto lunged for her. She was ready for the attack, landing on her toes as she sprung back from his meaty fist. Knees bent, she was ready for his next attempt to grab her, but he was faster than she anticipated. His vice like fingers latched on to her free arm and she tried to pull away, but his grip was too strong. He squeezed his muscular hand until she winced in pain. Gaining control of her senses she slashed her blade across his knuckles, forcing him to release her.

"Hurt!" Franto pulled his hand away and sucked on his bleeding knuckles. He looked at her over his bloody fingers. Anger, pure and unstoppable anger, slowly began to show in his childlike eyes. He lowered his hand leaving blood smeared across his face and teeth. With a roar that rattled her teeth, Franto swung his uninjured arm at Sterling, but she ducked and slashed her knife along the soft flesh of his arm. Blood immediately darkened his brown shirt. Franto began to howl in pain, outrage and frustration that tugged at the simple-minded man child.

"Hold it." Sterling froze when she felt the steel tip of Motego's blade pressing into her back. He took her own knife out of her hand and shoved it into his waistband. "You've caused us too much trouble, *vishca*. Now get in the back of the wagon." Franto kept howling, which immediately caused Motego to pick up a nearby stone and plink it at Franto's head. "Hush ye fool! She barely scratched you! Quit your crying or I'll give you something to cry about!" Franto immediately stopped, albeit with a few broken sobs and a small groan of displeasure. "Now that's a good boy." Motego slipped his dagger back into the sheath. "Now be an even better boy and put the pretty into the wagon, yes?" Franto nodded and started pushing Sterling toward the rear of the wagon.

"Let me go." She struggled to free herself, but his grip was too powerful. *How could this be happening to me?* Hemi was going to be furious if she got herself kidnapped. Sterling did not stop struggling, using every technique Hemi had taught her in self-defense, but to no avail. Franto pulled open the rear door of the wagon and pushed Sterling into the darkened interior. She fell to her knees as she struggled to free herself.

Sterling came to her senses when Franto wrenched her arm behind her back and she felt the rough fibers of a rope being wrapped around her arm. She reared back hitting Franto in the nose with the back of her head. He yowled in pain releasing her to grab his broken nose. Sterling jumped out of the wagon, but Motego was there waiting. "Where do you think you're going?"

"Motego! Look!" Franto yelled, still holding his nose with one hand pointed down the road toward Shee, a dust cloud plumed into the still air behind a troop of soldiers on horses.

"Damn it! It's the Severon!" Motego abandoned his quest to steal Sterling away and jumped into the driver's seat, slapping the reins hard against the horse's back. The wagon sped crazily down the road, its wheels bouncing on the uneven ground. The Severon galloped past her in pursuit of Motego. Sterling watched in horror as Motego lost control of the wagon and it skidded sideways and then toppled over, throwing Franto from the back.

What were the Severon doing this far north? Sterling picked up the bag of rabbits she had abandoned and quickly crossed the road hoping the Severon had not noticed her. She tried to even her pace so as not to look suspicious. She felt as if her heart were going to pound out of her chest. She was nearly to the path that led to the road that would take her to the orphanage. She hazarded a look over her shoulder and nearly tripped when she realized one of the Severon had broken away from the rest and was riding toward her. Why had she not worn her hood today? Of all days, why today?

"Hold there, miss," the soldier called out to her with a smooth aristocratic voice, but she pretended not to hear him and continued at the same pace. "Stop there miss, I have some questions for you." If she didn't stop he would become suspicious, but if she turned and faced him he would see her eyes. What should she do? Her heart painfully thumped in her chest.

She stopped as he ordered, but without turning she held up the sack of rabbits she caught earlier. "Please, milord, if I don't get these rabbits home soon they will go bad." Hoping her words would satisfy him she continued edging closer to the tree line. If she had to, she could make a break for it into the forest. The trees were thicker on this side of the road.

"Stop there and turn around." She could tell by his voice that his orders were not often questioned. But if she stopped he would see her eyes and the Severon were not ones to pass on any such abnormality. "Either you stop here, or I'll have you taken to Sionaad and I'll question you there."

She'd heard rumors of Sionaad and the torturous acts the Severon committed within its walls. She stopped for fear of angering him, but she kept her back to him. The leather of his saddle creaked as he started to dismount. This was it; this was the end of her. All he would have to do is look at her face and see the legacy of her mother looking back at him.

"Commander Engram!" one of the soldiers called out from the wrecked wagon. The other soldiers were trying to wrestle Franto to the ground. His enormous size seemed to be too much for them. It was then that Sterling realized Engram's attention was no longer on her. She quickly darted into the cover of the forest and ducked behind one of the trees as the Severon Commander returned to his men. Without a thought, he drew his sword and drove the steel through Franto's heart. The giant's struggles ceased immediately. She could hear Motego cry out in agony as his friend collapsed, but even his cries were cut short by the same blade that had taken Franto's life.

Sterling's breath left her lungs when the Commander turned back to where she had disappeared into the forest. His dark eyes had an evil behind them she'd not seen before. There was such malice in their depths that it was palpable. She fell backward away from the tree as if the force of his gaze had physically pushed her. She gathered the rabbits and her bow and ran as fast as she could toward home. The sound of ominous thunder followed her through the forest.

4

STORM FRONT

He hadn't seen her.

Sterling was thankful for that small favor as she walked through the Sarno toward home. Sterling hurried her pace, she had to be back before Hemi started missing her. She'd already been away far longer than what was normal. If Hemi found out about the Severon she was sure to be in trouble. He'd warned her dozens of times to be careful and avoid the Orom's personal army. They were known for their brutality toward prisoners. There were rumors they were just as brutal toward people they considered allies. Hemi had always been careful of this, having hidden her in the cellar of the orphanage every time the Severon had paid a visit to Mother Anwell. At her young age she thought it was merely a game, but as she grew older she understood the risk Mother Anwell was taking by allowing her and Hemi to stay at the Orphanage.

Sterling pulled herself back from her musings when a rumble of thunder reminded her of the pending storm. She looked up through the soft green canopy and could see the black and silver tinted clouds looming dangerously close. The storm was moving faster than she had expected. She quickened her pace, wanting not to be outside when the storm unleashed its wrath upon the earth. As she ran she dodged limbs and clambered over felled trees, something she had learned to do all too well considering how primal the forest around her could get at times.

Still, the going was difficult as she made her way to the small road that led to the Orphanage. Out of the dense trees the way was much easier, but now she was exposed to the lightning that splayed across the sky. She reached the crest of a hill and paused for a moment to catch her breath. Though at times she was thankful that the Lady of the Vale Orphanage was so isolated and remote from the prying eyes of civilization, yet at this moment she cursed the long hilly road that led to safety. She drew in a deep breath before continuing but stopped when she heard the faint sounds of youthful laughter.

Sterling furrowed her brow. What were girls doing out here and so far from the Hall? She looked up again to gauge the storm's fury as she headed toward the sound. There were girls of many different ages that stayed at the orphanage and most of them liked to sneak off and play in the surrounding woods. It was often Sterling's job to round the girls up for dinner. She knew of the clearing where the wild flowers grew and thought that may be were the girls were playing.

She made her way through the brush and came out into the clearing. She stood there for a moment watching. Elise and Grace, two of the older orphans of the Hall were dancing about arm in arm and laughing as they made themselves dizzy. They were unaware of Sterling as they collapsed in a fit of laughter. Sitting nearly engulfed in the yellow field of daisies was yet another of the girls, Brigit, one of the younger orphans by at least four years. She was busying herself collecting a bouquet from the flowers surrounding her, her small, yet surprisingly nimble fingers weaving and interlocking the stems into a very pretty wreath. Though she was listed as being seven, she was much tinier than even the toddlers, due in part to the illnesses she had endured in her early years. Sterling started toward the girls, "What are you three doing so far away from home?"

Elise and Grace's heads popped up from the knee-high flowers, smiles spread across their innocent faces. "Sterling!" They jumped up in unison and ran toward her. They nearly knocked her to the ground with their enthusiasm. "Brigit wanted to collect flowers, so we came with her."

"These are for you Sterling." Brigit stood and limped her way to Sterling with the wreath of mostly wilted flowers grasped tightly in her tiny little fist. She was such a sweet child, having been left at the orphanage by strangers who had found her swaddled along the road. They had wanted to keep her but were too poor to continue to look after Brigit. The deformity in her legs and her continuing poor health were too much for them to maintain. Despite her sickly constitution and the deformity of her leg, Brigit was energetic and carefree.

Sterling had been sixteen when Brigit arrived. She had fallen in love with the tiny child from the moment Mother Anwell brought her in. "Happy Birthday Sterling," Brigit beamed at her, showing Sterling a mouthful of gleaming white teeth.

Sterling's initial disgruntlement melted away the moment she took the flowers. "They're beautiful," she smiled down at her, "thank you Brigit."

Thunder rumbled and shook the peaceful clearing. "There is a storm headed this way, we all need to get back before it gets here, quickly now," Sterling half chided.

"It's a race!" both Elise and Grace yelled as they ran off hand in hand toward the tree line leaving Sterling and Brigit behind. Sterling watched as they skipped together singing and laughing, on their way back to the Orphanage. Those two had been inseparable since they both arrived at the Lady of the Vale five years ago.

"Come on, let us get back before this storm hits." She took Brigit's hand and started off toward the forest. Brigit held on tight as Sterling hurried through the trees and as they stepped out of the woods the rain began to fall. Thick drops the size of grapes pelted them as they scrambled up the steep hill. It was the last one before the orphanage, which lay just on the other side in a small valley. Lightning streaked across the sky followed instantly by a rumble that rattled Sterling's teeth. *We'll never make it at this pace*, Sterling reflected, *not with Brigit's limp.*

Brigit let out a giddy little squeal when Sterling lifted her up in her arms, shifting the bag of rabbits over her shoulder. Sterling chuckled despite herself as she raced down the hill, child in arm and making odd faces at Brigit as they both giggled at each other. The ground had already become slick with mud, and there were a few times that Sterling thought she'd end up slipping and sliding the rest of the way on her rump, but thankfully gained her feet and made her way down. The wind had picked up during the storm, sweeping fiercely over the hill and pushed Sterling from behind. The trees were swaying wildly, groaning under the sudden shift, sending loose green leaves spinning and dancing in the wind. Brigit screamed as lightning struck a tree, splintering it and sending smoking bits of bark across the hillside. Sterling stumbled and fell to her knees. Brigit slid out of her arms across the muddy path, almost landing on the bag of rabbits. Another bolt hit on the other side and the impact threw Sterling back.

"Sterling!" Brigit screamed as tears of fright rolled down her muddy cheeks. Her arms outstretched.

Sterling struggled to her feet, her body heavy after the impact with the hard ground. She scooped Brigit and the bag up in a running jog, trying to gain what traction the muddy earth had to offer and broke full out toward the safety of the orphanage. Mother Anwell and the others stood with awe and fear shining in their eyes as Sterling raced for both her and Brigit's lives. The storm was directly over the orphanage.

"Hurry!" Hemi stood in the doorway waving her to quicken her pace. She forced her legs to dig in and made a final dash for shelter. She collided with Hemi's solid body and turned to see a bright flash light the sky. A bolt of lightning hissed and cracked as it wound through the clouds and hit the ground where she and Brigit had last stumbled. A wave of shivers ran down her spine when she realized if she'd been a few seconds longer on the ground both she and Brigit would be dead.

"Are you hurt?" Hemi asked his voice gruff.

"No," she heaved a sigh of relief as she pushed muddy hair out of her face. "Just covered in mud."

"Sterling." Brigit's small hand tugged at her arm. "You dropped your flowers." She pointed out at the flowers that lay scattered across the muddy ground.

Sterling stooped down and hugged Brigit. "Don't mind, we'll go tomorrow, and you can pick another bouquet twice as big."

"All right," Brigit nodded.

"You're both filthy!" Mother Anwell stood towering over them. "Off with you now, clean yourselves. And let's get those rabbits on the fire, it's almost time for dinner."

5

HAPPY BIRTHDAY

The aroma of roasted rabbit wafted from the open kitchen window. Sterling could hear Sister Treva laughing with one of the junior Sisters who helped her in the kitchen. Sister Treva had been preparing for Sterling's birthday feast all week and had promised to fix Sterling's favorite dishes.

Sterling pushed open the door into the kitchen and her stomach promptly growled its anticipation.

"Such manners," Sister Treva scolded.

"What can I say?" Sterling laughed. "It reacts to the smell of good food," she added as she stole a crust of bread from a bowl on the work table.

"Oy!" Treva swatted at her with a large wooden spoon. "No stealing food before dinner."

Mother Anwell stood in the doorway a stern look aimed at Sterling, "Don't ever scare me that way again." Sterling smiled at the woman, happy that she ruled the orphanage with a firm, but kind hand. She'd heard those same words repeated numerous times over her life. It was always the same. She would do something stupid and Mother Anwell would scold her and tell her never to scare her again. To which Sterling would do something stupid and Mother Anwell would scold her, yet again. Sterling mused, she probably shaved at least three or four years off the poor woman's life due to worry and anxiety alone.

Still, she was thankful to the old woman for giving her and Hemi a place to live. They had arrived at the Orphanage when Sterling was just six. Hemi had found out about the caretaker job from the owner of the Scarlet Bull. They had been here ever since. Sterling had no memories of what happened before coming to the orphanage, only the few pieces that Hemi told her of moving around from place to place finding work so he could feed her.

"Take these to the table," Treva handed her a platter of roasted carrots and potatoes, "then call everyone to dinner." Sterling carried the heavy platter and placed in the center of the table that was already covered in her favorite dishes. Her stomach growled again at the sight before her.

"It smells good," Brigit said as she walked into the dining room.

"Yes, it does. Treva has outdone herself this time," Sterling said as she walked through the house to the dinner bell that sat on a table in the foyer. From the very beginning it had been her job to call the girls to dinner. As a child, she'd barely been able to lift the large bell, but now the worn wooden handle fit comfortably in her hand. She lifted her arm and swung the heavy brass bell up and down announcing that dinner was served.

"Happy Birthday Sterling!" The chorus of cheers rang out across the dining table. Treva's meal had been delicious as usual and Sterling was happily satisfied by the food. Brigit sat in her lap, her arms around her neck as she kissed Sterling on the cheek. "Happy

Birthday," she whispered into Sterling's ear. The younger girls all gathered around Sterling as Hemi told embarrassing stories of when she was a child. It seemed that her birthday celebration had turned into a recounting of all the embarrassing things Sterling had done over her lifetime. But it was because she felt comfortable in this setting that Hemi would tell the stories he told. He knew how uneasy she was in large crowds and having people stare at her.

At first, as a child, when new girls came to the orphanage they would avoid Sterling and her silver eyes. It pained Sterling to no end to have it happen. To be the social pariah, especially in an orphanage of all places, was something a child should never experience. But over time, despite her differences, she had made some friends. It was a vicious cycle when the girls had befriended her, only to be adopted by a family and never seen again. Sterling had to start over again with new friends repeating the same thing every time. It got to a point, as she grew older, that Sterling would be mean to the new girls just so she wouldn't have to go through the heartache of losing another friend.

Now, fifteen years later, here she sat with a gaggle of girls wishing her a happy birthday. She loved each one of them for the joy they brought, but it still broke her heart when one would leave with their new family.

"Sterling, promise you will help me pick a new bouquet tomorrow," Brigit said as she pulled at a strand of Sterling's dark hair.

"I promise." Sterling returned Brigit's kiss.

"Sterling." She turned when Hemi's gruff voice broke through the squeals and laughter of twelve girls gathered around her.

"Yes Hemi?" she replied softly.

"I need to talk to you for a moment." His tone was off. She knew immediately that something was wrong. He turned and left the dining room expecting her to follow him.

Sterling lifted Brigit off her lap and gave up her spot to the girl. She said her goodnights to Mother Anwell and followed the hall that Hemi had taken to the Mother's study. "Close the door,"

Hemi said, with his back to her. She could see his reflection in the window. There was a sense of nervousness she'd never seen expressed in his face before. His hands were clasped behind his back. He was a giant of a man that had been her rock since as far back as she could remember. He was always steady, never faltering.

"What's going on?" Sterling asked as she closed the door.

"Sit down." Sterling could feel the blood drain from her face. Had he found out about her confrontation with the Leyenese? She knew if he discovered it she would be in big trouble. It was best to face up to it now and get it over with than let his ire grow.

"About that," she started, "I know I shouldn't have gone so far sou-"

"I'm not your Uncle." His words cut into her explanation.

"What?" She laughed, thinking she had misunderstood him.

He repeated his words and she could tell by his tone that he was telling the truth. "I don't understand. Of course you're my uncle. Father and Mother died in a fire when I was a baby and you brought me here."

He finally turned to face her, "Your father was a Kai'Varian warrior, and I was his slave." Sterling's ears began to ring as Hemi's words sank in. Her father was Kai'Varian? How could that be? Hemi was a slave? *None of this makes sense*, she thought.

"Is this a joke?" The look he gave her told Sterling that he was not joking. There was pain in those stoic eyes. "You're not joking, are you?"

"No," was all he said. It was enough.

Sterling felt her knees give out and she slumped into one of the leather chairs that lined the wall of the study. "Your father, Khort Rin'Ovana, was a Kai'Varian warrior and a Veillen High Guard. I was given to him as a slave after my unit had been captured crossing into Kai'Varian territory."

"I don't understand." Sterling stared at Hemi's feet afraid to see the truth in his eyes, "Hemi, I don't understand any of this."

"On the day you were born, there was a fierce battle between the Veillen and the demon graekull, your father died protecting you and your mother. She-" He paused for a moment, "She died shortly after your birth."

"But why bring me here?" Sterling stood. "Didn't my father have any family to raise me?"

"Khort instructed me to hide you," Hemi shook his head, "but not from whom or from what. He told me to take the necklace," Hemi pointed at the necklace that hung around her neck, "so I did, I took it and you and I ran."

Hemi was interrupted when Sister Treva came bursting through the door. "Oh, thank the heavens I found you." She was out of breath and her face was devoid of color.

"What is it? What's the matter?" Hemi asked, his stoic face now fading into worry.

"It's bad. The Severon are here," Treva warned, her face white with panic.

6

CAGED

"They are looking for a girl with silver eyes." Both Hemi and Treva looked to Sterling. "Mother Anwell is keeping them occupied, we must hide you."

The Severon? Sterling's heart raced as she followed Hemi toward the back of the house. Was it the same cruel man that had killed Motego and Franto on the Merchant Road? How could they have found her? Especially here, of all places?

She was certain he had not seen her eyes that day. Had someone given her up to the Severon? No one in Shee trusted the Orom's army since they had purged the city of foreigners breaking up families in the process. She doubted they would willingly divulge her location.

"In here." Hemi easily pushed the heavy dining table out of the way and threw back the carpet revealing a hidden door. He pulled up on the iron ring, opening the way to the root cellar. She'd been inside the cellar once before during a visit by one of the Orom's envoys. She disliked the closed-in feeling she got in this room. *It is like crawling into my own grave*, she thought as she moved forward. But knowing that Hemi could get her out quickly once the Severon were gone made the decision less overwhelming.

"Hurry," Sister Treva urged, "Mother Anwell cannot stall them much longer."

Sterling slid into the dry root cellar and sat, pulling her knees close to her face. It was a long room that spanned the length of the house and the only other entrance was the cellar door that let out into the kitchen garden. She took one last look at Hemi and saw the fear and concern in his eyes. He winked one last time, then a smirk crossed his lips. *Forced*, Sterling thought, *but oddly reassuring nonetheless.* It was like he was telling her not to worry, that he would take care of everything just like he always had. Dozens of times before. Yet that tingling sensation of dread kept trying to crawl into her brain. He closed the door and replaced the carpet. Dust rained down on her as he pushed the large dining table back into place. And that sense of being buried alive began to bleed through her resolve.

The root cellar was pitch-black except for a few places where the slats of the floor had been worn away. Dust motes floated in the meager light that forced its way through the tiny holes. Sterling could hear the footsteps of the approaching Severon. Their boot heels struck the wooden floor with a decisive staccato. The softer footsteps of Mother Anwell followed the men into the dining room.

"I am Commander Remus Engram of the Northern Arm," the man said introducing himself. "There are rumors that you've been harboring a Devian. Rumors I tend to believe from a man who no longer has to worry about counting to ten."

Engram? Sterling recognized his name as the man she'd seen on the Merchant Road. The one that had murdered Motego and Franto. The one who had almost caught her.

"But Commander Engram, there is no one here. We are just a simple orphanage," Mother Anwell softly responded.

"And I am a simple soldier following the Orom's edicts. If you say there is nothing here, then you should not have a problem with us searching for what you say is not here."

There was a short pause, "Go right ahead Commander, we have nothing to hide."

"Then you have nothing to be worried about. Search this building from top to bottom. Every room, every closet. Every chest. You there, search the farmhouse and the grounds."

Several answers of, "Yes, Commander," were followed with retreating footsteps.

"You there, have we met before?"

"I do not believe we have, Commander," Hemi answered, his deep voice calm despite the chaos swirling around him.

There was a long pause before the Commander spoke again, "Mother Anwell, how many girls do you have living here with you?"

"We've twelve girls."

"And their ages?" Sterling had a sinking feeling come over her.

"They range from seven to thirteen." Sterling could hear the hesitation in Mother Anwell's voice.

"I'd like to see them, all of them. Bring them here before me."

"But, Commander the girls are asleep." There was nervousness in Mother Anwell's voice that was not usually present. She was a strong woman.

"That wasn't a request. You will do what I ask, or I will yank them all out of bed myself and the... pleasantries we are exchanging now will come to an end." A silence came over the room as the commander waited for the girls to gather.

Sterling carefully changed positions until she was directly below one of the cracks in the flooring not covered by the carpet. She could just see through it and into the dining room above her. Engram's hair was brown and he wore the full uniform of the Severon. He was sitting in one of the high-backed chairs that lined the room. He had an air about him that frightened Sterling. That cold, unfeeling killer instinct that seemed to twinkle in the light. He glanced down at the floor, but thankfully could not see Sterling through the tiny crack.

There was a long, quiet pause while Sister Treva roused the girls from their beds. Soft footsteps soon filed into the room along with confused questions. "But I'm sleepy," one of the girls said with a quiet confusion. Tears gathered behind Sterling's eyes when she realized it was Brigit's tiny voice, protesting being woken.

"Don't worry little one, you will sleep again soon." The kind voice belied the cruelty Sterling knew lay within the Commander. There were muffled voices and conversation, as several soldiers returned to report on their failed search for the silver eyed girl on the Orphanage grounds. Turning back to the girls, he asked, "They are all very sweet and innocent aren't they gentlemen?"

He stood, and his boot heels struck the floor with a quiet anger. "What is your name little one?"

"Brigit," Brigit answered, without any fear.

Sterling put her hand over her mouth to mask her quick, frantic breathing. Her heart was racing so fast she thought she would faint. *Oh, please don't hurt Brigit,* she begged silently.

"What a lovely name you have, Brigit," Engram said. "Such an innocent child." His voice grew louder; he must have stooped down to be eye level with the little girl. "Tell me Brigit, does someone live here with silver eyes?"

"Uh," Brigit hesitated. Mother Anwell had told all the girls to never mention Sterling's silver eyes to anyone. Sterling prayed Brigit would remember the rule. She covered her face with her hands, waiting on the little girl's answer. *Please, please, please.* "No, I don't know her." Sterling released a thankful breath at Brigit's answer. She'd remembered.

"No? That is most disappointing." Sterling shifted so she could see better as Engram stood and faced Mother Anwell. "It's quite funny really, I only asked the child if she'd seen someone with

silver eyes, but she seems know the person I'm looking for is a girl."
Sterling's jaws clenched tightly at the Commander's soft voice, "I see
I've been lied to. By both a child and a Mother. No more lies. No
more games. No more pleasantries. You are harboring a Devian, and
you will tell me where she is. Or you will be punished!"

"Please milord, she's just a child!" Mother Anwell pleaded
for Brigit.

"All the more reason for you to cease your lies."

"You're hurting me!" Brigit's tiny voice squeaked out.

"Tell me where the Devian is and I'll let this little one go. Her
fate is in your hands, Mother."

"Yes! Yes," Mother Anwell's voice cracked, "there was a girl
with silver eyes who lived with us for a time. She-she left two days
ago, said something about people looking for her."

"Where did she go?"

"East, last I saw. Through the woods. That's all I know, sir. Now
please, please let Brigit go."

There was a long, tense pause. Finally, the Commander let
Brigit go. "See? Was that so hard?" He looked gently at Brigit, deep
into those small, innocent eyes. He smiled lightly to her, cupping the
side of her head. "You should never lie to your elders, child. But you
knew no better." He patted her head once before resting his hand on
her small shoulder, "You are forgiven."

Sterling watched in horror as the point of a dagger punched
through Brigit's small body. Blood pooled quickly where the dagger
protruded from her tiny chest. Brigit's last breath was a gurgle as her
knees buckled. She landed hard, face first on the floor.

"*You bastard!*" Hemi roared above, as what sounded like a
scuffle ensued.

The girls' screamed in fright as the two men fought. A chair
toppled causing dust to rain down on Sterling. She covered her
mouth to keep from coughing. The sound of a sword being pulled
from its sheath preceded more screams from the girls.

"Hemi, no!" Mother Anwell keened. A loud slouching thump shook the boards directly above Sterling's head. Screams from the girls filled the room, almost drowning out the last words she would remember Hemi ever uttering to her.

"Sterling." Hemi's whisper reached her over the yelling, "You must go to Kai'Vari." He had trouble forming the words, his breath was shallow. "The Rin'Ovanas are family..." Hemi breathe rattled in his chest, "Fende...she help you..."

"You're still alive?" The question was followed by a pained grunt and the point of Engram's sword penetrating the floor board, nearly slicing into Sterling's hand.

Sterling covered her mouth to keep from screaming. *No.* She shook her head in denial. *Oh gods no.* This man was a monster. A butcher. Brigit, Hemi. No, no, no. They were only inches from her; on the other side of the floorboards was the man that had raised her. Her hand went up and touched the wood that separated them. Blood began to seep through the cracks, covering her fingers and dripping down onto her face. Tears mixed with the warm viscous liquid. He was her rock, the person that kept her world together when she fell apart. He was always there guiding her in the right direction when she veered. And dear, sweet Brigit. This child of ill-fortune, a pure soul that had never, ever caused harm to any living being in her life. They were both dead because of the Severon.

"Hemi!" Sister Treva's voice invaded the roar that had filled her head, "Hemi!"

"Where is the girl!?" Engram yelled.

I'm here! Sterling wanted to yell out, but the words would not form. If she revealed herself perhaps he would leave the children alone. But no matter how hard she tried to yell out, her voice remained silent.

"I know she is here somewhere and if you will not tell me where she is hiding then we'll simply smoke her out. Lock them in the chapel and burn it to the ground, burn it all to the ground," Engram ordered his men.

"Yes, Commander."

"No. You mustn't they are only children," Mother Anwell pleaded.

"I gave you a chance Mother, which is more than what I would have given even to my own blood. Your lies have doomed you all."

"But there is no one here Commander!" Treva continued to deny Sterling's presence.

"Enough," he said dismissively at Treva. His footsteps retreated followed by the tiny screams of the girls. Sterling could hear Mother Anwell and Sister Treva plead and beg and finally curse as they were pulled from the room.

She had to get out. She had to save the girls. If Sterling turned herself in he would surely let the girls live. Sterling tried pushing on the door hoping she could knock the table over, but its weight was too much. She'd have to use the doors that led to the kitchen garden. It was difficult to find her way through the darkness of the cellar. Only a meager amount of light seeped through the cracks in the floorboards. As she shimmied her way over the hard packed ground she knocked her head on the floor above her when the ground started to rise. She would have to squeeze through on her stomach.

Sterling exhaled and inched her head and chest through the small space, and finally, with arms out in front she pulled herself toward the opening. She was halfway through when the distinct smell of smoke reached her. It was then that she realized it was no longer light that seeped through the floorboards, but the glow of uncontrolled flames. *They've set the Orphanage on fire*, she thought. Her struggles to get out of the cellar were renewed. She'd burn to death in this dark lonely place if she didn't reach the cellar doors. She used both hands and feet to pull and push her way across the narrow opening. Her nails dug into the hard earth until finally she was free and tumbled into the larger area of the cellar. She was able to walk hunched over now, instead of crawling on hands and knees.

The smoke had thickened, and Sterling could no longer hold back the wracking coughs. Her eyes burned from the noxious fumes.

She wiped her tears and finally found the doors that would lead her to freedom. If she could make it to the chapel in time she'd be able to free the children. The door was heavy, but she finally threw it open and struggled up the stone steps and into the warm night. She lay there for a moment catching her breath as the smoke started billowing out of the underground opening. She pushed herself to her feet and leaned against the railing of a fence. Sterling took a deep, cleansing breath and started toward the chapel.

Somewhere in the smoke, she could hear muffled cries and screams.

Her feet started running, the urgency she felt was over-whelming. She reached the side of the house and ran into the open yard between the chapel and the main house. The sight before her brought her to her knees. Tears welled in her eyes and down her cheeks. No, no, no! she repeated to herself over and over. The roof had collapsed, and the walls had followed suit, burying everyone inside under the flames that engulfed the tiny building.

The uncontrolled sobbing shook her shoulders as the thoughts of Brigit entered her mind. "Brigit. Why? It's my fault. It's my fault," she whispered to herself. Sterling gasped for breath when a course of pain surged through her from the base of her neck. It felt like a thou-sand needles slamming into her, taking her breath. She punched the ground, nearly breaking her hand, "No!"

"Well, well, well. What have we here? It seems I've scared up a cellar rat." Sterling turned her head and looked over her shoulder. Engram stood behind her, one hand on the hilt of his sword. A smirk creased his lips as he looked down at Sterling. "This ends here little Devian. This ends tonight."

7

CLEVER GIRL

Dan'Ruok, 27th Ignis, 1021

Finally, after weeks of false leads, dead ends, and dead bodies, Engram could finally go home with his prize in hand. *It is tempting*, Engram thought to himself, *I could just slit her throat*. Even after tossing her across the back of his horse, her hands and feet bound, he was still thinking about doing it. But the Orom commanded her alive.

"Stop squirming," Engram sighed when the girl tried to escape yet again. "You were difficult to find, do not think it will be so easy to get away." She kicked her legs into the horse's side in an attempt free herself. Angered at her attempts, Engram pulled her head back by her hair, "Mind yourself or you'll feel my wrath."

He was met by a stare from her silver eyes and muffled curses behind the gag he'd stuffed into her mouth. "To think I had you in my grasp when we stopped that Leyenese man and his son. You are a clever girl."

"Commander," Phayo pulled his horse up beside Engram, "we've made camp ahead."

"Very well," Engram spurred his horse into a slow cantor. He took some delight knowing the pace he set was painful for the girl. Engram dismounted in front of the large tent his men had erected for his use. He pulled Sterling from the back of his horse and dropped her in a heap at his feet. "Deal with her," he ordered. Even though his men were busy with tending to their horses and erecting their own smaller tents, they jumped at the order.

He left her in the hands of his men and retired to his tent. He was exhausted from his travels and was thankful he could finally go home. To his family, to his people. *His* people, not this dirty, inbred rabble, but men and women of civilization. Intelligence. Order. Obedience. He would be home. Soon.

Engram yawned, removed his boots and sat down on the cot that was his makeshift bed. His thoughts turned to the pleasure he would have in turning the girl over to the Orom. Laying down he closed his eyes and was instantly asleep. He dreamed of the accolades he would receive upon his return to Sionaad. That was until he was woken by Phayo in the predawn hours that one of his men was dead and all the horses were gone.

"*How?*" He was furious. Every man within ear's reach cowered from Engram's anger. He was incensed that the girl had, somehow, in some way, escaped his grasp yet again.

Scoutsman Kerl was on his knees, his forehead pressed to the ground. "Forgiveness, Commander. I swear that I do not know how. But I shall find her." He'd been apologizing ever since they had found him unconscious next to the dead soldier.

Engram huffed, wiping the sweat from his forehead.

Clever, insolent little girl. How did you manage to unbind the ropes, and kill one of my men, an armed and armored man of war no less? You released all the horses so we could not follow you, and then somehow you managed to sneak past one of my best trackers without leaving any signs of passage? Not only have I lost my prize, but the Shard along with you.

"Phayo!"

"Commander?" Phayo said, bowing his head gently. His most trustworthy and skilled tracker knelt, ready to do as Engram ordered.

"Find her. You have leave to hunt. But I want her alive. However, if she travels with companions execute them. And make sure she watches."

"Yes, Commander, by your will." Phayo left the line, paused for a moment looking at the tracks and ran in the direction the girl had escaped.

Engram turned his attention back to Kerl. The man still had his face buried in the dirt, groveling and writhing in sheer terror for mercy. Engram stepped over the man, thinking, *a man who shows mercy shows weakness. A man who shows weakness shows fear. And a man who shows fear is a coward. A liability. A weak link. It was time to make the chain strong again, by removing the weak link.*

Engram stood behind his scout, tucking his hands behind his back. "Up, Scoutsman Kerl."

"Sir!" Kerl rose, straight-backed, his hands resting on his thighs.

Engram paced around the young scout, "Tell me Kerl, what do you know of the Devians?"

"Sir?" Kerl looked up at Engram, his confusion obvious.

"Do you know why we hunt the Devian, Kerl?"

"Because they know where the Shards are," Kerl regurgitated the exact reason all new Severon recruits are given.

"But do you know *why* they know where the Shards are?" Engram slowly walked around Kerl. The other men slowly stepped out of Engram's path.

"Uh…" Kerl had no answer for Engram's question.

"It is because, Kerl, they are descendants of the Elemental gods," Engram came to a stop behind Kerl. "The Elemental gods, Kerl, were created by the gods of Balance, Orla and Moraug." Engram pulled his dagger from its sheath and knelt behind the trembling Kerl. "And do you know why that is important?"

"No, sir." Kerl's voice was tiny with fear.

"It's important because the Shards are the very power of Moraug, and the four Elemental gods concealed their location. Devians are the only ones who know where the Elemental gods are hiding the Shards. And now you have managed to let this very important Devian escape."

Engram ended his explanation by thrusting his dagger up into the base of the unsuspecting man's skull. He gripped Kerl by his throat, steadying him while he struggled. As his blade punctured the man's brain, Engram seemed to take demonic delight as he twisted and turned the blade. While the light in Kerl's eyes slowly faded, Engram whispered gently in his ear one last time, "May the Orom forget your name."

He let loose of Kerl's throat, standing as he pulled his dagger from the man's head. With a quick kick, he sent Kerl's lifeless body to slam face first into the dirt. "Let that be your grave," he spat as he turned and headed back to camp.

I'm beginning to feel a little better already, he thought as he walked away from the body.

8

SLY FOX

Central Duenin
Twelve Days Later
Dan'Ruok, 9th Unda, 1021

The heat was unbearable. Sweat was dripping into her eyes, and she blinked furiously to relieve the sting. Even the shade here was no relief from the sun's brutality. Her mind wandered, and she longed for the cool mountain air of home. Reality settled in and she knew that she had no home to return to. Sterling wanted to sleep, but the images of Brigit and Hemi kept flooding her mind. There was Brigit in the center of the field of flowers holding up a bouquet of yellow daisies, a sweet smile on her little face. The light in her blue eyes faded as tears of blood streamed down her face. Then her little mouth opening in a silent scream as flames surrounded her, engulfing her.

My birthday, she thought, was a day of death. First my parents, so many years ago. And now, my friends. "I am a curse," she whispered.

She was exhausted. She'd been on the run from the Severon for two weeks, hiding and avoiding any village along the way. She'd fled from the Severon camp on a stolen horse with no weapon, no money, and only the simple clothes she now wore. She had managed to pilfer food from a few isolated farmhouses along the way. The pains of hunger gnawed at her stomach. If she was going to make it to Kai'Vari she needed to eat. And now here she was on the outskirts of Hemrac, hiding among the hedgerow that lined the nearly immaculate cobblestone road for any signs of the Severon.

The village sat in a shallow bowl in the land surrounded by fields of wheat and corn. The hedgerow she lay under sat atop one of the rolling hills overlooking and leading to the quiet village below. It was perfect for watching the comings and goings of the village inhabitants. She had stumbled upon this village the previous night during a storm and had hidden in one of the outlying barns for safety. She'd risen before the moonset and hid among the hedges before any of the citizens were up for their morning chores. She'd known that riding into any village on a horse branded by the Severon Militia was asking for trouble. Especially one with a saddle that no doubt had the seal of a Severon Commander.

She had left that horse at a farm and when the time came she would find a replacement. There had been no sign of the Severon or any other military patrols in the village this morning and now that the noon sun had long since passed she felt safe to emerge from her hiding place. Her body screamed in protest as she stood from her prone position. She itched from not having a proper bath. Wading in streams and rivers was not the same as relaxing in steaming water. She felt the weight of the gold in the pouch she'd taken from a traveling merchant while he slept at his makeshift camp. *Perhaps I'll treat myself tonight,* she thought.

Sterling made her way down the winding path until she reached the edge of the village. The main street ran from one end of the village to the other with smaller avenues veering off like tentacles. The main street was quiet after the long afternoon of bustle. She made her way toward the only pub in town. *The Crow's Head*, she weakly grinned to herself looking at the pub sign, *I'm almost hungry enough to eat a crow's head right now*. She paused before entering, looking over her shoulder for any followers. Satisfied she was alone, Sterling pushed the door open and entered the darkened interior. She'd made a habit of not making a flashy entry, but no matter how quiet her entrance she felt all eyes on her as the door swung shut behind her.

Sterling avoided eye contact with the other patrons as she scanned the pub. A booth in the far corner looked inviting. She walked the perimeter of the room keeping one eye on the pub's customers as she slid into the chair. Her back was to the wall, so she could see the entire pub. The smell of food cooking wafted into the dining room, enticing Sterling. She had not eaten a proper meal in what seemed like days, not since she'd caught a fish in one the of streams she'd crossed.

Hemi would have beaten her rear raw if he knew of all the things she'd done since she fled the orphanage. Stealing, lying, killing, taking things from good and innocent people. Her eyes lost focus as the thought of Hemi jumped to the forefront of her mind. He'd only been inches from her when he died. She swore that she would bring revenge down upon the Commander tenfold for what he'd done to Hemi. She missed them all so much she felt emptiness in her heart. Just breathing was painful when thoughts of Mother Anwell and Hemi and all the other girls came to her.

She missed Brigit most of all.

The waitress startled Sterling. "What can I get you, dear?"

"Uh, ale, I suppose, and whatever food you have." Sterling looked up into the plump face of the waitress. Her eyes were shining, cheeks rosy from the warmth of the pub. Sterling knew the instant the woman saw her silver eyes. The light behind her brown eyes vanished and the smile melted into a frown.

"We don't serve your kind here."

Frustrated by the woman's attitude Sterling plunked the bag of gold down on the table, "I have coin for food and a bed."

The wench simply scoffed and sniffed. "Your money's no good here. I don't care if you have the Orom's personal gold kurons in there." Slowly and forcefully, the waitress made her message as clear to Sterling as possible by saying the words slowly. "We don't serve your kind. Now get out of our inn."

"My *kind*?" Sterling narrowed her eyes and rose to meet the woman's glare. She was tired, she was angry, and most of all she was starving. The woman's attitude ignited Sterling's fury, "I'm not leaving until you serve me."

"We'll just see about that," the woman growled at Sterling as she stepped through the swinging doors of the kitchen. Sterling replaced the pouch of gold back on her belt and stared out into the dining room. She realized then that she'd gained the attention of the other customers. She felt exposed without her hood to conceal her eyes. She averted her gaze to a scratch in the wood table in front of her and tried to sink further into the darkness.

"A *what*?" Sterling jumped at the booming voice that came from the kitchen. It was followed by a burly man who pushed through the swinging doors. "I'll be damned if I serve a Devian at my inn. I don't need the eyes of the Severon on me." Sterling sat up straight, her eyes widening at the man that stood before her. He was a mass of blubber, hair and sweat. His shirt was stained with food and filth. His round face was red from the heat of the kitchen fire. Meaty hands were propped on his rotund waist as he stared down at Sterling.

She stared back into his eyes that were nearly invisible behind the folds of fatty skin. She was accustomed to fear and confusion when people saw her unusual eyes, but this man looked down at her with hatred in his. *What had she done to deserve this man's hate? Just because I'm a Devian?* Anger seeped into her skin as he looked down at her. She could feel her skin burning with the anger, muscles throbbing with the rising heat.

"What happened, did you eat the last Devian?" she egged the man out of anger.

Sterling blinked and realized she was on her feet, as the man effortlessly gathered her up one handed by the front of her shirt, pulling her toward him until she was inches from his face. The man snarled. "Yeah, although judgin' by your skin and bone ass, you'll jus' be an appetizer."

A new voice unexpectedly entered the conversation. "So much for Hemrac hospitality."

She turned her head to find a man standing next to her and the cook. He had his hands pressed between them, trying to separate them. She looked down and felt her cheeks blush when she saw his warm hand pressed a little too conveniently against her breast. The cook spat on the floor and dropped her back into her chair. *Great*, Sterling thought. *Try not to draw too much attention to yourself. The pub is the perfect place to lay low. Just another face in the crowd.* Sterling huffed and blew a stray strand of hair from her forehead.

"Like I told the girl, I'm not serving a Devian. They are bad luck and I don't need any of that," the cook said, wiping his hand on the blood smeared apron that barely fit around his rotund waist.

"Bertrand," the man had a smooth way of talking, though his accent was not Dueninian, "regardless of where she's from her money is no different than yours or mine." He had a smile on his lips as he winked at Sterling. "She's a customer, so therefore you need her, am I mistaken?"

Bertrand pointed a sausage like finger at Sterling, "I don't care. I'm not taking her money."

The man thumbed a single silver rina at Bertrand. "Then take mine."

Bertrand caught the coin with swift, surprisingly nimble fingers. He huffed and finally nodded. "Fine," he glared down at Sterling before he turned and retreated to the bowels of the kitchen.

"May I?" The man motioned to the seat across from Sterling. He seemed harmless enough with his blonde hair and blue eyes. She examined him for a moment before answering. She was wary, but he had come to her aid. Mother Anwell would scold her for not returning the favor and offering him a place to sit, but she told herself to be cautious. She motioned to the vacant seat and with a smile he melted his tall frame into the chair. "Name's Kellen, Kellen Leiten." He seemed almost too cheerful. His blue eyes sparkled in the darkness as if there was some inner light behind them.

"And you are?" He hinted for Sterling to give up her name, but she was too cautious to willingly divulge her name to this strange man. She continued to watch him from the corner of her eye. He had a constant smile on his lips and his teeth were strong and white. Sterling was mesmerized by the aura that surrounded him. He was like a prince that had stepped out of one of Brigit's fairy tales. His shoulders were broad and the white shirt he wore hung loosely on his muscular frame. He was so completely different than any other Dueninian she'd seen before.

"Berac."

Sterling shook herself from her daze long enough to say, "Hmm?"

"I said, I'm from Berac," he said, smiling slyly. That explained the crisp, throaty accent she noticed before. "Though, I've been here in Duenin for more than a year now."

"Why so far from home?" Sterling's curiosity got the better of her. Berac was to the far west and isolated by the Izanami Mountains. Sterling had only heard stories of Berac and its rolling hills of vineyards and the crystal blue water that ran along the coastline.

"I'll tell you if you give me your name?" He winked in amusement.

"I don't need to know that bad," Sterling responded trying her best to ignore Kellen.

"Fine, fine," he chuckled, "My father expected me to take over the family business, and, well, he and I disagreed about that course. So, here I am finding my own way in the great land of Duenin." He spread his arms wide as if the inn encompassed the entire world. "And you, you are not from around these parts either. What with those strange eyes of yours, I'd say you're from…"

"New Alden. I'm from New Alden," she lied. Her heart was racing. She did not want him to finish his words so she had cut him off and made up where she was from.

"A beautiful city indeed and one full of excitement." He stood when the waitress returned with a platter of food.

Sterling stared down at the plate of food, her sense of guilt caused her stomach to turn. "Sterling," she mumbled her name before he could retreat to the other side of the inn. "My name is Sterling."

"Well, Sterling I will take my leave then. Perhaps we'll see each other again."

"I doubt it," Sterling said around a mouth full of roast. Mother Anwell would have slapped the food out of her mouth for such atrocious manners, but her stomach was empty, and her need of food was far greater than any sense of decorum she may have once had. Peering over the rim of her cup, Sterling watched Kellen leave as she washed down the roast with the ale. *He is an odd man indeed. Was he too cheerful? Perhaps that was the way of the Beracians.*

She pushed Kellen Leiten out of her mind and focused in on the delicious meal that lay before her. Despite the grotesque appearance of the rude cook, he had a talent for cooking. The platter was filled with roasted beef, carrots, and potatoes. All of it was covered in a thick beef gravy that gave off the aroma of rosemary. The portion was huge, enough for a grown man to stuff himself, but she finished off the entire plate along with the bread that came with the meal. She washed it all down with the tankard of ale the waitress had brought.

The waitress was still wary of her when she returned to take the empty platter, giving Sterling a wide berth and side glances. She jumped when Sterling asked for a room. "There is one available, but it's the most expensive."

"I'll take it," Sterling said without hesitation. She was quietly thanking the rich merchant she pilfered the coins from.

The waitress eyed the gold then added, "It's the last room on the right at the end of the hall."

"I'd also like a bath brought up with hot water."

Sterling found the room the waitress had indicated and opened the door and stood dumbstruck. This was the most expensive? It was nothing more than an old worn out bed and a threadbare rug. There was a small table with a chipped wash basin. It smelled of old body odor along with other aromas that Sterling did not want to identify. Luckily the room had a window. Sterling bypassed the bed and pushed open the window. The night was warm, and it let in some fresh air. The room overlooked the stable yard of the inn. Just below the window a short roof jutted out that covered the back porch where the kitchen was located.

There was a sharp rap at the door, "Your bath miss." Sterling opened the door to two housemen who brought in a large copper wash tub and two buckets of steaming water. The tub sat in the middle of the room on the threadbare rug and took up most of the empty space. The first boy reached into his pocket and handed her a bar of soap wrapped in a thin cloth.

"Thank you," she said as she handed them each a copper berg. The light in their eyes told Sterling that the fat owner didn't give them much in the way of wages. They were thankful for the coins she gave them.

As soon as the housemen left and shut the door, Sterling threw off her clothes and shoes as quickly as possible and stepped into the tub. It was large enough for Sterling to sit down and have the water come to her chest, the sides reaching up over her shoulders so just her head was above the rim. The water was hot and soothed her tired muscles. The heavy pendant that hung between her breasts felt lighter in the water. She lifted the stone and examined it in the light. Hemi had told her it had once belonged to her mother and that it was precious to her. *What was so special about this stone?* All it did now was remind her of what she'd lost. She'd thought about selling it for gold but had stopped herself before going through with it. After all it was the only thing she had left from her old life. She let the stone fall where it slowly sank and lay once again against her heart.

She sat there a minute relaxing for the first time in two weeks. The Severon had dogged her the entire way. If she stayed in one place for too long they would inevitably show up and she'd be on the run again. But she hadn't seen them in three days and with no sign of them riding into Hemrac from her hedgerow hiding place, she felt confident for the first time that they had finally lost her trail.

Before the water started to grow cold she lathered the thin cloth with soap and washed the dirt and grime from her travels. Her skin was bright pink before she was complete, but once satisfied Sterling dunked her head under the water to rinse away the filth. She thought about what would happen tomorrow. She still had some ways to go before she reached Kai'Vari. Would she be able to stay ahead of the Severon? Sterling came up for air and turned her attention to her hair. Using the soap again, she washed the sweat and dirt from its long strands. Satisfied, she dunked her head back under the water to rinse out the suds.

Once again, she emerged from the water gasping for air. Soap ran into her eyes and she reached for the bath towel one of the housemen had provided. Eyes closed, she fumbled for the towel. Grasping the roughhewn cloth she stood, but the sensation of being watched suddenly sent a chill down her spine, goosebumps prickled her skin. She quickly wiped her eyes and gasped in shock when she realized she wasn't alone. Kellen Leiten was settled back on a stool, boots propped against the lip of the tub. That sly, handsome grin stretched from ear to ear, like a happy fox that had just gorged itself on a fat hen.

"What are you doing in my room?" She wrapped the small, oh so small piece of cloth around her body. "How long have you been there?"

There was a knowing smile in his eyes. "Long enough to know you can hold your breath for a very long time." Sterling could feel her cheeks start to burn.

She tugged at the bath sheet again and crossed her arms. "Show's over. Now get out," she growled. The smile in his eyes quickly vanished as he stood and advanced on her. Sterling's heart rate went up a notch as she prepared to defend herself. But when he didn't attack she was taken off guard. He went past her to the door. He opened it just a crack and listened for a moment. When he turned back to her he was a completely different person. His eyes were fierce, and the smile was gone. He was no longer the jovial man that had rescued her earlier.

"You may not have liked the way I came to tell you, but I thought," he said, looking over his shoulder at her, "you would be interested to know that the Severon are here."

The words he uttered drained the blood from Sterling's face. Her body went numb at the mention of the army that had doggedly tracked her like a hound. How had they found her? It had been three days since she last saw them. She'd been so careful to cover her tracks and to stay out of sight, not venturing into any villages and staying off the main roads.

"Quickly now, get dressed." She heard his words from a great distance, but she couldn't comprehend what he was saying. She just stood there and watched as he braced the lone chair in the room under the handle on the door. He must have noticed she was not moving and came over to her, placing his hands on her bare shoulders, "Sterling." He gave her a quick shake. Sterling blinked at her name and came out of her fog, "Sterling, quickly now. Get dressed, they are just downstairs. We can escape out the window, but you must get dressed."

Her body started to move on its own. Ignoring the fact that Kellen was there with her she dropped the sheet and quickly pulled on her clothes. She regretted that they were still filthy, she had wanted to wash them as well. There was nothing she could do about it now as she laced up her trousers. She pulled the leather vest on over her once white shirt then sat down to pull on her boots.

"Are you ready yet?" She could hear the impatience in his voice.

"Yes, I'm ready."

"Come on." Kellen left his post at the door and climbed out the window. He held a hand out for her, but Sterling was frozen in place as the handle on the door started to turn. "Sterling," he whispered with forceful urgency.

When the door failed to open there was a loud knock on the door, "You in there, open up."

"Sterling." Kellen reached back in the window and grabbed hold of her arm and yanked her out the window just as the door came crashing in.

Still in a fog, Sterling found herself being pulled toward two horses Kellen had waiting. The fog disappeared when Sterling heard a familiar voice behind her bark, "She jumped out the window!" Sterling's legs stopped on their own accord as she turned and saw the man that brought terror to her. Looking out the open window above her was the man responsible for the death of everyone she loved. Commander Engram. She felt a fire start in her heart, a fire of hate that filled her body and she started to turn back to the inn. No longer stopped in terror, she decided she was going to kill that man for what he'd done.

Pointing at her, Engram yelled, "Stop right there *Devian!*"

Kellen rode in front of her blocking her view of the window. "Sterling! Get on the damn horse!"

She came to her senses and mounted the second horse. As they rode out of the stable yard she took one look back, but the Commander was no longer there.

9

A NEW ALLY

Four Days Later
Dan'Idou, 13th Unda, 1021

"Can we please stop a moment?" Sterling called after Kellen. He seemed like such a jovial man, but he had set a brutal pace since they left Hemrac.

"We can't dawdle," he said as he slowed his pace, allowing Sterling a chance to catch up. Looking around warily, he pulled his reins and stopped. "Only for a moment," he cautioned.

Sterling sighed in relief, dismounted quickly, and found a dense patch of trees to relieve herself. She knew she should be embarrassed, but there was little time to think of decorum at this point in their journey.

Had it only been four days since they fled Hemrac? It seemed an eternity since Kellen had intruded on her bath and saved her from the clutches of Engram and the Severon.

"Sterling!" His urgency was evident in the tone of his voice as he called to her.

"I'm coming!" she called out to him. *Damn task master*, she thought, *at least give me a moment to stretch my legs.*

Mounting the horse Kellen had stolen from the stables at the Crow's Head, Sterling joined him. He glanced behind them again, but there was no sign of the Severon tracker that had dogged them since they left Hemrac. Following Kellen's lead, Sterling urged her horse into a quick trot. They wanted to put as much distance between the trackers as possible before night fall.

"We'll make camp tonight," Kellen called out over the sound of the horses. "There's a timbered thicket not too far from here that offers shelter."

Her muscles ached from the constant tension of not knowing if their stalker would ride over the horizon. They rode in silence, both looking over their shoulders when the feeling of being chased became overwhelming. Dread ebbed each time she glanced back and did not find the Severon.

The long shadows of the trees spread out before them as the sun slowly made its descent. Kellen had turned off the main road on to a small path just barely wide enough for the horses. The ground was uneven making their progress slow, not to mention the low hanging limbs that had her ducking to avoid being hit in the face.

They eventually exited the path to a small glade just the right size for their horses and for them to make camp. It felt like a cocoon of sorts, with the trees and brush surrounding them on all sides.

Sterling started to slide off her horse, but before her feet could touch the ground, Kellen's hands were on her waist easing her to the ground. "Thanks," she said, looking closely at the man who had saved her, "I probably would have collapsed."

Sterling was thankful for the respite. Four days and they were still far from the Kai'Varian border. Much of their time had been spent doubling back to hide their trail in hopes to evade the Severon.

"I'll catch us some dinner," Kellen replied as he slung a quiver of arrows over his shoulder. Sterling watched as he disappeared in to the forest. Except for the dried meat they'd pilfered from a farm, their food had run out yesterday and neither of them had eaten a real meal since. She was thankful for Kellen's help, had he not been there in Hemrac there was no telling what would have happened to her. The Severon were relentless in their pursuit and she still wasn't certain what it was they wanted from her.

She pushed the thoughts of Engram to the furthest reaches of her mind. If she thought too much of him her mood would plummet in to despair. *I'll just get the fire going and be ready for whatever Kellen brings back.* Sterling hummed to herself while she built a small fire. Its warmth ate away at the chill that had settled in her bones.

It wasn't long before Kellen returned, his face sullen. "You didn't catch anything?"

"Damn rabbits are too fast." Kellen leaned the bow and arrow against the tree and slumped to the ground in defeat.

"Seriously?" Sterling laughed, "you didn't catch anything?

Kellen started rifling through his pack, "I guess we'll be eating dried meat again."

"I'll be damned if I'll eat that again, I want some fresh food," Sterling said as she stood and gathered up the bow and arrow Kellen had discarded. *Dried meat, ha!* Sterling laughed to herself.

Kellen, sounding a bit wounded, said, "I'm telling you those little rodents are too quick." She heard him trip on a rock and scrape his trousers on a bush as he walked through camp.

Sterling stopped in her tracks and faced Kellen, "Perhaps if you weren't so noisy you wouldn't scare them away." With a smile she turned and pulled an arrow from the quiver. "Hunting rabbits is all about patience and quiet. Why do you think they have those big ears?"

"Good point," Kellen said quietly as he followed behind her.

"Get down," Sterling whispered when the rustling in the underbrush signaled her prey was near. She squatted behind a tree and waited patiently, while she nocked the arrow against the bowstring.

"They're too fast." A chill raced down her back when Kellen whispered the words near her ear.

"Quiet," she scolded him.

"Sorry." She could hear the laughter in his voice.

Sterling listened carefully to the rustling and followed the sound with the tip of the arrow. A fat rabbit hopped out from under the bush, its nose sniffing the air while its ears twitched about listening for danger. Sterling pulled the bowstring taut and aimed down the shaft of the arrow. Just as she was ready to release the arrow Kellen shifted, snapping a twig beneath his boot. The rabbit bolted at the noise. Sterling quickly stood while she continued to aim. She released the arrow just before the rabbit could disappear into the leaf litter and the underbrush of the forest. It let out a little squeak as it fell to its death.

Sterling retrieved the rabbit. She and Kellen retreated to the camp where she dressed the rabbit, skewered the meat with small sticks and propped them beside the fire to roast.

Kellen's stomach growled at the smell of the meat cooking, "I'm so glad we do not have to eat dried meat tonight."

Sterling glanced sideways at him, at his strong profile. He had high cheekbones and a noble nose. His hair was blonde with careless waves hanging about his face. When he looked at Sterling it was with clear blue eyes that pierced her with their intensity. Sterling wondered if all the men from his country looked like Kellen.

His Beracian accent was slight, but the throaty undertones were unmistakable. She had found that she loved to hear him speak and decided to try to start a conversation.

She looked over to him again and said, "So, you're from Berac. Aren't you awfully far from home?"

He was quiet for a moment, but a slight smile creased his lips to reveal white teeth. "Aye, I grew up in Berac, but left home when I was nineteen."

Sterling couldn't imagine walking away from her family. Hemi, Brigit, Mother Anwell. They were the only family she had, and now they were gone. But to leave the ones you love knowing they were worried? She responded, "Doesn't it bother you that they could be concerned about you? What of your mother or father? Surely they want you to come home."

Kellen shrugged, "Possibly, but my father was never an easy man and he showed little emotion over such things as family. When I told him I did not want to go into the family business we had a huge fight and I left." He smiled at Sterling, "That was five years ago and now here I am with you, running from the Severon for some unknown and mysterious reason."

Sterling reached out and turned the rabbit. They sat in an awkward silence until Kellen asked a question she'd been asking herself, "Why are the Severon after you?"

"I didn't get a chance to ask them while they were murdering my family," Sterling responded tersely. "Sorry," she felt guilty for snapping at him, "it's because of these," she said, pointing at her eyes.

"They are unique," Kellen said, then added, "and beautiful."

"D- do you think we lost him for good?" she stuttered awkwardly, unaccustomed to being complimented.

"Probably not," Kellen surmised. "That tracker of theirs is insanely good. We should stay off the road and avoid towns and people as much as possible."

"We?" She was surprised by his comment. She hadn't expected him to stay with her all the way to Kai'Vari, "You don't even know where I'm going."

Kellen laughed at her surprise, "It is easy to tell you're not from Duenin. Dueninians are pasty white and with that tan skin and silver eyes of yours I'd say you're headed south to Kai'Vari or possibly Paard."

Your father was a Kai'Varian warrior. Hemi's words kept swirling around in Sterling's head. She was a Kai'Varian as was her father, Khort Rin'Ovana. She said her full name out loud. The words sounded strange on her lips as she repeated them again. "Sterling Rin'Ovana." It had a nice ring to it, but it would take time for her to get used to not saying Sterling Rhesida. There was a family waiting for her in a new land, a place where she could start over and heal. And then one day she would get her revenge. She would hunt down Engram and dole out the punishment he deserved.

"Is it done yet?" Kellen's question brought her back to the task at hand.

Sterling handed the roasted rabbit to Kellen and his delighted sigh made Sterling laugh. She took a bite of the meat and reveled in the deliciousness of not having to eat dried meat and bread again.

"From now on, you're hunting for our dinner," Kellen said around a mouthful of rabbit.

"We'd starve if I left it up to you," Sterling quipped. She took another bite then stated, "We'll make it to Kai'Vari. I'm sure of it."

"We have to lose that tracker first," Kellen said, "the Severon are not ones I want to tangle with."

They sat in silence for what seemed like hours as the night sky filled with stars, with only the sounds of the night echoing through the trees. She couldn't contain the long sigh of relief after eating her fill.

Kellen's expression changed, a furrow etched in to his brow, "The Severon will be watching the main roads, so we should stick to the smaller, secondary roads." He thought for a moment then added, "Knowing the Severon, they'll be watching the secondary roads as well. We should try to avoid traveling during the day. There are tiny hamlets that even the Severon would ignore, we'll head south skirting those small towns."

"It sounds impossible," Sterling laughed, but there was no humor. Kellen's words sunk into her heart darkening the mood.

Kellen stood and looked down at Sterling, "Don't worry, we'll make it to Kai'Vari. We'll find your family." He picked up his sword then said, "I'm going to check out the area, make sure no one saw us."

Sterling watched silently as Kellen's broad back disappeared into the darkness. She was thankful for this forested area and its respite from Duenin's flat landscape and the relentless early summer heat. Sterling leaned her head back against the bark of the tree and closed her eyes for a moment, just until Kellen returned.

The green, swampy water bubbled in the deep ruts along the trail like a festering wound. The sky's angry clouds were reflected in the water's dark depths. Sterling looked up and watched the roiling clouds darken as lightning lit the inside of the cloud, thunder rumbled like a massive heartbeat of some wild beast. The sun struggled to keep the dark clouds at bay, its ray shining through the darkness giving her hope that the storm would pass.

It was the same as it has always been. Ever since these dreams started the landscape of the valley changed, but the walls remained the same. This time the valley was a flat plain with sunken ruts that dug deep in the small road that cut its way through the dream's lowlands. Sterling knew if she followed the road it would end at the edge of a wall, with no way out.

The few trees that did dot the landscape, swayed in the increasing wind. Their shadows danced upon the ground like a pagan ritual, praying to the gods that held court in this desolate valley. Their shadows slowly faded as the darkness swallowed the last vestiges of the sun's rays as the sky opened and the rain started. Thunder growled in the depths of the storm just after a streak of lightning raced across the sky and struck a tree. Sparks flew in all directions, lighting the area with a bright flash.

The energy gathered in the clouds again as another streak shot across the sky and landed closer to Sterling. She stumbled backward but kept her footing. The clouds seemed to growl at her as another bolt shot from the sky, one after another in rapid succession they seemingly chased Sterling across the valley. The tall cliff face loomed over her as she pressed her back into the rock. A deep growl gathered in the darkened sky as it prepared to release another bolt upon her. As the sky flashed again, Sterling put her arms across her face as a voice boomed in her head, "*Othail gee Elementals!*"

Sterling jolted awake as the expected bolt of lightning struck her. She gasped for breath for a moment trying to gather her wits.

Where am I? She realized she was in the same secluded spot. The stars dotted the night sky.

Sterling glanced around in the soft moon light and found Kellen leaning against the tree beside her. "Bad dream?" he asked, his eyes still closed.

"Something like that," Sterling responded behind unexpected tears.

Without saying a word, Kellen's arm wrapped around Sterling and pulled her to his side. She leaned into his warmth but held all the emotions that wanted to escape in check. It would do her no good if she let the emotions come flooding to the forefront. He held her gently. "Crying is not a sign of weakness," Kellen said softly.

She wanted to cry for those she had lost and for the feeling of hopelessness that had gripped her since the Severon had taken away her family. She wanted to cry, but instead repeated the words said to her more times that she could remember, "Crying doesn't solve problems, it only makes your eyes red and your nose runny."

Kellen took a deep breath and shifted, pulling her closer. He offered no words of comfort, for no words would ease the pain in her heart. He simply held her until the pull of exhaustion was too strong. She gave up her struggles and fully nestled into Kellen's warmth, closing her eyes to the stars above.

10

HONEY

Thirteen days Later
Dan'Idou, 26th Unda, 1021

The fire was warm. Sterling leaned closer to the flames, her hands out trying to absorb the fire's warmth. Goose pimples raised the hairs on her skin as a damp chill took hold. They had been caught in a sudden and vicious storm and were barely able to make it to a shallow cave before the large hail stones pelted the forest, ripping leaves and limbs from the surrounding trees. Thankfully the storm had passed quickly, but they were both soaked through and through and with the cool spring night air they were both chilled.

"Here," Kellen said as he draped a blanket over her shoulders, "get out of your wet clothes before you catch a cold." Kellen turned his back to offer more privacy.

"Thanks," she said. Her cheeks turned red at the thought of undressing so close to Kellen. He usually left their campsite when she needed some privacy. But she knew the last thing they needed was either one of them sick with a cold.

Somehow, they had kept ahead of the Severon and the persistent tracker that had dogged them since Hemrac. They'd made a few mistakes along the way, like wandering too close to a village and discovering bounty posters hung along the gates to a village. Fortunately, they had managed to leave the area before any of the villagers were up and about their morning routines. Since then they had avoided the main roads and stayed out of any villages. The fewer people they encountered, the better.

Kellen had artfully navigated the landscape, so their trail was difficult to pick up. For three weeks Sterling had followed every order he'd barked at her and they had finally managed to outwit that dog of a tracker. Sterling laughed silently, *had it only been three weeks since Kellen saved her at the Inn in Hemrac?* It seemed as though they had been running for months. But despite all their efforts at hiding their tracks, the anxiety of being caught was wearing heavily on Sterling.

She huddled under the blanket and peeled the wet fabric from her arms. Hungry, she was distracted by the smell of roasting meat and it caused her stomach to growl with displeasure.

"Are you done yet?" Kellen's voice reached her under the blanket. His voice had a way of pulling her out of her thoughts. "I've seen you naked. You don't have to huddle under that blanket like a shy virgin."

It embarrassed her that Kellen continued to bring up the fact he'd seen her naked. He thought it funny to see her cheeks redden at their second meeting. She pulled off her boots and struggled to pull the leather pants down her damp legs. She managed to get them half way down, "I'm stuck," She laughed out loud.

"Need some help?" She could hear the laughter in his voice. "Here, give me your feet." Before she knew what was happening he'd grabbed hold of her bare feet throwing her onto her back, flipping the blanket up and over her head in the process.

"Wait!" she shouted, as she tried to pull the blanket around her, but he had her legs up in the air and her pants off before she could cover herself, leaving her with only the short braies for modesty.

Their eyes met for a brief second until Sterling realized she was lying before him, her chemise pressed to her damp skin. She scrambled backward, covering herself in the process. Kellen turned away and busied himself with laying her clothes out to dry. He had pulled his shirt off and laid it next to hers. Sterling couldn't take her eyes off him. His back was broad, though he wasn't a large man, he was lean and muscular. She watched as the muscles flexed under his tanned skin. He had an air about him that brought light into her world. It seemed he instinctively knew when she was thinking of Brigit and Hemi, it was then he would do something crazy or silly, ultimately lifting her spirits.

She'd told him very little of what had happened. She had only mentioned that Engram had murdered her family. The details were still too raw for her to speak of.

Sterling was thankful for his company. Without him there was no telling where she would be right now, probably locked up in the dark belly of Sionaad. The Severon prison was notorious for being inescapable. Even tales of the towering white fortress had reached as far north as Shee.

Kellen stood, grabbing a dry shirt from his pack and pulling it over his head. "I'm going to scout the area and make sure our tracks are covered." He stared at her for a moment. A soft smile touched his lips as he turned and vanished into the darkness.

Sterling watched Kellen as he faded into the night. She was accustomed to this routine now, but the first time Kellen had left her he'd been gone for hours. She'd thought he had abandoned her to the lonely night. She'd been near tears when he emerged from the darkness. She'd not felt such relief in a very long time. Now, Sterling was used to Kellen being gone while he scouted the area to make sure there was no hint of the trail leading to their camp. But tonight, he seemed more solemn than usual. He didn't have the sparkle in his eyes that normally reassured her.

"Is everything all right?" She asked as he reappeared out of the darkness.

"Huh?" He seemed surprised by her question, "Oh, yes. Everything is fine, the trail is clear and there was no sign of that *dog*."

"Maybe we lost him for good this time." Sterling let out a pent-up breath she hadn't realized she been holding.

"He is persistent if not anything else." Kellen crouched by the fire and warmed his hands. "I'm starved," he added, as he turned a rabbit so the uncooked side was facing the fire.

They fell silent as they ate one of the rabbits Sterling had caught. Only the crackle of the orange fire broke the intense quiet of the night. The meat was delicious and as she took a bite the juice ran down her chin. Sterling quickly wiped her face and licked the remainder from her fingers. She looked up to find Kellen staring at her intently. She could feel her cheeks blush as their eyes connected over the dancing flames. Sterling quickly averted her gaze and pulled the blanket tighter across her shoulders.

"That pendant that you wear, it is quite odd, but it suits you," he said, breaking the awkward silence.

"Oh this?" she said as she lifted the pendant from between her breasts and held it up to the firelight. "It belonged to my mother, but I don't know anything else about it." Sterling examined the black-ish-gray stone that had been with her since she was a child. It was a luminescent gray with flecks of silver mixed in, giving the stone an almost ethereal effect in the light. It was a narrow cylindrical shaped pendant that was the length of her fingers. "My uncle always said that as long as I wore this pendant my mother would be close to my heart and she would protect me from harm," she said. She let the pendant fall back between her breasts as they fell into silence. "A lot of good it's done me so far."

"You're still alive, aren't you?" Kellen poked the fire. "So, what will you do once you get to Kai'Vari?"

She'd asked herself that same question hundreds of times since she fled the orphanage. Hemi had told her that her father was a Kai'Varian warrior, but he also mentioned that Khort had instructed him to hide her, but from who? The question had swirled around in her head since Hemi had revealed the truth to her. "I suppose I'll look for my father's family, though all I have is a name."

"You should start in Sela'Char, the capital. I hear they keep a record of family names." Kellen laughed, "You never know, you may even be *nobility*."

Sterling giggled at his remark, "I seriously doubt that. My father was a warrior, a soldier, there is no way a soldier would be nobility."

Kellen offered her a piece of the second rabbit that had been roasting alongside the fire. "Your highness," he bowed with an over exaggeration, "may I present to you a fine feast of wild rabbit, the taste so delicate it will bring tears to your eyes?"

Sterling pulled a bare arm out from beneath the warmth of the blanket. She took a generous bite of the meat, "A fine feast indeed," Sterling quipped. "What about you? Where will you go?" she asked around a mouth full of food.

He was silent for a moment, "I haven't decided, but I've heard rumors of a treasure located in Du'Gald. I might try my hand as a treasure hunter." He laughed at his own comment.

"What kind of treasure?" Sterling was curious.

"Supposedly a treasure of gold was hidden in a volcanic cave."

"Hmm, sounds interesting." She sat back and finished off the rabbit.

"You should come with me," Kellen said after a brief silence.

"What?" Sterling thought she'd heard him wrong, "Come with you?"

"Forget about Kai'Vari, come with me to Du'Gald. The Severon will never find you there."

Sterling was silent for a moment then shook her head slowly, "No, I need to find my family."

If he was disappointed, Kellen hid it artfully behind his blue eyes. "Well, if you change your mind…," his words trailed off as he took another bite of rabbit.

The food was delicious and once her belly was full Sterling could no longer contain the yawn. The rain had stopped, but the cold night air had seeped under her skin. The warmth of the blanket combined with the fire could not keep a shiver from racing down her spine. She looked longingly at her clothes, still drying.

"You better get some rest. The morning will be here soon." Kellen stood and cleared a space for her to lie down, "I'm afraid we've lingered longer than I would have liked."

Sterling lay down, while Kellen busied himself with checking their packs for the next day. The rhythmic dancing of the fire drew her attention and she had a difficult time looking away. She watched as the flames danced to a silent rhythm. The movement was mesmerizing and the longer she stared the more she was pulled into the dance. The sounds of Kellen rummaging through his pack faded away. The night sounds of crickets and frogs dimmed until all she could hear was the hiss and crackle of the dancing fire. Sterling lost all awareness of her surroundings until it was only she and the flames that remained. Her eyes widened as the flames began to shape and form into familiar images. Tears formed when a tiny image of Hemi appeared in the center of the fire. He stood there looking back at her, hands on his hips as if scolding her. The flame cracked and the image of Hemi was replaced with Brigit. Her tiny visage, just about four inches tall, skipped and hopped about in a circle and then stopped and smiled at Sterling, her little hand waving with exuberance. Brigit reached her hand out as if asking for Sterling to follow her. Tears rolled down her cheeks as she pulled her arm out from the blanket and reached for the little girl's hand.

"Sterling! What are you doing?" Kellen's fierce words brought Sterling back. He was holding her hand, stopping her just inches from placing her hand in the flames. "Are you trying to catch yourself on fire?"

Sterling could feel the dampness the tears had left behind still on her face. The feeling of loneliness had left her heart empty and dry. She missed her family so much and the fire had been so kind to let her see them once again.

"Your hands are like ice and you're shivering. We've got to get you warmed up." Kellen pulled the blanket back and wrapped himself around Sterling before covering them both, "Why didn't you tell me you were so cold?"

"What are you doing? Get off me!" Sterling tried to push Kellen away. He was too close, his arm wrapped around her holding her flush to his chest.

"Be still. Our combined body heat will warm you in no time."

Sterling's face was blazing hot from embarrassment. The length of her body was pressed against Kellen's as their feet entangled with each other. She could feel every fiber of the cotton pants that were pressed against her legs. There was no inch of her that could not feel the warmth that his body offered. Kellen wrapped his arms around her, moving her face into his neck. His heartbeat thumped strongly beneath her hands, pressed against his bare chest. He held her like that until she no longer shivered. The heat of his body had seeped into hers, relieving the pain the cold had brought on.

He relaxed his arms until she was lying on her back, his arm her pillow. She stared up at the fire lit ceiling of the cave unsure of what to do or say next. "Thank you." Sterling blushed, how silly the words sounded.

Kellen smiled as he pulled his arm from beneath her and propped his head on the bent arm. "What did you see in the fire?" he asked as he pushed a strand of hair away from her face.

Sterling stared up at the ceiling of the cave searching for the right words, would he understand if she told him what had happened? "Memories," she said as her eyes returned to his. She was taken aback by their intensity and their intent. She drew in a breath as he leaned toward her. Her heart beat exploded in her chest as she felt his warm breath against her lips.

"I've never met anyone like you before," he whispered just before his lips touched hers. His lips pressed against hers as he deepened the kiss. A shiver ran down the length of her body as his hand wandered up her side to pause alongside her breast. Her body tightened at first, but it relaxed as he pulled her in close to him and deepened the kiss further. A groan escaped his mouth as he rubbed his body along hers. His leg pushed its way between hers as he leaned in to her. His hand was gentle as it caressed her breast. With unexpected pleasure, she felt she would burst out of her skin.

His hand left her breast, for a moment, to cup her cheek as the kiss deepened yet again. The taste of honey filled her senses as he slipped his tongue between her lips. The feeling of his body pressed against hers was like nothing she'd felt before. She moaned into his mouth and ran her hands through his hair, holding him close to her, deepening the kiss.

For a mere moment, their eyes locked. A look of recognition, or remembrance, perhaps, briefly crossed his face.

Sterling was surprised when Kellen pulled away abruptly, breathing heavily and obviously affected by her kiss. His pupils were dilated, and his eyes had a hint of anger shining in them. He turned over, without saying a word, presenting his back to her. "Kellen?" The sudden change confused her. "What's wrong?"

He mumbled a terse, "Go to sleep," without turning back toward her.

She muttered, "I don't under…"

Cutting her off, he said, "Go to sleep Sterling, we've a long day ahead of us tomorrow."

She was confused by his actions and hurt by his dismissal. "Good night, Kellen," she whispered as she rolled over with her back to him. She lay for some time staring at the flames hoping the images of Hemi and Brigit would return to console her, but the flames never returned to their dance.

She had trouble falling asleep, her body still tingled from Kellen's touch. *Why had he turned away from me?* Had she angered him somehow? He seemed to be enjoying the kiss as much as she had, so why turn away? Her face flushed as she thought back to the moment his tongue had pressed against her lips, he had tasted of honey. Sterling thought that odd as her eyelids drooped and she eventually fell asleep.

The nightmares came without delay.

11

DUPLICITY

Dan'Ruok, 27th Unda, 1021

"Wake up." The words came from a distance booming from the ravaged sky of the valley. Sterling looked up into the unending rain. "Wake up." The voice was familiar as it echoed throughout the valley.

Sterling squeezed her eyes shut for a moment and when she opened them she was staring up at the ceiling of the cave. Kellen stood over her with an impatient look in his blue eyes. "We need to get out of here before they find us." He dropped her dried clothes into her lap. "Get dressed." She watched as he left her alone in the cave.

Why was he so angry? The kiss they shared flooded her memory and caused her cheeks to burn. "What was I thinking?" she said aloud as she stood and pulled her clothes on. The fabric was stiff from drying overnight, but she was thankful for the warmth. Kellen had already extinguished the fire and readied the horses for travel, but he had not returned by the time she'd finished dressing. She sat down and waited.

She tried not to think about the kiss they'd shared. Why had he turned away so abruptly? Had she angered him somehow? She couldn't think of anything she had done wrong and he seemed so… *eager*. She had enjoyed his touch and had not wanted him to stop. If he hadn't turned away would he have made love to her?

Sterling sat up with a start as a thought came to her. *Am I in love with Kellen?* She wouldn't deny the feelings that had grown in her heart toward him. The past weeks they had spent together had felt good despite the Severon on their heels. *Do I love Kellen?* she thought again. She wasn't sure she was ready to call the feelings she felt love, but she thought that given time she could fall in love with him. His smile brought light to her darkest moments.

"Are you ready?"

Sterling jumped when the disgruntled words reached her. She stood and wiped the dirt off her trousers, "Yes."

"Let's go, the Severon would not have stopped through the night."

Sterling couldn't help the scowl that formed. "Well, good morning to you too," she said under her breath.

"We don't have time for pleasantries."

Kellen mounted, but did not wait for Sterling to mount before he rode off down the sloping hill toward a rutted trail that would lead them south through the forest. She pulled herself into the saddle and rode after him. *He is being an ass*, she thought as she caught up with him. Mimicking one of the younger children at the orphanage, she stuck her tongue out at him. The gesture somehow relieved some of the pent-up anger that had been brewing inside her.

"How long will it be until we reach the border?" She urged her smaller horse to ride alongside his so she could hear his answer, but he ignored her. "It's been almost a month since we left Hemrac, it couldn't be that much further could it?" Still nothing. His eyes never veered from the road ahead of them. She tried again, "Another week, do you suppose?"

Finally, he glanced at her. She was taken by the hostility that looked back at her. "We will get there when we get there." He kicked his horse and rode ahead not looking back.

Sterling felt the blood drain from her face. His words had hurt. She felt a pain in her chest as she watched him get further away. The blood quickly returned as anger replaced the hurt. *How dare he treat me that way?* she fumed to herself. Playing on her emotions and then throwing her aside like yesterday's trash.

A pain started radiating from the base of her skull as her anger grew. *Great,* she thought, *he's given me a headache.* She kicked the horse into a gallop until she was riding next to him once again. "What is wrong with you?"

"Nothing," he said, not looking at her.

The pain increased as her anger grew. "What do you mean *nothing?* The kiss we shared last night certainly wasn't nothing."

"You should just forget about last night."

"I will," she said, pulling on the reins so she was no longer beside him. Had she really thought she loved him? For the remainder of the time they spent on the small trail she glared at his back. The pain at the base of her skull had increased as the minutes passed.

Eventually Kellen turned off the path when they reached a dry river bed. "This is a short cut and will throw them off our trail."

The pain that had started in the base of her skull had nearly engulfed all her senses. She could see 'that Kellen's lips were moving, but the words did not reach her. She desperately clung to the horn of the saddle to keep from falling. It took all her control just to stay upright.

"Kellen." Her words barely made it past her lips before they evaporated into the morning air.

He must have sensed something was wrong. Kellen stopped along the dry bed and turned in the saddle to look at her, but he made no mention of how she looked or how she was struggling.

Instead he dismounted, "We'll stop here for a moment. My horse seems to have picked up a rock."

Sterling was thankful for the pause. She gripped the pommel and somehow swung her leg over the saddle and slid down the side of the horse. She leaned against the weight of the animal, drawing in deep breaths hoping to ease the pain that had now encompassed her entire body. Every inch of her throbbed in time with the pain centered at the base of her skull, "Kellen, help." Her words were barely audible.

I must get to Kellen, she thought, *he will help me.* She carefully pushed away from the horse, holding on with one hand. She started walking toward Kellen, who was bent over examining the front hoof of his horse, his back to her.

The morning sun was blinding as it topped the tree line along the banks of the dried river bed. Sterling put her hand up to shield her eyes from the painful light. "Kellen," she spoke softly. She took another cautious step toward his bent head, but still he did not hear her. The pain continued to radiate throughout her body, but it had somewhat lessened in intensity. "Kellen," she said his name again as she came up beside him. "Kellen, help me." *Why can't I speak louder?* she thought. *Why can't he hear me?* She looked over his shoulder just as he released the hoof. "Kellen, my head," she gasped as the pain intensified to the point she thought she'd black out.

Kellen turned to face her but avoided eye contact with Sterling. Instead, his eyes were focused on something behind her. As she started to turn to see what had his attention the world around her went black as a bag was thrown over her head. The pain that had consumed her suddenly vanished releasing her body from its paralyzing effects. Her hand went up and tried to pry the dusty fabric from her face. However, the more she struggled the more difficult it was for her to breathe with the dust that filled the bag. A fit of coughing erupted from her lungs.

"Stop struggling." The thick fabric of the bag muffled Kellen's words. He took hold of her hands and wrapped a rope around her wrist, the coarse fibers abrading her skin. She tried yanking her hands out of his, but he pulled them back and finished tying her hands together. He released his hold, but he did not step away. She could feel the warmth of his body as he stepped closer to her, his hands went to her shoulders as he leaned into her, his mouth beside her ear. "I am sorry," he whispered to her. He pushed back, ripping the chain from around her neck as he stepped away.

"Why? Why are you doing this?" There was no response to her question, "Kellen! Why?"

"You've done a magnificent job, Kellen." The blood in Sterling's veins went cold at the voice that complimented Kellen, "Perhaps we'll do business again someday." The sound of a pouch of coins being tossed and then caught rang through Sterling's head.

As suddenly as the bag had been thrown over her head it was yanked off, the morning sun blinding her for a moment. She raised her bound hands to shield her eyes. Standing before her, with an evil grin spread across his face was Commander Engram. The man who had murdered everyone she had loved in this world, the man who had taken everything away from her. Without a thought Sterling lunged toward him, her bound hands beating his chest. He fended her off easily, knocking her to the ground.

"Take her to my horse." Engram turned his back on her and said something to Kellen before he mounted his horse.

"Kellen!" Sterling yelled across the distance to Kellen's retreating back, "Kellen!"

Two of the Commander's men lifted Sterling to her feet and started carrying her off. Sterling struggled and pushed one away, looking back over her shoulder to find Kellen riding away, "I curse you Kellen! I curse the day you were born. I'll find you and cut the heart out of your chest!" Anger like she had never felt before consumed her. Her vision blurred as it was filled with a hatred that she would never forget. "If I ever see you again I'm going to kill you!"

Engram stepped into her line of sight, blocking her view of the retreating Kellen. He was close, so close that she could smell honey on his breath. Realization struck home as Kellen's betrayal became clear to her, *the two had shared a drink.*

"Would you please just shut up?" Engram barked at her. His hand connected with Sterling's face, knocking her to the ground. Her head struck a rock and pain raced down to her toes. Her vision blurred as she watched Kellen fade into the darkness.

"Now that's better." Engram stepped over her and it was his face that filled her vision as it went completely black.

12

BY ANY MEANS NECESSARY

Nine Days Later
Dan'Yin, 7th Solum, 1021

Engram stood at attention within the interior chamber of the Orom's personal quarters. His heart was beating so fast he found it difficult to breathe. The Orom was furious. The former king sat back in a fine leather chair, his fingers interlocked in a judgmental manner, "I send you on a simple errand. An errand that could bring me one step closer to the end of a lifetime of struggle. And you manage to completely miss the fact that the one item I expressly requested you bring back is missing."

Engram swallowed hard, every muscle in his face suddenly was made of stone as he tried to speak. "Milord, the bounty hunter hired to track her must have taken the pendant without anyone knowing."

The Orom scoffed. "Excuses. All I hear from you are pitiful little excuses. I grow tired of excuses. Especially from you, *Commander*." The old king sat back in his chair, a heavy sigh escaping his grizzly looking frame. "Have your men found this Beracian yet?"

"I've sent my best tracker after him," Engram nodded curtly. He prayed Phayo would find Kellen Leiten soon. His life, and Engram's life for that matter, depended on it. Engram felt like a bug under a boot as the Orom stared at him. Vaan Tydar, the 35th Orom, was not a man given to patience. He was unforgiving when crossed and did not abide disobedience in his subordinates.

Younger than any previous man to hold the title, the Orom was a very strong man that stood head and shoulders above the army that served him. Many speculated he was in his late sixties, but no one in the Severon ranks was certain of the Orom's true age. He had hazel eyes and pale skin all topped by a head full of shockingly white hair. His fingers were long and had a powerful grip, a strong grip Engram had seen used on servants that had not reacted quickly enough for the Orom's taste. He expected his orders to be carried out without question and he demanded results. Engram had witnessed many of his fellow Severon fall to the Orom's rage. Engram had risen through the ranks of the Severon army by following every order handed down without question and completing each task with perfection.

But this bounty hunter, Kellen Leiten, had ruined his perfect record. The Beracian had contracted with the Severon several times to hunt down Devians within the Duenin territory, and he had come through repeatedly. Until now.

Kellen had left a trail for Phayo while he had been with the Devian. Engram had simply been patient while the bounty hunter led the girl closer to Sionaad and his waiting arms. The man truly was worth the price he charged for his services. Sterling was completely caught off guard when Kellen handed her over.

"As you know, Commander, I will not tolerate failure in my ranks." The Orom's desk was placed just in front of a sweeping wall of windows. The bright light coming in from the windows concealed the Orom's expression.

"Yes, my lord. I am aware," Engram bowed at the waist.

The Orom pursed his lips and stood. He waved Engram over to follow as they made their way to the main audience chamber. "You have been a valuable asset these past fifteen years," he said as he walked slowly beside Engram, who he himself made sure to stay but one step behind and to the right of his liege. The Orom's long black and red robes trailed behind him, his deep-set eyes glittering in the dark spaces of the hallways as they walked. "It would be a shame for this one blemish on an otherwise perfect record be your downfall, and," the Orom paused, turned to look at Engram while a snarl played upon his face, "more ambitious men than you have already felt my wrath. You would be no different."

Orom Tydar's hazel eyes pierced Engram to his core, with unabated menace behind them. Engram bowed his head submissively. *Damn it Phayo, you better come through*, he thought, adding, *I would like to keep my head.*

"Yes, my lord," he answered respectfully, while his hand went instinctively to his own throat. The Orom stepped away to gaze out the wall of windows that overlooked the wide, sweeping entryway to Sionaad. The gleaming white towers of the Severon headquarters held reign over the surrounding countryside.

"Have you interrogated the girl yet?" the Orom asked as he continued to glance out across the kingdom he had forged, quite literally with fire and sword.

"For two weeks, my lord. She is," Engram paused, "proving to be rather resilient. She has not revealed the location of the Shards."

The Orom grimaced. "She is a Devian, is she not? They're all the same. Stubborn until the end. You simply need to find the right method to... motivate her into talking. Then she'll tell you anything you ask.

It was true the girl was a Devian, but from what Engram had gathered she had been raised in the orphanage near Shee. But he knew Devians and he knew their bloodlines. They instinctively understood where the Shards were located. "She will," Engram agreed, "and we will utilize everything at our command to pull the information out of her."

"Good, good," Orom Tydar nodded, as he seemed to study every brick, every cobblestone in this kingdom. He turned his head toward Engram, "The Devians are hard to come by, we must not squander this gift before us, by any means necessary accomplish the task."

With that simple command said, he waved a hand in dismissal. Engram clicked his heels together, bowed, and let himself out of the Orom's chambers. A sigh of relief rushed from his lungs as he rubbed his neck again. He was lucky his head was still attached. Death by beheading was not something that he was looking forward to as his... retirement.

Engram made his way down the long stairwell that led from the Orom's chambers at the top of Sionaad to a nondescript door that stood in a dark hallway. Two guards stood at attention on either side of the door. The Orom's final command tumbled around in Engram's mind. *By any means necessary...* He stood there for what felt like an eternity as those words seemed to ring in his head. He shook himself out of his stupor, straightening himself gently and clearing his throat. "I've come for the prisoner."

One of the guards pulled a set of keys from his belt and with a soft thud the lock was released. He opened the door and stepped aside to let Engram by. Engram stopped and looked to the guards, "Bring me a bucket of water."

"Yes, Commander." Engram followed the guard down the narrow stairway. The atmosphere changed the further he descended, going from the clean affluent air of the Orom's chambers to a dank musty air that was filled with pain and regret.

The sounds the guard made as he pumped water into a bucket echoed up the stairs, becoming louder as Engram reached the bottom. A narrow hallway of cells lay at the foot of the long staircase. This prison was not part of the main dungeon at Sionaad where normal prisoners were held. This hidden prison was reserved for Devians. In each of the six cells were Devians waiting for his presence. They were a stubborn lot and did not give their secrets up easily. Many had gone to their grave with their secrets still held to their chest, but it was from these Devians they first learned of the Union Key and of a possible second location in Du'Gald.

He paused for a moment and examined the wall filled with the tools he needed for interrogation. Knives, whips, straps, razors, and various saws and hammers were hanging closest to where he stood. He smiled to himself and selected a riding crop with a metal tipped end. He continued to where the guard waited outside Sterling's door, grabbing the bucket of water on his way.

Engram peered through the tiny window. Sterling lay huddled in the corner with her arms covering her head. *How pathetic*, he thought. She was stronger than any other Devian he'd met. She refused to speak and when he did enter her cell she glared at him with those damned silver eyes.

Engram turned the key in the lock and stepped inside, emptying the bucket of water on her head. She gasped and quickly sat up as she was doused in the icy liquid, her eyes widening in shock. Once she gained her senses and realized what had happened she backed herself even further into the corner of her cell. The cell was dark, save for the meager light from the torch that just barely lit the hallway. He could just see the tips of her toes and the silvery gleam of her eyes shining in the darkness like tiny moons against the night sky.

Chills inched down his spine as depravity slowly took hold. Never, never in his life had a Devian affected him like this. It made him angry that she had that much power over him. *By any means necessary*, repeated over and over in his mind. He heard, and he obeyed. "Get up," he said, as he walked toward her in the tiny cell. His command was rejected with a growl.

"No!" She spat at him as Engram slammed the door behind him. "No!" she yelled again as Engram strode two more steps and hefted her up by her hair.

"I told you to get u-" Engram's rage was blindsided by a sharp kick to the shin. Despite her small size, the girl nearly broke his leg with that kick. Engram was furious. "You little bitch!" he backhanded Sterling so hard she was forced back against the grey stone wall, her head bouncing off the rock with a loud wet thud.

She was dazed by the hit and no longer struggled as he tied her hands together. Engram forcibly lifted Sterling by her bound hands and looped the rope around a hook that hung from the center of the cell. She stood on the very tips of her toes, her arms extended above her head in an uncomfortable position.

Engram stepped back, his breathing heavy, every muscle tense. Every fiber of his being wanted to simply strangle this woman and be done with it. The sting in his shin had become a dull throbbing sensation compared to the fury that was fueling his hate.

By any means necessary to accomplish the task.

Coming to her senses she stared at him with those defiant silver eyes. Those eyes had invaded his dreams at night igniting a lust he dare not admit to. His desire was overwhelming and it disgusted Engram, it angered him that she had this much control over him. In a fit of rage Engram lunged at her, tearing away at her clothing revealing the soft tender skin beneath. The orange flame danced, highlighting her exotic olive skin.

Sterling screamed, or at least Engram thought she did, as he began to force his body closer to hers. She cursed at him, he knew that much. He didn't care. He deserved every word that escaped her lips. But the dark lust that had plagued his dreams suddenly overtook him as he began to force himself on her. As he began to violate everything that was this woman, this Devian. Beyond this dark and violent wave, he knew nothing until the act was done.

By any means necessary.

13

PAIN

How many days, how many weeks of pain had she endured?
She had tried to keep count, but after so much pain and confusion
she'd lost track. What she thought were days and nights bled into
one another until the time seemed to drag on endlessly. The only
real passage of time was the sound of the guards when it was time to
change shifts. The ringing of their voices echoing off the stone walls
sent Sterling's body in to a panic. She knew she was not the only
prisoner in this dark pit. She could hear, despite the stone walls, the
screams and wails of other prisoners.

Engram had stripped her of her clothes leaving her naked
with nothing to protect her from the cold air that seeped in to the
cell. After these days and weeks, it seemed the cold had moved past

her muscles to her bones. She was stiff and found it difficult to move. But the cold stone soothed the heat radiating from her battered and lashed back. Sterling huddled in the corner forcing her body as far away from the door as possible, but no matter how small she made herself the damp walls of the cell seemed to close in on her. She shut her eyes, praying when she opened them she would wake up from this nightmare. But she knew this was her reality because when she slept the true nightmares began.

Kellen's betrayal had left a horrible and bitter taste in her mouth. She prayed daily to any god that would hear her for revenge upon his head. He had deceived her, making her think he cared for her when in the end, he had been leading her to the Severon all along. The kiss they had shared meant nothing to him. For her, it had been the beginning of love. She'd felt it whenever he happened to glance her way. The tightness in her chest had only grown the longer they spent together. She swore if she ever saw him again she would kill him, she would drive a knife through his heart. *I wonder if he even has a heart?* Sterling thought, as she pushed her back into the stone.

Her nightmares had continued to grow increasingly vivid, filled with images of Engram and Kellen. No matter where she turned in the unending dream valley, Engram and Kellen would be there mocking her, laughing at her attempts to escape the nightmarish landscape. She forced herself awake to get away from their demon eyes only to wake to the reality that was, itself, a nightmare.

She closed her eyes and rubbed the back of her neck. The tingling that had started the day of Kellen's betrayal had continued to plague her. No matter what she tried, nothing would alleviate the coursing pain that radiated from the base of her skull. The throbbing radiated from her neck and down her back reaching as far as the soles of her feet. This constant ache fought for dominance over the other pain that now suffused her body. The agony had only worsened from Engram's visits as he violated her repeatedly, tormenting her from head to toe, making her skin hypersensitive to the smallest of touches. *Was there no relief from this misery?*

The sound of the lock being turned jolted Sterling from her musings. As quick as she could she pushed herself from the cold floor to stand. If she wasn't quick enough the consequence would be an icy cold bucket of water. The door swung open and Engram stood in the opening, a bucket at the ready in case she was still on the floor.

"I see you've finally learned," he said, setting the bucket down. He stepped into the cell and closed the door behind him. Engram came to stand in front of Sterling, raising his hand to her cheek. He ran his fingers down her cheek to her shoulder, pushing the long hair out of the way. He lowered his hand to her breast, pausing as he cupped, then squeezed the tender flesh. Sterling flinched at his touch, which brought a smile to Engram's face. He ignored her disgust and slid his hand down to the raw skin of her bottom that had received a lashing not two days ago.

"Beautiful," he whispered as he lowered his mouth to her neck and placed a delicate kiss where her shoulder met her neck.

Sterling desperately swallowed the bile that suddenly rose.

"Have you decided to tell me what I want to know?" he whispered in her ear, his voice menacing.

If I tell him, would he leave me be? Sterling thought. She opened her mouth, but thought better of it, *no, he would know I was lying.* Instead she said the same words she repeated every time he asked the question, "I don't know anything about your Shards."

Engram stepped back, his brown eyes filled with anger, as he started to remove his jacket, "If you would only tell me the truth you would not have to endure the pain."

"I don't know anything," Sterling shook her head, "I've told you already, it's the truth."

"You lie!" Engram raised the riding crop in the air and swung it down slashing Sterling in the face, slicing open her lip.

"No!" she yelled as she tried to protect herself, but he was too powerful, and the crop came down again and again. "I don't know, I don't know!" she repeated the words, but to no avail.

PAIN

"Tell me the truth or I'll leave you in this pit to die!" The beating continued until Engram was out of breath and Sterling barely conscious. The sting where the crop had lashed her skin fought for dominance over the needling pain that prickled its way down her spine.

Engram wiped the spittle from his mouth when he paused in the door way to the cell, "You'll rot in here until you tell me what I want to know."

14

ISOLATION AND
LOATHING

One Hundred Eight Days Later
Dan'Kell, 29th Cadere, 1021

Sterling could feel her skin crawling with filth. For so long now she'd gone without a bath, left in this darkness to wallow in the dirt and grime of torture. She couldn't remember what fresh air smelled like or how good a gentle warm breeze felt against her skin. The sun's rays as they speckled the forest floor were lost to her, as were the sounds of laughter from Brigit as she frolicked in the field of wild flowers.

When did I last sleep? She had long been judging the days and nights by Engram's visits, but he had stopped coming to her cell. *Just as he had promised, he has left me here to die.* Sterling sat up, the fear of being alone gripped her heart and made breathing difficult. *Am I alone? Where is Engram?* She loathed the fact that she needed to see his face, that seeing him would bring her some relief from this loneliness.

Her only companion in these dark days since Engram had stopped coming was the constant pain that enveloped her body like a blanket. It reminded her she was alive, but also an endless reminder of those she had lost to the Severon. Despite the loneliness she felt, Engram's absence meant she had some relief from the constant questions and beatings. Her back was starting to heal and constantly itched. She had no doubt the wounds that crossed her back were infected.

Sterling laid on her side, her head was propped on her bent arm. Her eyes over the last days, weeks, or months had adjusted to the darkness so that she could see the edges between the stones. Her hearing had become acute and listened for the tiniest of sounds. The whimpers and pleas for release from the other prisoners bounced throughout the darkness like a wailsome melody.

As she lay there she listened to the silence that surrounded her. Her heartbeat sounded like a thundering beast in her ears. She'd taken to counting the beats. Inevitably she would lose count and have to start over at one. *10,645... 10,646... 10,647... 10,649... wait, no, it was 10,648 then 10,649.* Sterling tapped on the stone in time with her heart as she counted, *10,650... 10,651...*

The sudden clank of keys in the lock caused her to jump. *Engram!* She loathed the broken happiness she felt at seeing his face. But her loneliness was unbearable. Somehow, she forced herself, through the pain, to stand. She stood with her back to the far wall and waited for Engram to enter the cell. The door slowly opened with a long groan like a yawning beast. The torches in the hall were like the bright sun to her causing her eyes to squint. The light backlit the man standing in the doorway. It took her no time to realize that the man standing before her was not Engram. His frame was much shorter and thinner than Engram's lean muscular frame. His hair, highlighted by the orange flames was a dark brown and cut close to his scalp. He stood there for what seemed like ages just staring at Sterling, but because his face was in the shadows she could not see his expression.

"Where's Engram?" Sterling searched for her tormentor

"He was right," he said as he stepped into the cell, "you are insolent, but no matter. We will take care of that attitude soon enough." He stepped close to Sterling and took her chin in his hand and turned her head from side to side. "Such lovely eyes, you Devians are truly magnificent."

Sterling wrenched her face from his hold and glared up at him, "Who are you?" She asked again. "I want to see Engram." Sterling could feel the bile forming in the back of her throat at having to ask for Engram, but this man had a different feel about him. He seemed... cruel, sadistic.

The pain that had stayed with her suddenly increased, causing her breath to catch.

"I am Duke Helios." He ran a gloved hand down the side of her cheek to her neck where his grip tightened just enough to punctuate his words, "I'm here to get out of you what Engram could not."

Sterling felt a shiver of fear race down her spine as the pain in her neck increased. "I've told Engram everything I know, which is nothing."

"The Orom grows weary of your refusal to divulge where the Shards of Abaddon are located. Engram has failed at pulling this information out of that little mouth of yours, but I will succeed where he has not." He smiled down at Sterling, but there was no humor in his eyes, "Now then, why don't you tell me where the Shards are located."

"I don't know," Sterling shook her head, "I've never heard of these Shards. I keep telling Engram, I was raised away from any other Devians. *I do not know anything.*" Sterling was tired of repeating herself and growled the last few words through gritted teeth.

"You continue to tell lies." Helios's voice never wavered, "Devians by nature are drawn to the Shards of Abaddon, they are after all descendants of Moraug and Orla. The Shards are a part of them, what created them."

"I cannot tell you," Sterling gritted her teeth, "what I do not know."

"Royce!" he called out, never taking his eyes off Sterling.

"Here, milord." Helios stepped aside as a second man came into the cell. He wore the apron of a blacksmith and carried an iron pot filled with hot glowing coals. He placed the pot just inside the door and moved back out of the cell. His eyes never left the floor, as if he were afraid to look upon her.

Pain. The pain doubled as a second Severon stepped into the cell.

"Hold her," Helios commanded his subordinate.

Sterling attempted to dodge the guard, but in her weakened state she stumbled and was quickly overpowered. He grabbed her hair, forcing her head back at the same time he twisted her right arm up and back. "Please," she whispered in desperation.

She hated herself for begging. To be taken so low by these barbarians. She hated herself for this weakness. Tears gathered in her eyes as the pain radiating from her neck intensified beyond measure causing her vision to blur. Through the haze Sterling watched as Duke Helios pulled a glowing iron rod from the coals and walked slowly toward her. "Devians have such beautiful eyes. It would be quite a shame to destroy such beauty, but when one does not obey they are punished no matter how beautiful they are." He never took his gaze off her as he slowly moved the iron up her arm, "Perhaps this will motivate that tongue of yours."

Sterling's eyes widened, and a scream was ripped from her mouth as Helios pressed the length of the white-hot metal into the soft flesh of her forearm. Her body jerked away in reflex, but she was held in place by the second Severon. "I shall ask this only once. And you will answer. Or you will suffer. Simple. Now, where... are the Shards?" Helios asked in an impatient tone.

"I don't know," Sterling sobbed. Her body was lax, head hanging. "I don't know."

Duke Helios simply shook his head. "I do not believe you."

Sterling came out of her daze when Helios took hold of her other arm, "No." The words were a mere whisper never reaching beyond her lips.

Helios laughed as he pressed the hot iron into her other arm, scoring a mark from her wrist to her elbow. The breath rushed from her lungs, but it wasn't the pain from her arm that took her breath away, no it was the pain in her skull that radiated down her back to engulf her arms, her legs – every inch of her body was throbbing with the intense pain. It was all she knew, this pain until she could no longer control her body.

From a great distance, she heard Helios asking her once again about the location of the Shards. She felt her head being pulled back. Her vision went black as Duke Helios raised the hot metal to her eye.

Fire. An all-encompassing fire. That was the last thought, this dreamy memory in her head before Sterling lost herself to the black. A swirling, raging conflagration of fire. Like a tornado. One that swept through her body, engulfed her, but did not harm her. Screams. Men screaming in terror. In agony. The smell of burning flesh. The acrid taste of ash in her throat. Vengeance personified. Given form. Or a dream of the orphanage. At that moment, as the darkness of nothingness took her, she did not know.

It was in the great black darkness of solitude when she realized that the pain had disappeared. Her body felt odd without the constant pain heightening every pore. Sterling brushed the hair from her face and tried to push herself up from the floor. Had it all been a dream? Helios? Engram? Were they just a part of her nightmares? As she struggled to sit up, the throbbing pain from where Helios had branded her told Sterling it was not a dream.

She lifted her head and opened her eyes, blinking to clear the fog. At first, she was unsure of what she was seeing, but quickly realized the sightless eyes of Duke Helios stared up at her. She scurried away from him, his body covered in blood. Sterling looked around and found the second Severon. He lay dead, the metal iron shoved deep in his chest. His dead eyes stared unseeing at the ceiling of the tiny cell.

What happened here?

The last thing she remembered was the pain engulfing her.

Sterling scanned the cell. It was covered in blood; the walls were splattered with it and it pooled on the floor. Her naked body was covered in dried blood, and her hair dripped with the thick viscous liquid. A scream threatened to escape and she quickly covered her mouth with both hands trying desperately to contain it.

Where were the guards? Who had killed Helios, but left her alive?

The door stood open, the light from the torches illuminating Helios's sallow complexion. Using the wall for help, Sterling stood on shaking legs. She inched her way across the tiny cell to the door. She scanned the hall and fell backward when she saw one of the guards hanging from the wall. He had been impaled on one of the hooks that held many of Engram's torture implements. Another guard was slumped against the wall with his sword piercing his heart.

They were all dead.

A muffled sound caught her attention and she peered down the dimly lit hallway, at the end, in a dark corner, the blacksmith Royce, huddled with his arms around his legs and tears streaming down his face. His eyes stared blankly down the short hall as if waiting for something to come and get him. When their eyes connected he yelled out, "Stay away! Stay away from me."

Sterling turned quickly to see who was behind her, but she was alone in the hall. "Stay away you monster!" Unsure of what to say to the man she ducked back into the cell. There was no way she was going to stay and wait for the changing of the guards, but she couldn't make a run for it as she was now. Sterling quickly examined the two men in her cell and found Duke Helios was the smaller of the two and set about removing his uniform.

Despite his smaller size, his uniform swallowed Sterling. She rolled the sleeves up several times just so her hands were free. The rough fabric rubbed against her fresh wounds sending pain up her arms. She tucked the excess fabric into the boots that were far too large for her tiny feet and then tied the laces around her legs so the boots would not fall off. Sterling cinched his belt as tight as she could around her waist. The long sword nearly hitting the floor.

Sterling prayed the heavy uniform would not become too cumbersome. She took one last look at the cell that had been her prison. The blacksmith's quiet sobbing echoed down the hall and mirrored Sterling's own feelings. Her heart sobbed at all she had lost to the Severon. Sterling frowned, as she had never been one to feel sorry for herself. She hardened her heart and swore she would take her revenge upon the Severon. She would destroy them no matter the cost, they would pay for the crimes and the wrongs they had committed against those she had loved.

Sterling stood for a moment in the hall, looking at either end, unsure of which way to go. She'd been unconscious when they brought her to Sionaad, waking in the dank cell. She glanced back at the blacksmith. *He would know the way out*, she thought. Sterling started toward the cowering man and nearly tripped as a white, emaciated hand reached for her from under one of the heavy doors to the adjacent cell, "Help me," a feeble voice called out, "don't leave me here." The plea was joined by others from the long row of cells. Their chorus of cries sent Sterling into a panic. She couldn't leave them here to the same fate as she had endured.

"Where is the key?" she begged the blacksmith.

The blacksmith's eyes widened, "Stay away from me!" His cries echoed off the stone walls and most assuredly up the staircase.

The sounds of footsteps on the stairs sent Sterling's panic into a frenzy. "Give me the key," she begged again.

Sterling's heart stopped when the echoing of footsteps grew closer as they reached and began to descend the main stairs. The blacksmith hesitated, looking hopeful at the entrance, as if the new guard would be his salvation.

"Please," Sterling whispered. "Please."

His eyes shifted to Sterling and then back to the stairs. Taking pity on those locked away he handed her a set of keys that shook in his trembling hands. There were numerous keys on the ring and she fumbled to find the one that fit the door. Nervous, she dropped the keys with a loud clank.

The footsteps grew louder as the guards neared the bottom. She was out of time. Guilt scorched the pit in her stomach as she dropped the keys yet again, "I'm sorry," she whispered to the pleas of the other prisoners.

"Where does this lead?" Sterling asked Royce.

"St- stables," he stuttered.

Sterling ran up the stairs to freedom. She knew at once when the guards arrived at her cell. Footsteps scurrying around and the cell door hitting the wall as it was slammed open. "She's escaped!" one yelled out. "Duke Helios, he's dead."

Sterling reached the top of the stairs and pushed open the door that separated her from freedom. It was night and the stable yard was deserted. Torches lit the walkways and there were lights on in the barracks but save for the horses that were corralled, the yard was empty. She could not linger any longer. She pushed her way past the door and ran across the yard. The heavy uniform slowing her escape. The distance seemed to grow and lengthen. Just as she neared the gate the two guards emerged from the door. "There!"

Sterling climbed the wooden fence, but as she reached the top a guard grabbed hold of her foot. Sterling looked back and kicked with all her might, connecting with the man's nose. She heard the soft crunch as his nose spurted blood.

"Stop her, she is escaping!" The second guard made such a racket that men started emerging from the buildings. "Stop her!"

Without hesitation Sterling threw open the gate and jumped onto the back of one of the many horses that clamored for freedom.

She yelled out, kicking the giant beast into a full gallop and the remaining horses followed behind.

Sterling glanced back, her heart stopping as her eyes connected with Engram. He stood in the center of the yard, men and horses running about around him. But he was completely oblivious to the commotion. His eyes held such anger and hatred that Sterling could feel it in her bones. They were eyes of retribution and of steely resolve. She knew he would not let her go, and that no matter how far she ran he would find her. That's what she saw in those cold eyes.

Sterling turned away from her captors and leaned into the horse that now galloped with full force. The cool night air streaked past her face as tears of joy were lifted and carried away by the wind. She refused to ever look back again.

15

KAI'VARI FOUND

The sound of birds chirping merrily seemed to come from a great distance. Their melody was muffled by the throbbing in her ears. *Where am I?* she thought, opening one eye in a squint and then the other. Sterling's head felt as if it had become a great drum being played, though this pain was different than the overwhelming pain she'd felt in Sionaad. *My head*, she thought, *did they catch me?* Confused, looking around, she saw fields to her left, and a great, lathered, strong horse that appeared to be nearly dead to her right. Then she remembered. She understood the throbbing was from knocking her head against the hard ground when her horse collapsed from exhaustion. As the horse stumbled, Sterling had gone flying and

landed in a heap among the tall wheat grass of Duenin's southern plains.

She needed to get up, keep running, but her weakened body would not respond. The Severon had been on her trail since she escaped Sionaad and that had been nearly six, no eight days ago. She'd managed to lose them at one point when she raced her horse through a bustling village where the foot and horse traffic concealed her tracks. Somehow, she had managed to stay ahead of them the rest of the way. Stopping only for a moment at a time to steal what food she could. Her body was starting to feel the effects of eating only scraps of food.

Sterling stared up at the vast cerulean sky. White puffy clouds billowed above her as if watching her escape from on high. The tall grass danced in rolling waves as the breeze swept across the plains. Sterling raised her arm and blocked out the sun's rays with her hand. She welcomed the sun's warmth for the air had turned chilly in the late autumn day. *Autumn?* Could she really have been in Sionaad for six months? It had been the middle of spring, in late Unda, when Kellen had handed her over to the Severon, and now the air was filled with the smells of autumn. *Six months of her life was gone.*

Sterling lightly touched the burns scored into her arms, they were red and angry. *Are these my hands, my arms?* Sterling thought as she examined how thin and frail she had become.

The exhausted horse tried to stand, but its legs gave out as it collapsed back on its side. Sterling felt guilty for riding the beast so hard, but she refused to go back to Sionaad. She'd rather welcome death than the walls of that dark pit. Sterling sat up and looked around. She was in the middle of nowhere in a vast field of wheat grass. The last village she'd passed had been two days ago and since then nothing but a scattering of ruins dotted the landscape.

Sterling grimaced as she forced herself to stand. The woolen fabric of the Severon uniform pulled at her wounds that crossed her back and the burn marks. They throbbed constantly, but there was nothing she could do about it until she found safety in Kai'Vari. On

wobbly knees Sterling scanned the horizon to the south. Somewhere the border between Duenin and Kai'Vari waited for her. She'd prayed every day that it would just be over the next ridge, but her prayers went unanswered as another sweeping plain after sweeping plain had met her.

Sterling approached the horse and tried to urge it to its feet but it lay with its head amid the grass, "Come on," she said as she tried to get it to stand, "you've had enough time to rest." But the horse refused to budge. When it refused again and morosely whinnied, she gave up and sat down with her back pressed against the animal. "I'm sorry," she absently apologized to the beast before standing. *I am cursed. Yet another being who has helped me and been hurt*, she thought. *This animal has given me it's all.* Being around horses all her life, she knew it was exhausted, but that it should recover. But it would take time she didn't have to wait on the horse to regain its strength. "You will be fine in a bit," she told the great animal as she leaned over to place a kiss on its head. "Thank you for helping me." She stood and started in the direction of Kai'Vari.

The boots she'd stolen from Helios were heavy as she trudged through the tall grass. Too big, they had rubbed her feet raw causing blisters to form. But she could not risk taking them off, else she feared she would not be able to get them back on.

As she walked the sun slowly edged its way closer to its zenith. *How many hours have I been trudging through these damnable fields?* Would she make it to Kai'Vari before it sank below the western horizon? She was begrudgingly thankful for the uniform she'd taken. It had kept her warm during the cold nights. She wanted to discard the heavy clothing, the mere thought of having it against her body disgusted her. She knew what she really wanted more than anything was a bath.

As if her prayers were answered from the heavens the sound of running water reached her ears. A smile cracked her parched lips as Sterling quickened her pace toward the sound. She was running by the time she reached a small stream that meandered across the wide plains, and nearly fell head first into the shallow water. It was just narrow enough for her to jump across. She knelt along the bank and dipped her hands in the icy stream and scooped up a mouth full of clean, cold water. The cold liquid slid down her throat calming the thirst that had dogged her since she left Sionaad.

Sterling examined her hands – dried blood was caked under her fingernails. *So much blood, it still clings to me days after leaving that place,* she thought. She scrubbed her hands in the water, but the caked-on blood was stubborn and was difficult to wash away. *Helios's blood.* What had happened in that cell? All she remembered was the pain and then waking up to find them dead. Their bodies had been mangled as if some great beast had thrown them across the room.

She tried hard to ignore what had happened in her prison, but her continuing nightmares would not let her forget. Each night Engram would visit her in her dreams, and even though she had escaped the walls of the prison, as she slept she was still locked away in the dark. No amount of rest would ease the anguish she felt. Her body and her mind ached and all she wanted to do was sleep, but she knew with sleep came nightmares.

Sterling sighed, no amount of scrubbing would cleanse her hands of the blood. She pushed away from the stream and stood, for as far as the eye could see was an ocean of brown grass. The vastness of the Dueninian plains made her feel insignificant. She looked back across the limitless horizon and where she had already walked was a trail cut through the grass. She could see the path weaved back and forth aimlessly. It was hard to judge progress in the fields of wheat, but looking back she realized how far she had walked since leaving the horse behind. Sterling turned her back on where she had come from and faced forward toward Kai'Vari.

The land began to rise under her feet until she reached a small ridge. Once at the top the sight before her took the breath from her exhausted lungs. She had fully expected another in the unending series of grassy plains. *Is it true? Can this be?* She excitedly thought to herself. She couldn't contain the smile that creased her dry, cracked lips.

KAI'VARI FOUND

The Kai'Varian border lay before her – the Sandori Forest spread across most of northern Kai'Vari standing guard against any invaders that dared to cross the border. A rush of excitement and a renewed burst of energy coursed through her broken, tortured body. A glimmer of hope nudged in as well, a feeling she hadn't had in quite some time.

Hemi had told her of the immensity of the forest, but never in her dreams did she imagine this. The tall trees of the Sandori spread out before her with no end in sight. She started down the ridge when she felt the shaking of the earth beneath her. She looked back over the ridge and her blood turned to ice. Severon – half a dozen in their menacing black and red uniforms were galloping full on toward her position. She ducked back down below the ridge line and thought. *I only have one chance to make it to safety.* If she hesitated they would be upon her in no time.

She pushed off from the ground and started down the shallow incline at a full run. She knew the moment they saw her, as they spurred their horses. *Damn my luck*, she thought as she sprinted toward the safety of the border.

Sterling dared one more glance over her shoulder. The demon among the Severon, Engram, was leading the charge – whipping his horse into a frenzy in his attempt to run her down. Sterling stumbled but regained her footing. Her lungs burned as she struggled to run in the heavy uniform. Her blistered feet screaming at every step, but no amount of pain would slow her down. No, not when she was this close to freedom.

Frantic, like a wild animal, she ran and scrambled and leapt and crawled and ran again. She pulled strength from a place she didn't know she had. *I would rather die like a fox with the hounds, than have that foul, evil man touch me again*, she thought. The tree line seemed to get farther away the more she ran toward the safety of the Kai'Varian border. She could hear the hoof beats closing in, and she imagined the hot breath of the war horses touching the back of her neck. Stumbling for a second, she feared exhaustion was near, but the thought of the terror filled night, that first night, when Engram had first tortured her, spurred her forward in a sprint.

Engram was almost on her when the blessed safety of the trees swallowed her and he was forced to pull up or risk injuring his mount. She darted between the wide trunks of the trees that stood watch over the land of her father. The forest was thick and her pursuers had a difficult time keeping up with her.

"Come out Sterling!" She'd lost sight of them but Engram's voice echoed through the dense forest. "There is nowhere for you to hide."

Sterling stood with her back to a tree, breathing in deep breaths hoping to steady her heart rate. "No matter where you go we will find you." His voice seemed to come from every direction. She edged around a tree looking over her shoulder checking for the evil man. As she started forward she walked into a uniformed chest. A Severon stood in front of her, a vicious smile on his thin lips. He held her upper arms in a vice like grip, "Found you."

Sterling struggled to free herself, but his grip was too strong. "Be a good girl and behave," he whispered maliciously in her ear. Anger welled up in Sterling. Anger at every hurt the Severon had caused; anger for every time Engram had taken her unwillingly. Anger at the death of those she loved and anger at Kellen's betrayal. With all her strength Sterling brought her knee up into the man's groin.

"Let go of me, you bastard," she spat out at him. He instantly went to his knees clutching himself. He let out a mouse like squeak as he toppled over onto his side, eyes rolling back in his head. She ran, pushing through the brush, her hair catching on twigs and pulling painfully at her scalp. Tears of frustration blurred her vision. She could hear her pursuers charging after her. *Will I ever be free from the Severon?*

16

BROM DA'GAIHEN

Northern Kai'Varian Border
Pan'Dale Hold

The graekull hunted, sniffing the air for its prey. *Ironic*, Brom thought, *because today, demon, you are the prey.* Brom silently tracked the monster through the Sandori forest to this root filled clearing. This graekull was all that was left of an attack that started two days ago. The hunting pack of five graekull had emerged from a deep well, wreaking havoc on a small village that was nestled along the border between the Pan'Dale and Da'Gaihen Holds. The Manuk horns had sounded throughout the forest and Brom, along with other Veillen guards stationed in the lookout towers, had managed to kill all but this last one. It had split off from the rest of the pack and had slaughtered a farmer and his family while they worked their land.

Brom had been traveling with Gavin Da'Gaihen, the second prince of Kai'Vari, and Conal Fal'Barbner, a Master Archer and second in command of the Regular army. The three of them had been riding toward Pan'Dale from Sela'Char. Along the way they had come up on a group of Veillen battling the hunting pack of graekull. Brom had ordered Conal to take Gavin away from the battle to a safe distance. The young Prince had argued that he wanted to stay and watch, but Brom had put his foot down with his cousin. While Conal and Gavin retreated to safety, Brom had lured the remaining graekull away from the village. Now it was caught in Brom's trap.

Brom breathed in slowly, filling his lungs with air. He stood perfectly still, waiting for the graekull as he spoke the ancient words that called to his Velkuva, Raiken.

"*Kerbodia for'velki,*" Brom spoke, the ancient command of his forefathers calling the Velkuva.

I will be with you, Raiken's deep voice resonated in Brom's mind as he responded to Brom's request.

Brom slowly faded into the Veil. The sun glowed with an eerie blue brightness. The sounds of the forest were muffled as he completed the fade. In this realm of the dead, Brom's senses were heightened and his movement speed was increased threefold of a normal human. But he dared not linger in this realm. His body was screaming for release from the spirit world where only the dead should ever walk. He would remain here in the Veil until he spoke the words that would end his hold on Raiken's power.

The graekull lumbered through the forest, paying no mind to the trees before it. *He's a big one,* Brom noted.

Watch those claws, Raiken warned.

The graekull's claws were indeed impressive. The long black nails were cracked and broken by a myriad of unseen battles. But the claws alone were not the graekull's only weapon. Teeth, green and sharpened by the countless humans and animals it had eaten. Raw. That's how they liked it. Its gray mottled skin was pulled taut over powerful lean muscle and bone that was exposed where the skin was charred away. Those powerful arms could fell ten men in one swipe. Large trees that would impasse any man, this graekull simply pushed them out of the way.

The blued sun highlighted the sinew and bone that were exposed where the flesh was charred and curled, leaving visible holes in its skin.

The demon beast stopped just a few steps in front of Brom, sniffing the air through its blunt nose; eyes closed trying to find Brom's scent that lingered in the forest. Though he couldn't image how the beast could smell anything past its own putrid scent.

Brom silently reached above his head and unsheathed Tryg, his bloodsword. Razor sharp, the bloodsword was made to slice through graekull flesh with ease. Brom raised Tryg, ready to strike, when a whirlwind of arms and legs came barreling into the clearing colliding headlong into the graekull. Both graekull and girl went tumbling to the ground. The beast was the first to recover. Lumbering to its feet it stood over the girl and growled, baring a mouth full of grotesque teeth. The girl who appeared to be young, perhaps fifteen summers, crawled backward from the monster, scrambling in the dirt and tried to stand and run. Before Brom could react, the graekull grabbed hold of the girl's leg and flung her across the clearing and into a stand of trees. She hit a branch, then the trunk, and collapsed at the base of a tree, limp as a child's doll.

"*Klute'wer.*" Brom said the words that would release his hold on Raiken and emerged from the Veil, yelling out to get the graekull's attention off the girl, "Here!" It turned at the noise and watched Brom for a moment before charging. Long arms ending with sharp claws reached out for Brom, but he deftly side stepped the ungainly beast and brought Tryg down, slicing through the beast's flesh. Roaring in pain the demon quickly turned on Brom, its red black eyes watching Brom as they slowly circled one another. Attacking a graekull head on was a potentially lethal move that brought death to many young Veillen warriors. Its claws could slice through flesh with little effort. Brom had witnessed many warriors make the mistake and pay the price of having limbs severed or their chest opened. Or both.

Brom goaded the beast, "Come on, dull stone. What are you waiting for?" He doubted the demon understood the words, but he had to keep the monster's attention off the girl. The graekull growled, bits of spittle and debris flew through the air as it lunged toward Brom. He swiveled out of the way and in one fluid motion drove Tryg deep into the graekull's back. The point of the blade was so sharp it sliced through bone and sinew. The graekull roared in pain as black blood seeped from the deep gash in the demon's back. Brom quickly withdrew his blade and retreated before the demon could swing its arm around. As the demon spun, its arm outstretched, it struck one of the large bareq trees that made up the Sandori. Wood and bark went flying as its claw gouged the tree. Those claws were indeed deadly.

Taking a stance, Brom raised his sword and eyed the demon down the length of the blade. Brom circled the beast slowly, waiting for the moment when it would charge again. It followed Brom with its dark eyes, and as Brom circled around to its back the demon turned to face Brom. With a violent roar, it pounded its chest and charged. Brom, in turn, charged as well and just as they were about to collide Brom evaded the massive claw and sliced Tryg through the demon's arm severing it at the elbow. It howled in pain and lashed out with its uninjured arm. Brom raised Tryg and deflected the demon's claws, then went on the offensive. With a quick move he spun around and drove the blade into the graekull's chest, piercing its heart with ease. The beast collapsed to its knees, but even mortally wounded it was still dangerous. Brom pulled Tryg from the leathery flesh and in Veillen tradition he raised his bloodsword high in the air, swung it downward with might and precision, and sliced the head off the graekull. "*Vare takk.*" He thanked Raiken as he wiped the blood off the blade.

Well fought. Raiken responded to Brom's words.

He turned his attention to the girl. Brom stepped over the monster's corpse, which would soon disintegrate into the soil, and hurried to the tree where the girl lay limp. Stooping, he brushed dull, matted hair out of her face. *No broken bones, that's good.* He was surprised by the amount of dried blood that covered the girl. He carefully rolled her over on to her back, *a Severon uniform?* The jacket had come unfastened and the large white shirt had pulled away, revealing a smooth olive shoulder. Upon further inspection Brom could see a myriad of scars, both old and new, crisscrossing the tender flesh. "What happened to you?" he asked as he checked her pulse and found a strong beat. *Alive,* thought Brom, *despite having been slammed against a tree. The impact alone should have killed her.*

Brom pulled the shirt and jacket into place and noticed an angry mark on her forearm. He pushed the sleeve further up and found a long, slender brand burned into her forearm from wrist to elbow. He pushed the other sleeve up and found a matching brand on her right arm, "Damn Severon." Brom spat the name.

His head came up as the sounds of footsteps drew closer. "Hand over the girl, she is Severon property."

Brom stood and faced the intruders. Five Severon stood in the clearing, their brushed silver buttons contrasted against the deep black and red of their uniforms. Each man stood before Brom with sword drawn, a stance that would be their last if they choose to attack.

"Any ownership you may have had ceased the moment she stepped onto Kai'Varian soil," Brom said as he sheathed Tryg. The Severon's irritation evident in their scowls when they realized he did not fear them. After all the Severon fed off the fear of their victims.

The middle Severon took a step toward Brom, raising his sword to Brom's chest. A sneer curled his lip, "Listen savage, I am Commander Remus Engram, Severon Commander of the Northern Arm and Emissary of Orom Tydar, we have tracked this girl for more than a week from Sionaad. She is an escaped prisoner wanted for the murder of two Severon and that of a dozen orphans. She will be punished for her crimes."

"It appears as though she has already been punished beyond measure," Brom said, stepping forward so the tip of Engram's blade pierced Brom's skin. Blood pooled at the tip before dripping to the leaves below. The other four soldiers took a step back at Brom's bold action. He glanced at the sword piercing his chest. "Whatever crimes she may have committed in Duenin do not exist in Kai'Vari," Brom said as he placed his hand around the blade hilt, forcefully removing it and pushing Engram back three steps.

Brom quickly stepped back, away from Engram and spun around while unsheathing Tryg. In one motion, he held Tryg to the Severon's neck that had tried sneaking up behind Brom. But Brom had been aware of the man's presence even before Engram's glance had given the man away. Brom forced the man toward his fellow Severon with the tip of his blade. "Leave now before I have you executed for trespassing on Kai'Varian land."

"Executed?" Engram scoffed, "On what authority? Yours? You are nothing but a savage."

"On my authority," Gavin, Brom's cousin, answered the Severon as he rode into the clearing.

Brom sighed and glared at Conal. "He insisted," Conal shrugged.

"And who are you?" Engram asked.

Normally an immature fifteen-year-old, Gavin put on a haughty air and looked down his nose at the Severon, "Gavin Da'Gaihen, Second Prince of Kai'Vari."

Engram frowned, taking a moment to size up the boy. Brom saw the moment he dismissed Gavin as unimportant. "We are not leaving here without her," he said, pointing his sword at the unconscious girl. "She is a criminal and will answer for her crimes against Duenin." Engram spread his arms, "As you can see we outnumber you, throw down your weapons or we will be forced to kill you."

"You are a fool if you think to attack us." Brom had grown tired of this man's pompous attitude.

"Very well," Engram motioned to his men. Brom laughed at their attempts and dodged the first attacker letting the man's momentum carry him off balance, the second attacker brought his sword down and Brom easily blocked the man's attack and countered with an elbow to the man's nose.

Brom quickly brought Tryg up and shoved the sword backward through his arms. The first Severon gurgled as Tryg went through the man's heart. Brom turned and pushed the man off his blade with his foot, the Severon falling to his knees and to his death.

He turned back to Engram and the remaining four, "Would you like to try again?"

Engram's eyes narrowed and filled with the fire. He motioned for another attack. The next two tried to attack in unison. They came at Brom with swords drawn, approaching him cautiously. Brom simply watched them with his body relaxed and ready. They charged together, but Brom blocked the first sword and kicked the second man in the knee, breaking his leg. His screams of pain overshadowed the sound of metal hitting metal. Brom focused his attention on the remaining attacker. Brom backed the man into a tree with the tip of his sword held to the Severon's throat.

"I surrender," the Severon mumbled as he dropped his sword, his hands shaking uncontrollably as he lifted them.

Brom shoved the man away and turned back to face Engram once again, "Take your dead and wounded from our lands before you also feel my blade." Brom took a step to the side as the Severon with the newly broken nose fell to the ground with an arrow in his back. Brom glanced over his shoulder at Conal.

"What?" Conal teased, "I thought he was going for his dagger."

"I've suffered your presence long enough Remus Engram of the Severon. Leave now before I lose what patience I have left." Brom sheathed Tryg, "Do not return to our lands for if I see you again or any Severon on Kai'Varian soil I will not hesitate to kill you or the rest of your men." Brom kept his eyes trained on Engram's. The anger that emanated from their core was palpable. *Who was this man?* Brom thought. *To enter unfriendly territory for this scrap of a girl was truly bold if not crazy.* Engram growled a command to his remaining men.

They gathered their dead and helped the wounded to stand. Engram, all the while stood staring at Brom.

"What is it they call you?" Engram asked.

Brom hit his chest with a clenched fist, "Brom Da'Gaihen of the Veillen High Guard. Wielder of the Bloodsword Tryg and slayer of the graekull hordes," he looked to the dead Severon, "and I suppose I should add Death's Wing to Severon Fools stupid enough not to tuck tail and run when they had a chance."

Engram nodded slowly. "It is not a name that I shall be forgetting anytime soon, Brom of the Veillen High Guard. Not a name that I shall be forgetting *ever*."

Brom turned his back on the retreating Severon, a sign of disrespect in Kai'Vari that went unnoticed by the Severon. To show an enemy your back was telling them that they were no threat and easily dismissed. If Engram had been a Kai'Varian, Brom would expect an attack at any moment, but the Severon commander retreated with his men.

Brom turned his eyes to Conal and wordlessly the man knew Brom's wishes. "Death's Wing? Are you serious?" Conal laughed as he followed the Severon to make sure they returned to their own soil. Brom turned his attention back to the girl who remained unconscious.

Gavin had dismounted and knelt by the girl, curiosity lighting his eyes as he examined the dried blood and the uniform. Brom worried over his cousin and his lack of experience on the battlefield. The boy had been coddled all his life and was now being thrust into a millennial old war. "Who do you suppose she is?" Gavin asked as he brushed blood encrusted hair from the girl's face. Blood, mixed with grime, covered her face making it impossible to tell her age.

"Gather some firewood," Brom instructed Gavin.

"Aye," Gavin set about gathering wood. "I wonder why the Severon wanted her back so badly." Gavin continued his incessant questions. He was an avid questioner and Brom knew if he answered one the questions would never stop. No, it was best to ignore the boy's curiosity.

Gavin dumped the wood in a heap and Brom set about starting a fire. He placed a lump of peme in the middle of the fire pit and ignited it with his knife and flint. The hard and oily lump quickly caught fire and the flames spread to the firewood. All the while Gavin droned on and on about the girl, asking endless questions. Where she came from, how old was she, why was she covered in blood? Brom had learned to tune out the boy's constant jabbering. He looked over his shoulder and sighed, "To be a Veillen Guard you must be intimate with silence."

Gavin looked confused for a moment, but Brom could tell when his words finally sank in. Gavin said a simple "Oh" and stood. He left the girl's side and started to remove the saddle from his horse and untied the bedrolls. Brom sighed at the blessed quiet.

Satisfied with the fire, Brom started on Tor's saddle and placed it on the ground. He untied the sheep's bladder and tossed it to Gavin. Gavin understood the silent command and left the camp to fill the waterskin. The stream was not far from the camp, but it would give Brom enough time to move the girl without Gavin's constant questions.

Brom spread a blanket close enough to the fire so the girl would stay warm. He lifted her into his arms, surprised at how light she was. The borrowed uniform concealed her petite size. Not only small, she appeared to be malnourished. Brom could feel her bones through the thick Severon uniform. Blood stains covered the material.

He examined her face as he laid her on the blanket. A large knot had formed on her head where she'd undoubtedly hit it when thrown by the graekull. Brom suspected she'd have a monster of a headache when she woke. Dried blood caked her hair and eyebrows. It looked as though she tried to clean her hands but there was still blood under her fingernails. Brom removed the heavy jacket and tossed it aside. The once white shirt beneath was now brown with dirt and grime. He untied the laces that wrapped around her legs and pulled the too large boots from her slender legs. Brom winced at the blisters that covered her toes and heels. Where she had laced the boots around her legs there were deep red marks that must have been painful.

Brom hesitated when she groaned but continued once she settled down. She wore nothing beneath the shirt. Brom could not help but notice the appealing shape of her breasts and the scars crisscrossing the tender flesh. He eased her arms from the sleeves and could feel his blood begin to boil at the number of wounds covering the girl's body. The brutality of the Severon was rumored, but these scars were evidence that the rumors were true. Brom spread a second blanket over the girl when he heard Gavin's footsteps. The boy would never learn to quiet his steps.

Gavin stopped short upon entering the camp. "You undressed her? That's why you sent me away?" Gavin handed the full bladder to Brom, "I'm not a child Brom, I've seen naked women before."

"Your nursemaid," Brom said under his breath taking the bladder from Gavin and poured a small amount of the cool liquid onto the corner of the shirt. He wiped some of the grime from her forehead, exposing the tender skin beneath the layer of filth. He cleaned the blood from her eyebrows next, revealing a soft brown color, next her high cheekbones. Her dark lashes lay against the olive skin. A tiny cut was carved into her upper lip.

There was a mixture of old and new scars on her stomach, chest, and arms. He gently rolled her onto her side and grimaced at the network of scars covering her back. He returned her to her back and examined the burn marks on her arms. The twin marks appeared to be newer burns that seemed on the verge of becoming infected. The skin surrounding the wounds was red and swollen, warm to the touch.

Brom gently washed the dirt and blood from the burns and cuts and applied a small amount of droglin salve into each wound. His efforts would at least keep any more dirt from entering the damaged areas. He'd leave the rest to Moira. Satisfied with his work, he threw the uniform shirt and jacket at Gavin. "What am I supposed to do with these?" the Kai'Varian noble asked.

"Throw that damn jacket in the fire, and the shirt? Clean it."

"I'm a prince Brom, not a laundress."

"Out here, right now, you are whatever I say you are."

Gavin stood there for a moment weighing Brom's ire. "Fine," he sighed as he sulked away, mumbling about how princes should not be maids in the middle of a hunt. Brom grinned and turned his attention back to the girl. He shook her slightly to wake her, "Wake up lass." When there was no response he lightly tapped her on the cheeks, but her eyes remained steadfastly closed. There wasn't much he could do with her matted hair; he'd leave that for Moira to tend to.

Conal returned shortly after Gavin left. He dismounted and pulled his saddle from Riorn and placed it next to Tor's saddle. He stopped next to the girl and examined her for a moment, "She looks familiar."

Brom peered down at the girl. Her eyebrows formed dark slashes atop almond eyes. Her cheekbones were high, and she had a smallish nose. He thought about all the nearby Tohms but couldn't place where he'd seen her. For the moment, however, he simply put it away in his mind for later thought.

Conal chuckled, "Pretty women all look familiar until you're trying to remember their names after too much a'kel."

Brom shook his head. "I suppose you're right." He put the matter to rest and laid down on his own bedroll. Tryg was beside him, as always, within reach. His arms behind his head, he thought on everything he had to do before journeying to Var'Khundi. This girl was an unnecessary burden he did not have time for.

"Gavin has returned." Conal commented minutes before the boy stepped into camp. "If you make as much noise hunting graekull as you do stomping through the woods, you'll make a horrible Veillen." Gavin shrugged his shoulders and spread the wet shirt over a branch to dry.

"Did the Severon give you any resistance?" Brom asked Conal.

"One thought to charge me."

"What did you do?" Gavin asked as he plopped himself down next to the fire.

Conal grinned and chuckled, "Let us say, they will be planning another funeral."

Gavin edged closer to the girl, "Do you think she really did what they accused her of?" Gavin peered at the girl, "I mean, she's so tiny. I don't think she could harm a puppy."

"Looks can be deceiving," Brom responded. "You never know what is in a person's heart that may lead them to kill or destroy."

"Do you believe them?" Gavin's curiosity was avid.

"Brom, believe the Severon?" Conal laughed, "When the fires of Du'Gald go cold."

Gavin laughed nervously, "But why chase a girl across the border? She must be very important to them."

"Or hated," Brom said, his eyes closed. "They wanted her back, but I doubt it is because she killed someone. More like she has or knows something they want."

Brom watched Gavin behind his half-closed lids. The boy's endless curiosity would get him in trouble one day. Gavin's young hand reached out and started to lift the blanket to peak under at the girl's body, but before he could look the girl's eyes suddenly flew open.

Gavin jumped back in shock as the girl scrambled to her feet, pulling Gavin's short sword from its scabbard. She took advantage of Gavin's confusion and held the sword to his throat, using him as a hostage.

Both Brom and Conal were instantly alert and on their feet. Brom held Tryg in a loose grip while Conal had his bow at the ready, an arrow nocked.

"Let me go, do you know who I am?" Gavin spit and sputtered at the shock of being taken hostage by a scrap of a girl.

"Who are you?" The girl asked peaking around Gavin's shoulder.

BROM DA'GAIHEN

Brom opened his mouth to answer, but the words would not come. His body was frozen at the sight before him. Staring back at him were the silver eyes of a Devian.

17

DEVIAN

A *Devian?* Raiken's shocked question echoed Brom's thoughts. It had been twenty years since he'd seen the silver eyes of a Devian. It made sense why the Severon had followed her across the border into Kai'Vari. They were obsessed with capturing every Devian they could get their hands on.

"Brom, do something," Gavin said, his voice wavering.

"Easy there, lass," Brom said, his hand up trying to calm the girl. The last thing he needed was for Gavin to be injured or even killed. "No one is going to hurt you."

"Where are the Severon?" She demanded, pulling Gavin a step backward as Brom took a step forward. Despite her short stature, she was surprisingly strong to be able to hold Gavin, who was a half a head taller than the girl.

"They're gone," Brom took another step forward. "They won't be able to touch you here."

"Stay back!" She yelled at Brom as he took another step toward her.

"Easy," Brom took another step, closing the gap between them so only a few steps remained.

"Just say the word," Conal said softly, his bow taut and ready to release an arrow.

"Who are you people?" She asked, her eyes darting between Brom and Conal.

Kerbodia for'velki, Brom spoke the command silently in his mind to Raiken. Brom faded into the Veil and through the blue haze he could see the girl's eyes widen in shock as he disappeared from her sight. She pulled Gavin backward and pressed the sword to his neck. A thin line of blood beaded on his neck.

"Where did he go?" She frantically searched for Brom, while pulling Gavin backward with her.

"I'm right here," Brom said after releasing his hold on Raiken. He grabbed hold of her arm that held the sword to Gavin's neck and easily pulled the weapon from her frail and emaciated hand.

She fell backward with a squeak as she scrambled away from Brom's sudden appearance. She pressed her back against the rough bark of a bareq tree, she must have just realized her chest was bare for she quickly covered herself with her arms and glared at Brom with eyes that could melt steel.

"You're..." Brom started but was interrupted by Gavin's outraged tantrum.

"How dare you threaten me!" He turned on the girl, his arms flailing about like an apoplectic toddler.

"Gavin," Brom pulled the boy away from the girl who was staring daggers at Gavin's youthful outrage, "get a hold of yourself." He shoved Gavin toward Conal and slowly crouched so he was near eye level with the girl. She quickly covered herself with the blanket he offered to her.

"You're safe here," he started, "the Severon have left with fewer men than they came with." Brom paused while the girl absorbed his words. "You're in the Pan'Dale Hold region of Kai'Vari."

She looked from Brom to Conal, then Gavin, "I made it?" She asked as her eyes darted back to Brom. *I really made it.* Sterling couldn't help the tears that gathered behind her eyes as the realization that she was no longer where the Severon could touch her.

"I made it, I'm really in Kai'Vari?" she asked again as if she needed the reassurance she was truly in Kai'Vari.

"Aye," Brom nodded, "you're safe."

Sterling felt a tremendous weight lift off her shoulders as she stared up at the man who had disappeared before her eyes and reappeared next to her. He was large, at least six feet with broad shoulders and long brown hair that touched his shoulders and was partially pulled back in a leather strap. His beard was scruffy and showed bits of red in the stubble. He was bare chested with an intricate tattoo spread across half his chest and down his right arm.

The other two were standing back watching her. One with the bow was elbowing the younger one and teasing him about being taken hostage by a mere girl.

"I'm Brom, Brom Da'Gaihen," Brom said as he reached out his hand for the girl to help her stand. When she placed her hand in his he could feel tremors that shook her body. He helped her to her feet where she wobbled for a moment. "What is your name, lass?"

She looked at him briefly, her eyes glazing over, "I'm…" she paused, her hand going out to steady herself, "I'm Sterling, Sterling Rin'Ovana."

Brom's breath caught in his chest at the name she threw at him. Rin'Ovana? *That's impossible*, he thought. He opened his mouth to speak his thoughts but stopped when she collapsed. He caught her, lifting her in his arms, her body limp with exhaustion.

"Did I hear her correctly?" Conal asked. "Did she say Rin'Ovana?"

Brom closed his eyes for a second to gain his composure before responding, "Aye, she did indeed." Brom laid Sterling down and covered her with the blanket. She seemed to be resting peacefully despite the wounds that ravaged her body.

"How is that even possible?" Conal asked. Brom stood and backed away from Sterling, the same question and more were in a jumble in his head. *A Devian, but she couldn't be more than fourteen or fifteen summers.*

He needed answers, and the only person who could provide them was asleep. Brom took a deep breath and settled his thoughts and his nerves, "There won't be any answers for the time being." Brom took Tryg off his back and set the sword down beside his bedroll and stretched out his body. Both Gavin and Conal followed suit and they lay there in silence listening to the crackle of the fire. Brom closed his eyes, but sleep did not come easily. Dreams of his past swirled around in his head. Memories of silver eyes, laughing with love and tenderness occupied his sleep.

Brom, Raiken's voice jolted Brom awake. His Velkuva's voice only came to him when there was danger.

Brom scanned the campsite, but the night was too dark, the moon hidden behind thick clouds and the fire was nothing but ashes. *Ilunpetan argia*, Brom whispered the command to Raiken. All at once, where the darkest shadows loomed, Brom could see as if it were in the middle of the day. Brom averted his gaze from the brilliant light of the coals that were still red. *Ilunpetan argia*, the command for Dark Vision, allowed the Veillen to see clearly in the dark.

Scanning the campsite again, Brom cursed under his breath. Sterling was gone. Brom silently stood and scanned the ground and quickly found her tracks which led to where Conal lay sleeping. *She's taken his bow,* Brom noted.

He followed the tracks out of the camp and to the north. *What are you planning girl?* Brom had a sinking suspicion and hurried his steps in the event he was correct.

Her tracks were easy to follow, she made no effort to conceal them. At one point she must have tripped and dropped the bow and quiver for a few of the arrows lay scattered across the ground.

He was almost to the border between Kai'Vari and Duenin when he heard the voice. He slowed his pace and listened for a moment.

"You could have avoided all this if you'd only told me what I wanted to know." It was Engram's voice.

"Go rot in Abaddon!" Sterling's voice returned. Brom could hear the anger mixed with tears as she shouted the curse.

"Come now, is that any way for a lady to speak?"

As Brom stepped out of the forest, the clouds covering the moon were pushed away by a wind that swept across the wide-open plains of Duenin. He released Raiken with a quick *Klute'rean*, so he would not be blinded by the moon's rays.

Sterling stood just north of the tree line, but still on the Kai'Varian side of the border. She'd donned the white shirt again and stood with her feet apart and with Conal's bow pulled taut, an arrow nocked in the bow string. He was amazed she was able to draw the bow. Conal's bow had one of the heavier draws since he would often join on hunts for graekull.

"You're a monster!" she yelled back. The bow wavered, and she quickly regained her control.

"The true monsters are those Kai'Varians," Engram's words were smooth, and slithered off his tongue. "They practice witchcraft among other atrocities."

She growled and released the arrow, but it wobbled in the air and landed harmlessly at Engram's feet. She scrambled to pull another arrow from the quiver. She fumbled and dropped one while trying to pull another. Engram suddenly started running toward her.

Brom reacted instantly and was at full run as well. Sterling let out a shocked squeak as he stepped in front of her just as Engram reached her. Brom grabbed the other man's arm and easily tossed him to the ground, "You were told never to step foot on Kai'Varian soil again," Brom threatened the man as he pulled Tryg from its sheath.

Engram quickly stood and backed away until he was on Dueninian soil again. He glared at Brom, "Even if we lose her, there are still other Devians that will tell me what I want to know."

"You bastard!" Sterling yelled, stepping around Brom and aiming another arrow at Engram's back. When it fell short she nocked another and released it, only to have it wobble and fall at her feet. "You bastard." She struggled to get the words past the tears of frustration as she collapsed in the dirt, her shoulder's shaking.

When Brom stooped to comfort her, she pushed his hand away, stood and nocked the last arrow in the quiver. She took a deep breath, drew the bow as far back as she could, and steadily aimed down the shaft of the arrow. She exhaled as she released the arrow and it flew straight and true at the retreating Engram's back. Had it not been for one of his men warning him, the arrow would have pierced the back of his head. Instead Engram spun and dodged the arrow just as it razed past his face leaving a long think cut on his cheekbone. The guard let out a scream of pain as the arrow lodged in his shoulder.

As Engram approached his man, he unsheathed his sword and in a fit of rage killed the man with a piercing strike to his heart. Engram glanced over his shoulder one last time as he wiped the soldier's blood from his blade and replaced it in its scabbard. He continued over the ridge and disappeared at the same time clouds again covered the moon.

Brom was watching Engram when he heard the bow crash to the ground. He turned just in time to catch Sterling as her body crumpled. Brom picked up the bow, and lifted Sterling into his arms and started back to camp. Whether he liked it or not he was stuck with this little Devian until he could get her to his sister at the Pan'Dale Hold.

18

PAN'DALE

Dan'Idou, 7th Turcia, 1021

"Do you think she's really a Rin'Ovana?" Gavin's question still lingered in Brom's mind. It was the last thing Gavin had said before he and Conal had left for Pan'Dale Keep. He'd sent them on ahead once the morning sun crested the horizon.

Brom had instructed Gavin to keep the information to himself for the time being. At least until they could confirm her claims. Brom examined the girl who still lay asleep. She had turned on her side and was curled up like a baby. Her hands were folded together under her left cheek and the blanket, sometime during the night, had been thrown to the side. The Severon uniform swallowed her tiny frame and made her look more like a child than she already was.

Once Brom had led Sterling back to camp from her failed attempt to kill Engram, Conal had bemoaned the fact she had lost all his arrows. His complaining was only halfhearted when Brom explained what had happened. Conal had been amazed that she could draw his bow even a tiny bit, let alone shoot an arrow with precision.

Brom was still amazed at the level of exhaustion the girl had reached, but he understood. He had seen it a few times in soldiers who had been held prisoner, and who had survived horrific torture.

She's strong, Brom thought nudging her shoulder. The sun was above the trees and he needed to get her and himself to Pan'Dale. "Sterling," he said, softly touching her shoulder. "Sterling," he repeated.

She moaned in protest of being woken and rolled to her other side, her back to Brom. Brom's mood took a turn in the wrong direction. *Did she just turn her back on me?*

Brom stood, took a deep breath. "Wake up!"

Sterling jolted into a sitting position at his bellowed words. She glanced around, wiping the sleep from her eyes. She looked up at Brom who was standing over her, his arms crossed in front of his chest. "You're too loud," she said with a scratchy voice before collapsing back onto the bedroll, pulling the blanket up and over her head.

Brom could feel his anger building. Fever or no, wounds or no, he would not be ignored by the likes of this... child. "It's time to get up," Brom said as he bent and pulled the bedroll out from under Sterling. She rolled a good three feet, the blanket twisting around her legs causing her to trip when she tried to stand.

She stared at him for a long moment. Brom wasn't sure if she was sizing him up or just unsure of what to say or do. He couldn't help himself from staring at the silver eyes that were framed by dark lashes. She cleared her throat when it was obvious his gaze had lingered longer than it should have.

Brom turned and busied himself with saddling Tor and replacing his bedroll on the back of the saddle. She stood there watching him the whole while, with her arms folded across her stomach.

"I...," she started but her voice cracked. She cleared her throat, "I want to thank you for saving me from the Severon."

Brom paused and looked over his shoulder, "Anytime the opportunity comes to kill a few redshirts," he mumbled and returned to his task. "We've a day's ride to the Pan'Dale hold," Brom explained, pulling a bit of bread and jerky from his saddlebags, "so we've not time for a proper breakfast."

When he handed her the food her eyes lit up like a child on Unity Day.

"Thank you," Sterling said, her mouth full of bread.

"Here," Brom threw the waterskin at her and she nearly drank the entire bladder full of water. He imagined she could eat and drink more from the look of her. He'd noticed the night before that her ribs were showing.

Brom mounted Tor and offered her a hand, "Pan'Dale is just a day's ride from here. My sister is a healer and will be able to help with those burns."

Tor turned his massive black head to see who dared to ride him besides Brom. Sterling was nimble, and putting her foot on Brom's, she climbed up on Tor's back sliding in behind him. *She's not afraid of horses,* he was thankful for that small favor. Tor was, after all, an intimidating war horse that most avoided.

Brom guided Tor through the Sandori, west toward the Pan'Dale Keep. It was slow going at first, this portion of the forest still untamed. It was a tangle of overgrown brush and vines that threatened to ensnare weary travelers. This portion of the Sandori was also home to the shadow bear. A gigantic bear that could easily take down a horse Tor's size. It would be unwise to let his guard down. It was not only the bears that wandered this forest. Graekull could appear at any time from an abandoned well or a deep ravine that had tunnels leading from Abaddon. Brom's Manuk horn was always at his side in case a graekull did appear.

"You should hold on to me," Brom said when Tor hopped over a fallen tree. He thought Sterling would fall off, but she stayed seated.

"I'm alright," she said, her words muffled against his back. She was a very still person, she made no unnecessary movements and kept the space she took up very small, "Say," her voice almost a whisper, "why don't you wear a shirt?"

Brom was taken by surprise at first but laughed at the question. "We Veillen display our tanak, these markings. It would be rude to hide our victories."

"You're a Veillen?" her voice rose with the question.

"Aye," Brom answered. He expected her to say more, but she fell silent as they continued through the Sandori.

Brom was thankful the morning's chill had faded away by the time the sun had reached its midday zenith. It had been arduous navigating the dense Sandori with Sterling at his back, but they finally reached the Arevelyan Road. Once a magnificent example of Kai'Varian engineering, the long ancient road stretched from the banks of the Furiosa River in the west to the eastern shores of Kai'Vari. On its way it ran through the heart of the capital, Sela'Char. All that was left of the road were a smattering of ruins from the long war with Duenin, when Kell Wrenkin thought to invade Kai'Vari.

Brom's thoughts were on their neighbors to the north when Sterling tapped him on the shoulder, "Can we take a break?"

Brom reined in Tor and offered his arm to Sterling. She dismounted with an experienced deftness. She bent and stretched her legs, then wandered off behind one of the bareq trees. She returned after only a few minutes and was walking toward Brom when the sound of a wagon came rumbling down the road. It was Berk Pan'Dale, a local farmer who seemed to have a perpetual smile on his weathered face.

Brom watched Sterling as her eyes widened and she hurried back to his side. She quickly vaulted off his foot to land behind him.

"Brom, what has you out here?" Berk pulled the wagon to a halt alongside Tor.

Brom glanced over his shoulder, "Found this one running from the Severon."

Berk looked at Sterling, who stared back at him, "Wowee, a Devian, would you look at that." Berk whistled his amazement. "I haven't seen one of your kind in many a year. You nothin' but skin and bones girl," Berk laughed, "I have chickens with more meat on their bones than you do."

Brom chuckled, "I'm sure once Moira gets her hands on her she'll be fatter than one of your pigs."

Berk laughed, his sparsely-toothed smile etched deep laugh lines in his weathered and tanned skin, "Isn't that the truth." Berk slapped the reins against the horse's back and rode alongside Tor. "You got some new nors this time around?" Berk asked without taking his eyes off the road.

"Aye, three this time. Gavin, you know and Gregor should be arriving with the other two, Tibal Ar'Bethnot and Oramek Fal'Barbner."

"Ar'Bethnot, you'll have a time with him," Berk laughed, "The whole lot of them think they're better than everyone else. And a Fal'Barbner, that's a hard working Tohm. He'll be an asset to you Veillen."

Brom agreed with Berk's opinion. He did not look forward to training a snobbish Ar'Bethnot and Gavin, he feared, would be too naïve to make it in the ranks of the Veillen. *The Fal'Barbner on the other hand...* He was optimistic about Oramek. As a Fal'Barbner himself, Conal knew the boy and had nothing but praise for the lad.

Now that they were on the main thoroughfare Brom wanted to increase their speed. As it was, the sun would be setting by the time they reached Pan'Dale. "Come sit in front of me." Tor came to a stop at a mere squeeze of Brom's thighs. "Come along," he urged Sterling.

"I don't want to," she said, her voice like a petulant toddler. "I'm fine back here."

Berk laughed, slapping his knee, "You got a spitfire in that one." Berk cracked the reins again and waved goodbye to Brom and Sterling. As much as he liked Berk, the man's toothless laughter raked his skin.

Brom heaved a sigh. "I do not," he said as he turned in the saddle and forcefully lifted Sterling and dropped her in his lap, "have time for your tantrums."

Sterling was shocked when she was suddenly sitting in front of Brom. She purposefully elbowed him in the side as she situated herself more comfortably.

"Don't test me girl," Brom urged Tor into a gallop and they quickly passed Berk as he ambled down the road. Brom could still hear Berk's laughter as they continued toward Pan'Dale.

Being near this man does not make my skin crawl, Sterling thought, and realized she was thankful for some small favors. On her escape from Sionaad, whenever she encountered men along the way her skin would crawl and itch if they got too close to her. The thought of having someone touch her made her want to vomit.

It was late afternoon when the walls of Pan'Dale and Menarik village rose to greet them. As they rode through the streets, Sterling could see that the village was winding down as evening approached. Many of the villagers were in their homes, but those that still wandered the streets greeted Brom as he neared the Keep.

The road leading toward the Keep was narrow and dropped off steeply on either side. It was the only path that led from the village to the Keep. It was a strategic design put in place hundreds of years ago that had managed to protect the Pan'Dale stronghold from invaders.

"This is Pan'Dale, and the village is Menarik," Brom explained as they continued up the road. "My sister lives here with her husband the Arl, Orrven Pan'Dale. My sister is a healer and will tend to your wounds."

Pan'Dale, the name, was synonymous with power. Orrven was now the Arl of the Pan'Dale family which had defended the border for nearly five hundred years. Orrven led the Vesperrin whose warriors were tasked with protecting the border between Kai'Vari and Duenin. Brom had great respect for his brother-in-law. He was one of the few people that could hold his own in a hand-to-hand fight with a Veillen.

The sun's rays cast a dark shadow across the courtyard where they crossed the lowered drawbridge and moved into the stable yard. The stables were abutted against the thick wall that encircled Pan'Dale Keep. Tor, a seasoned warhorse, shook his head knowing he would soon be able to rest. Brom shifted his weight back and Tor came to a stop in front of the stables. They were greeted by Otto, the stable master, "Well, look what the cat caught."

"Otto," Brom said in way of greeting. He dismounted then helped Sterling down from Tor's back. Her demeanor had changed drastically since they crossed the bridge. She seemed timid and almost afraid.

"Where'd you find the urchin?" Otto asked, staring at Sterling who had somehow maneuvered herself so that Brom stood between her and Otto.

Otto was nearing his sixties but had the strength and stamina of men half his age. Brom could understand Sterling's timidity toward the man, but he really was harmless. "This is Sterling, she escaped the Severon." Brom was hesitant to mention her Tohm name just yet.

"Well stop your hidin' and let me get a look at ya," Otto said as he tried to peer around Brom, but Sterling evaded Otto's gaze and circled around Brom to keep Otto on the other side.

"What are you hiding from?" Brom grew irritated by Sterling's behavior and solved the problem by stepping out of the way. Left standing alone Sterling looked helpless in the oversized uniform, with her hair hanging in matted tangles. She kept her gaze down, hiding her eyes from Otto's inspection.

"Bastards, the lot of them," Otto spat on the ground when he took in Sterling's condition. "Did you kill 'em?"

"We left a few of them alive." Brom responded, leaving Sterling to untie the pack from the back of the saddle.

Otto joined him and nudged him in the shoulder then whispered, "Be careful of that one Brom. She's got the look of someone who has been fighting to survive for a very long time." Brom knew what he meant and had already witnessed her ability to protect herself.

If in a desperate situation, she would not hesitate to fight to survive even if it meant harming someone who had been kind to her. *Even someone who had saved her life*, he thought.

"Where is my sister?" Brom asked, turning toward the Keep.

"She should be preparing for the evenin' meal," Otto answered.

"Come on," Brom motioned for Sterling to follow him, but when she remained in place he stopped and looked back at her. The look on her face was one of fear and uncertainty. He could understand her doubt, "There is nothing to fear."

She looked at him for a long moment before taking a step out of the stables. Brom turned and started toward the Keep. She followed him at a distance, but as they got closer to the main building the number of Pan'Dale warriors increased. He couldn't help but notice that she clung to his back like a cloak, her hand wrapped around Tryg's scabbard.

The warriors were milling about, freshly bathed and clean. His sister would never abide an unclean warrior stepping foot in the Hall for dinner. It had been a standing order since she married Orrven that no man would be served dinner if he had dirt under his nails or smelled of sweat.

Pan'Dale had a full army at its disposal. Men from all over Kai'Vari came to Pan'Dale to be part of the Vesperrin. Brom knew many of the warriors that were stationed at Pan'Dale, but despite having fought alongside them, many were still cautious of him. He was used to their whispers and side remarks, but it seemed this time the girl at his back was gaining more attention as he waded through the throng of warriors.

He could feel her trembling and wondered what had her so afraid. He paused and looked down at her. She was huddled at his back, her head lowered so no one could see her eyes. She'd managed to shrink her size down to as small as possible. When he glanced around he realized why she was acting the way she was. The warriors were huddled around like a hulking great beast and she was the tiny mouse that was its prey.

"Brom got himself a woman," one of the warriors called out, which caused the whole group to press in closer to see the girl. She flinched when one reached out, "Let's see the beauty that snared the great Brom Da'Gaihen."

In a move he suspected was the sheer will to defend herself, Sterling pulled the short blade that was nestled at Brom's back and sliced out at the men who were too close for her liking. Before she could do any damage Brom plucked the knife from her hand, sheathed the blade and let out a bellow that silenced the mob, "Move." The men split revealing an open path for Brom. He took hold of Sterling's hand and pulled her behind him. *I don't have time for this.*

"Brom!" His sister stood at the end of the path, a smile on her face at seeing him. Her dark green dress complimented her hazel eyes and brown hair. Her cheeks were flushed with the afternoon sun as she examined each warrior at the door to make certain they were clean before she allowed them to enter her home. With a stature taller than most women, she was a warrior in her own right. She commanded the warriors of Pan'Dale just as much as her husband.

"Moira." Brom greeted his younger sister, pulling Sterling to stand beside him.

Her eyes immediately went to Sterling, filled with curiosity. "It's a girl," Moira stated but stopped when she noticed the silver eyes of a Devian staring back at her, "She's a Devian," she added with a bit of surprise and confusion in her voice.

Brom sighed, "Your statement of the obvious is mind-boggling." He loved his sister, but sometimes, he just… He sighed again, "This is Sterling."

"Hello dear," Moira started with a smile which quickly faded when the wind shifted, "Oh my, you smell like a dead rat."

Brom quickly stepped in when Sterling opened her mouth, unsure how Sterling would respond to the comment. "Moira, Sterling is in need of you care."

"Well why didn't you say so?" Moira groused and motioned for them to enter.

They followed Moira while she moved up the curving stair-case to the portion of the Keep reserved for the Pan'Dale family and their guests. Sterling followed close behind Brom, her hand seeming to be permanently attached to Tryg's scabbard. *She's becoming too attached to me*, Brom thought. *I've too much to do to worry about this child.*

Moira stopped in front of a door that was adjacent to the one she'd set aside for Brom's use. Normally, when visiting other Tohms he would sleep in the barracks with the other Veillen, but Moira refused to let him sleep anywhere but in a guest room in the Keep.

"In you go my dear," Moira opened the door and stepped aside to let Sterling enter, "I'll be right with you." Moira closed the door and turned to Brom. He knew what was coming and he braced himself for the avalanche of questions.

"Where'd you find her?"

"Where'd she come from?"

"She's not diseased or anything, is she?"

"How old is she?"

Brom crossed his arms over his chest and leaned against the wall, waiting for his sister to finish.

"Sorry." A soft blush highlighted her cheeks, "Go ahead."

"I didn't find her." Brom answered her first question, "She barreled her way into a graekull I was hunting. She was fleeing Duenin and the Severon." Brom debated telling his sister that she claimed to be a Rin'Ovana. "She escaped the Severon and they followed her across the border."

"The Severon? They were here, on Pan'Dale land?"

"Yes."

"Oh dear," Moira was rubbing her hands anxiously. She knew if Orrven found out he'd be hunting them down in an instant. "What did you do?"

"I took care of them." There was no need for him to expand his explanation.

"Oh," The tension eased from her shoulders.

Brom brought the conversation back around to Sterling, "Aside from a worrisome fever, she has several wounds that have started to fester and a knot on her head," he said, tapping Moira on the head where Sterling's knot had formed.

"I'll tend to her Brom. You go eat with the men. Besides, Orrven is anxious to see you."

"What has him concerned?" Orrven was the epitome of a rock. He worried little because he had confidence in his army and knew that they could handle anything that was thrown at them. If Orrven was anxious it was mostly something beyond his control.

"There has been an increase recently in the number of graekull attacks."

Just as Brom had suspected. Orrven would need to request more Veillen troops from Var'Khundi if the sightings had increased.

Brom was just about to leave when Moira stopped him, "Brom, when you see Cinri, please have him bring my kit, and some hot water."

Brom nodded and started toward the Hall. The enticing aroma of food wafted up the stairs teasing Brom's senses. He stopped Moira before she could open the door, "Moira,"

"Yes?"

"She claims to be a Rin'Ovana."

"Truly?" Moira's enthusiasm was plastered to her face.

"Aye, but promise me one thing though," he said to his sister in a serious, hushed tone... "Keep that Rin'Ovana detail close to your heart as long as you can. The last thing we need are prying eyes wandering our way, even here. The less eyes the better in this case, yes?" Moira clamped both hands over her mouth, nodding gently. Still, her ruby cheeks stretched underneath and gave away the delightful smile still playing across her face.

19

HEALER

Moira watched Brom as he descended the stairs. Once alone, she took a deep breath and steeled her nerves before turning the knob and entering the room. *I can't believe she's a Devian* was all she could think about, *and a Rin'Ovana on top of that.* Moira was excited.

Pushing the door open she stepped in to the room. *Sterling,* Moira said the name to herself, *Sterling Rin'Ovana.* Moira thought the name suited the girl. She advanced into the room to find Sterling just standing in the center as if she was unsure of what to do.

"Are you all right, my dear?" Moira asked, approaching Sterling.

"I'm afraid to touch anything." Sterling said, her cheeks flushed. Moira expected her flushed cheeks were more from a fever than from embarrassment.

"Never you mind," Moira said as she rummaged around in the wardrobe for a nightshirt to replace the filthy clothes Sterling was wearing. "Whatever gets dirty can be washed," Moira continued with her head in the armoire. *Here it is!* Moira thought excitedly.

Moira pulled a long nightshirt out of the drawer and turned to Sterling who continued to stand in the center of the room, unmoving.

"Milady," Cinri's voice was followed by a small knock on the door, "I have your kit."

"Oh, splendid." Moira hurried to the door and took the box from Cinri. "Thank you Cinri."

"I shall be right outside, if you need to call for me."

Moira was sure it was Brom's instructions to Cinri to remain close. Her brother was ever the warrior and always cautious.

"All right, come here my dear, let's take a look at you."

Sterling hesitated for a moment. This was the first time in a very long time that anyone had been kind to her. She felt a relief wash over her and all she could do was follow Moira's instructions. She felt detached from her own body as Moira pulled the cotton uniform shirt over her head.

Sterling thought she heard Moira gasp when she noticed the network of scars that were scored into Sterling's chest, back and sides. The marks that Helios had burnt into her skin throbbed with a dull pain. *I'll forever be reminded of my time spent in Sionaad,* Sterling thought.

"Come sit," Moira pulled the padded stool from the vanity and instructed Sterling to sit. She examined each of Sterling's arms before reaching into a medium sized box that seemed to contain all manner of vials and bits of gauze. "We need to clean these wounds before they become any more infected than they already are."

Sterling sat patiently while Moira took out a small piece of cloth and soaked it in a strong-smelling liquid. Sterling was unprepared for the pain she would endure when Moira pressed the cloth to the open scrapes and cuts on her back.

"Ouch!" Sterling tried to dodge away from Moira's ministrations, but Moira held her still.

"Just bear with it," Moira's jovial manner was gone. Her brow was furrowed as she examined the lash marks inflicted by Engram.

She grew quiet as she worked her way around Sterling's body. Sterling became accustomed to the sting of the liquid and accepted the fact that it would hurt, but the salve Moira smeared on each wound had a numbing affect that seemed to erase all the pain.

Moira worked quietly as she examined Sterling's arms. She smeared a thick paste on the burns and then wrapped them in a thin gauze. "May I ask you a question?" she said while pulling the night shirt down over Sterling's head. She helped her get her arms in the sleeves.

Sterling nodded in response.

"How long were you a prisoner?"

Sterling thought about it for a moment, "I was taken to Sionaad on the 30th of Unda."

"The 30th of Unda?" Moira repeated, in shock. Then she said, "Today is the seventh of Turcia."

The amount of time Sterling had lost to the Severon hit her squarely in the chest - *six months of my life is gone*. Half a year wasted in a dark prison cell.

"Well," Sterling could hear the tears in Moira's voice, but she cleared her throat before continuing, "you are safe now. The Severon will never touch you again."

Sterling doubted she would ever get rid of the Severon. They followed her into her dreams.

Moira pulled a large bottle of out her box and poured a small amount of its contents, an amber liquid that smelled of lavender, into a small glass, "This is a mixture of valerian root and lavender, it will help you sleep."

Sterling took the glass and sipped the contents. It wasn't too terrible, *flowers with a slight hint of pine*. She drank the rest of the liquid.

Moira pulled another glass bottle from the box. She uncorked it and poured two tiny pellets into her hand, "This is feverfew. It will help with your fever." She filled the small glass with water and handed the two pellets to Sterling.

"What am I supposed to do with these?" Sterling asked rolling the two tiny round pellets around in her hand.

"You swallow them," Moira laughed. "Place them on the back of your tongue and take a big gulp of water and they'll wash right down."

Sterling was skeptical, but she followed Moira's directions.

"Come now," Moira helped Sterling to her feet and led her to the bed. "Let's get rid of those disgusting trousers." Sterling held the night gown up while Moira unfastened the belt Sterling had cinched tight around her waist. Sterling heard the slight gasp from Moira when she saw the scars that slithered up and down her legs.

"The Severon are very thorough," Sterling couldn't help the words that slipped past her lips.

"They should all rot in Abaddon," Moira's voice was angry, but she was gentle as she removed the trousers. She helped Sterling into the bed and looked at the blisters on Sterling's feet. She gave them the same care as her arms and wrapped her feet and ankles in gauze. "In you go," Moira smiled as she pulled the duvet back and directed Sterling to get into the bed.

"But I'm filthy," Sterling said. She did not want to get the white sheets dirty.

"Don't mind," Moira said, "you just lie down and get some rest. When you wake up we'll get you all cleaned up."

Sterling wondered if this is what it felt like to have a mother to care for her. She could feel herself sinking into the soft mattress as Moira stoked the fire. Moira watched over her until the draw of sleep was too much for Sterling and she drifted into nothingness.

20

GATHERING STORM

Dinner was in full swing by the sounds that echoed up the stairs. Tables were lined with men from Pan'Dale as well as those from other Tohms. The combination of food and drink was causing an all-out raucous of toasting their lord and cheering. Brom's stomach growled in response to the aromas that lingered in the air.

"Brom!" His brother-in-law strode across the great hall to greet him. Orrven was a man among men. With his tall, lean frame he was just slightly taller than Brom's six-foot, three-inch height. Three years older than Brom at thirty-four, he had met Moira in Sela'Char and fell in love. They'd wed when Orrven was twenty-four and Moira just eighteen. Orrven had become the youngest Arl in Kai'Vari and commanded both the Vesperrin and the respect of the other Arls. Blue eyed and blonde, many of the Kai'Varian women had vied for his attention, but he had eyes only for Moira. Brom was pleased that Orrven had been the one to woo and win his sister's heart. There was no better man for Moira.

"How was your hunt? Did you find your graekull?"

"That and more," Brom answered as he and Orrven headed toward the main table that stood at the head of the great hall. "We encountered a small group of Severon on the way back."

"Tell me of this girl you found," Orrven leaned over and whispered, "Conal tells me she is a Devian, is that true?"

"Aye, they claimed her a fugitive, but she'd been tortured." Brom sat in the large chair to Orrven's right, "They alleged she killed two of their own and some orphans, though I doubt that part to be true."

Orrven chuckled, "She's more a hero than a fugitive then."

"It would seem." Brom looked around, "Where is my cousin by the way?"

"He was at the range earlier. Conal was teaching him how to use the sendoa bow."

"How did he do?" Brom couldn't contain the chuckle that escaped. The sendoa was the most powerful of all the Veillen bows. It took immeasurable strength and years of training to use the sendoa. Conal had been trying to fully draw the string for as many years as Brom had known him and despite being a Master Archer, he could still only draw the large weapon about three quarters of the way.

"Oh, he was able to draw it, but not even a quarter back," Orrven grinned.

Brom snorted, "That's more than I expected. I suppose I owe you a coin."

Orrven laughed lightly as he sipped upon a mug of a'kel. "Indeed, I need it to help pay Conal back five." Brom eyed Orrven for a moment. There was a silence before both men erupted in laughter.

Brom's stomach growled in great protest as soon as a covered platter was placed on the table. Orrven let out another laugh. "When the cook found out you were coming she prepared your favorite dish. And judging by the way your stomach just roared, I'd say I'd be hesitant to take my fair share without pulling back a nub." Orrven uncovered the platter placed before them to reveal a succulent roast accompanied by potatoes and carrots. Brom's mouth watered at the sight.

"Your Veillen comrades left yesterday after word of another graekull was spotted west of here."

"Moira mentioned there had been an increase in attacks. Has Streegar requested more troops be sent from Var'Khundi?"

Orrven shook his head, "Streegar said he'd travel to Var'Khundi himself and request more men and that they wouldn't be back for a while."

Brom's stomach suddenly soured at the news.

"I was surprised when he left with all of his men," Orrven continued.

"Aye," Brom agreed, "he should have left at least one of his men behind." *That damned Streegar*, Brom thought, *leaving Pan'Dale without a Veillen to protect it from a possible attack.* Brom was happy when Streegar Fan'Gorn had been assigned to the Pan'Dale Hold. He was a talented warrior when it came to fighting, but in manners of business he had little common sense. Brom could see the concern in Orrven's furrowed brow.

"It's concerning," Orrven said around a mouthful of potatoes, "the number of graekull attacks has increased recently. Normally we may have had one or two a month, but just two weeks ago we had two groups of three attack. Of course, that is on top of this most recent onslaught."

"It's not just here in the west," Brom informed Orrven, "I've heard the Manuk several times on my journey here from Sela'Char." Brom had indeed heard the wailing of the Manuk horns echo across the Kai'Varian forest and plains. The horns were from the Manuk that lived in the canopy of the Midori. The horns were the perfect tool to pass the word along of an attack. "I'll not leave you and Moira without protection," Brom added, "I'll remain here until Streegar returns, or reinforcements arrive."

Orrven nodded, "You have my thanks." He chuckled but there was no humor in the sound, "My men are fearsome, but I doubt even our strongest of men could protect us against more than one of those demons."

Brom silently agreed with Orrven. In fact, Brom doubted that Orrven's men could even hold one graekull for more than just a couple of minutes. Veillen existed solely for fighting the demons that escaped Abaddon.

"Brom, you made it!" Gavin called out as he ran across the hall and sat cheerfully next to Brom, his face red from exertion.

Conal nodded at Brom, "He has potential, but needs training, a lot of training."

"I was able to draw it nearly halfway," Gavin boasted.

"Halfway?" Conal scoffed. "You barely pulled it a quarter of the way."

"Well, it's still better than what Orrven can pull." Gavin pointed at the Arl.

They all laughed at Orrven's expense, "Not even a quarter?" Brom laughed as well.

"Where is my wife?" Orrven bellowed around a mouthful of meat, trying to divert the unwanted attention.

"She is tending to Sterling," Brom remarked. The mood turned somber at the mention of Severon. "She is covered in wounds that needed attention."

"Brom, every time you come to my home you manage to occupy your sister's time with some needless task. I forbid you from coming here again," Orrven smiled.

Brom grunted and dug into the roast. He'd forgotten how much he enjoyed food not cooked over an open flame. He motioned for the servant and another platter was placed before him. He was halfway through when he saw Moira enter the hall. He stopped, fork halfway to his mouth. She was pale, too pale. He put the utensil down and stood.

"When do we leave for Var'Khundi?" Gavin asked.

"Master Brom," Cinri approached Brom with a sealed parchment, "this just arrived from Sela'Char."

Brom took the parchment and examined the wax seal to find the Veillen cross. Brom broke the seal and read the missive. "It seems we are staying longer than expected," Brom tossed the parchment to the side, "Gregor and the other two nors are held up in Sela'Char."

"When are they expected?" Gavin asked.

Brom ignored Gavin's inquiry and made his way over to Moira. The room was filled with the entire Pan'Dale army, but no one paid any attention to Brom as he headed toward his sister.

"What is wrong?" he asked her. She had tears in her eyes.

"Oh, Brom." She wiped away a tear that escaped down her cheek.

"What is wrong Moira?" Brom had a sudden fear that Sterling had somehow harmed his sister. Had he made a mistake leaving Moira with Sterling, who was still an unknown?

"There are so many scars," Moira said, around a sob. "What she has endured I would not wish upon my enemy." She leaned into Brom with her head down. "They are truly evil," she mumbled.

Brom put his hand on Moira's shoulder. He felt awkward and clumsy as he consoled his sister. "She is out of danger now. She will be safe here."

Moira nodded, "Her fever should pass soon. The droglin paste helped and I've given her some feverfew."

"Good, now go see to your husband. He is angry that I have kept you from him." Moira blushed and pushed past Brom and ran to her husband's side. He watched as she kissed Orrven on the lips and took her place beside him.

Moira was an excellent healer and she had seen plenty of wounds inflicted by both man and demon, but he hated to expose her to the Severon's brutality. He had protected her until she had married Orrven – now it was Orrven's job to see to her safety. Many men had wooed Moira when she came of age, but Brom had declined them all until Orrven demanded her hand. There was no hesitation on Brom's part in accepting the Pan'Dale Arl's proposal. It did not hurt that Moira had fallen madly in love with Orrven.

Brom gave one last glance at his sister's smiling face and exited the great room. Though the food was delicious, it was not in him tonight to deal with the chaos that was the evening dinner. He was exhausted from the hunt and filthy from travel. The draw of sleep was calling to him, but first he needed to wash the dirt from his tired body. In the coming days he expected the arrival of Gavin's fellow nor'Veillen. He would start their training here at Pan'Dale while he waited for Streegar's return.

Brom made his way to the bathing chamber below the kitchens. He leaned Tryg against the wall and disrobed. Before wading into the deep water, he sat on a low stool and scrubbed the filth and grime from his tired and sore muscles. He dumped a bucket of warm water over his head and scrubbed soap in to his hair and beard. His hair had grown longer while traveling to and from Sela'Char, perhaps he should have it cut before heading to Var'Khundi. Two more buckets rinsed away the soap along with the dirt.

Happy with the results, Brom lowered his body into the warm water until all but his head was above the surface. His aches eased away as the warmth soaked into his bones. The hot baths were the one thing he missed the most when he traveled across Kai'Vari. *And the cook's roasts,* Brom thought as he patted his full stomach, smiling.

Brom closed his eyes and leaned his head against the stone that ran along the edge of the bath. He had few opportunities to relax and he planned to take full advantage of this rare occurrence. The sound of heavy footsteps echoed down the stone steps to the bath. Brom opened one eye to see who it was that was disturbing his peace.

"I knew you'd be here," Conal said as he appeared from the dark stairwell.

Brom grunted and closed his eye.

"Gavin finally crashed after eating two platters of roast." Conal completed his own pre-bath ritual and slipped into the bath across from Brom. The water rippled across the large pool and lapped at the stone.

"He has always been full of energy." It was true that Gavin went non-stop, always chattering about something. His exuberance exhausted Brom.

"Perhaps you can channel his energy into his training."

Brom chuckled, "We can only hope."

"What are you going to do with the girl?" Conal inquired.

It was a question Brom had asked himself several times. He wanted to leave her in Moira's care, but the fact that she was a Devian and a Rin'Ovana made the decision a difficult one.

Brom stood, stepping out of the bath. "How long are you on leave?" Brom asked, drying himself before stepping into his pants and fastening the belt at his waist.

"I've a month before I have to return to Sela'Char," Conal replied. "But I'm leaving for the Fal'Barbner Hold in a day or two."

Brom picked up Tryg from where he'd placed his faithful sword and strapped the weapon to his back. "If you stay here too long Orrven will set you to work training his young archers," Brom said as he retrieved his boots and turned to leave.

"I refuse!" Conal's response bounced off the thick walls. "He'll have to contend with my wife if I stay any longer." Conal was the highest-ranking archer in all Kai'Vari and trained the young warriors sent to Sela'Char to serve in their King's army.

"Orrven would never survive," Brom chuckled as he left Conal in the bath and made his way upstairs toward the living quarters. The hour had grown late, and the great hall had emptied of its revelers. The Pan'Dale warriors had retreated to their barracks located just outside the main building. Streegar and the other Veillen had their own barracks separate from Orrven's men, but the building stood empty with Streegar having left for Var'Khundi.

Brom entered his room and closed the door behind him. He was exhausted after being around so many humans. *Humans.* He was a human, wasn't he? He'd been born a human, but how many years had he fought the demons that emerged from the deep recesses of the earth? *There are times,* he mused, *that I feel half dead and half demon.* How many times had he faded into the Veil, into the realm of the dead? No human had the strength that he and the other Veillen possessed.

Is this really your will for us Orla? Brom wondered to himself. For the Veillen to protect the helpless humans from the demons that found their way out of Abaddon? Without Moraug's seal the gate stood open. Orla had tasked the Veillen with keeping the graekull in check and it was a task they had perfected, but when would the task end? It had been over a thousand years since Wrenkin had killed Moraug. When would the gates be sealed forever and the Veillens' task be done? How many more warriors would he see die at the hands of the corruption and greed that filled men's hearts?

Brom sat on his bed and situated his boots against the wall. He placed his sword on the bed next to him and laid back on the soft mattress and put his hands behind his head. Exhaustion pulled at him and made his eyelids heavy. He'd been on the road for over a month and the feel of the soft mattress surrounding him stripped away the last barrier to sleep.

A loud thud in the adjacent room brought Brom out of his haze instantly. He stood by the door to the adjoining room and listened. After a moment he turned the handle and pushed the door open. It was dark save for a single candle that struggled to illuminate the large room. The flame sputtered, threatening to go out, but the little flame held on and sparked back to life. Brom walked silently across the room and paused when he found the large bed empty. The shutters to the windows stood closed to the night air. Sterling had to be in the room.

A sob caught his attention and he peered around the opposite side of the bed. There, huddled in the corner, he found Sterling. She was curled up into a tight protective ball, with her arms wrapped around her legs and her face tucked into her knees. A single tear reflected in the flickering candlelight. Another low and heartrending sound escaped her cracked and dry lips as she gripped her legs tighter to her chest. Her arms were covered in bandages as were her feet. Behind the fabric of the nightgown, Brom could see Moira's other handiwork with the bandages that swathed the girl from nearly head to toe.

Brom sighed. *This girl*, he thought, *is more trouble than she is worth*. He scooped her up, her skin icy cold, and placed her in the center of the giant bed. She remained in her protective ball as he pulled the heavy duvet up to her chin. He stood there, watching her, until her body relaxed, her grip loosening so her legs could stretch out. The bed was so large she appeared as a child. She seemed calm, but every now and then her body would twitch and her brow furrow. A mumbled '*no*' would escape her cracked lips as if she was trying to fend off an attacker. Did she dream of Engram and the Severon?

Resigned to the fact that he could do nothing about her nightmares, Brom turned to leave, but stopped when icy fingers touched him. He looked down to watch her wrap her fingers around his much larger battle worn hand. Her eyes were still closed, but he knew it was not a restful sleep. Her furrowed brow relaxed as her fingers tightened around his. Brom sighed again and gently pried her fingers open, but as soon as he released himself from her grip the worried look on her sleeping face returned. Her hand moved about in a frantic search for something to grasp on to. A moan swept past her lips as her jaws clenched. "No." The sound was a mere whisper, but the desperation in that single word was enough for Brom to take hold of Sterling's hand again.

The moment their skin touched, the stress in her small body seemed to flow away. Relaxed once again, she fell into a restful sleep.

"Damn it," Brom groaned beneath his breath and sat down on the bed beside Sterling, the mattress dipping under his weight. He was exhausted. He had hoped once he handed her over to Moira he could wash his hands of her. He leaned his head against the massive headboard and closed his eyes. "When did I become a nursemaid?" he asked the question of the dark room.

He sighed and looked down at her for a moment and noticed her forehead clammy with sweat. Her long brown hair was matted in places and clung to her damp skin. He found the washing basin by her bed, the water now long cooled. With thick calloused fingers, he pulled out the small shred of cloth and wrung it gently. Taking a moment to brush the stray strands of hair away from her forehead, he began to gently wipe away the sweat still clinging to her face. He smiled gently for a moment, before wetting the cloth once more and gently brushing it against her face.

And did so throughout the rest of the night.

21

CLEAN

Dan'Ruok, 9th Turcia, 1021

Sterling sat up, pushing her hair out of her face. She was in a massive bed in a luxurious room. It was like nothing she had seen before. The walls were a soft blue with white accents that reminded Sterling of the afternoon sky. The furniture, the bed and night stand were fashioned of dark wood and the mattress was thick and plush and firm pillows surrounded her. Two chairs sat against the opposite wall with a small table between them. A bouquet of white flowers adorned the table.

Sterling felt a great weight lift off her shoulders the moment she and Brom had ridden across the bridge to Pan'Dale. The Severon could not reach her here, at least she prayed they could not. She'd given her trust to Kellen only to be betrayed. How did she know she could trust these Pan'Dales? Sterling looked down at her gauze wrapped arms and remembered the care she had been given.

Sterling eased herself out of the bed and onto the plush rug that covered the wide planks of the wood floor. She winced as she put her full weight on her legs. Despite the gauze and the ointment Moira had spread across the blisters, her feet ached, as did her legs from running.

She gingerly wandered the room, looking out the windows that were covered by a soft sheer fabric. She was surprised to find that when she pushed on the glass, the panes opened, and a breeze rushed into the room. She took a deep breath filling her lungs with the fresh air and expelling the dank air from her prison. Sterling glanced down and found herself to be on the second or third floor of the Keep. Below her, a wide training field stood empty in the early morning. A tall stone wall ran the perimeter of the Keep and beyond the wall Sterling could see a forest that spread out below them. Adjacent to the wall were several two-story stone buildings. Sterling wondered what their purpose was.

A wardrobe stood against the wall opposite the windows. It was a wide, grand piece of furniture. Curious, Sterling opened the two sturdy doors and found a selection of dresses and shoes that stood at attention on the floor of the wardrobe. Sterling's lip curled at the dresses and she closed the doors with a click. Next to the wardrobe, she noticed a second door from the one that led to the hall. *A closet perhaps?* Sterling walked across the room and reached for the handle. The door opened and on the other side was a similar room to her own, but with more rugged and sparse furniture.

"That's Brom's room," Sterling jumped at the sound of Moira's voice and quickly closed the door. Moira stood in the doorway with a tray of food in her hands. Moira laughed, "I thought you might be hungry."

Sterling's stomach growled in celebration. Moira laughed and carried the tray to the table that sat between the two chairs. On the tray was an assortment of fruit, ham, a large pile of steaming scrambled eggs, and a glass of fresh milk. Sterling couldn't help but gobble down the food as fast as she could. It had been so long since she had a real meal.

"Slow down or you'll have a stomach ache."

Sterling glanced at Moira over the glass and shook her head, "I don't care," she managed around the food.

Moira laughed at Sterling's delight in the simple fare Vita had prepared for her. While Sterling ate, Moira stood near the windows that overlooked the training grounds. The morning was bright, and the sun was warm. Moira threw open the windows and a gentle breeze tickled her cheeks. Below, Orrven and his men were at their daily routine of sparing and sword training.

She glanced back at Sterling who was in the process of wiping her mouth with the back of her hand. Moira rolled her eyes, "You know, there was a napkin there for you to use."

"Sorry," Sterling said around a mouthful of eggs.

"Come see," Moira waved Sterling over when she laid the fork down and gulped the last bit of milk. Sterling approached the window and Moira pointed to Orrven. "See there, that is my husband Orrven, the Arl of Pan'Dale. His men protect the borders of Kai'Vari from Duenin."

On the other side of the field Moira spotted Brom as he stood silently listening to Gavin, his arms crossed in obvious annoyance. Moira could only imagine what their cousin had gotten into this time. The poor boy was never going to become a Veillen. Moira looked down and found Sterling's eyes fixated on Brom. "You've already met my brother, Brom."

Moira watched Sterling as she watched Brom. She seemed to be transfixed by Brom. Her eyes never wavered from his unyielding form. It was true Brom was sought out by many Arls for marriage, but he had already dedicated his life to Orla. Brom, with his heightened senses must have felt their eyes on him. When he turned his gaze upon them Sterling drew in a breath and stepped back out of sight.

Another breeze pushed through the room, moving the odorous scent of sweat and filth from the training grounds. Moira turned and looked down at their guest. "Oh my, Sterling, you stink." The words were out before she could stop them. Moira giggled at Sterling's embarrassment, then said, "Let us get you in to a bath and get rid of that smell."

A bath! Sterling didn't think she'd been this excited about a bath in her entire life. "That sounds amazing," Sterling said with a smile. She started to pull the night gown over her head, but paused when Moira gave her an odd look, "What?" Sterling asked.

"What are you doing?" Moira laughed.

"I'm getting ready for a bath," Sterling responded.

"Silly," Moira smiled, "we have communal baths in Kai'Vari." Moira took Sterling's hand and led her into the hall and down a narrow set of steps that led directly to the bathing chamber. As they descended, the air steadily grew thicker with the heat and the humidity. "Watch your step," Moira cautioned, "the steps get damp from the moisture down here. We're directly below the dining hall." Moira gestured upward before she pushed open a narrow wooden door and entered the chamber. A large recessed round pool sat in the center of the room, steam from the water wafted through the air and caused an otherworldly glow from the torches that lined the walls. Four pillars stood to support the chamber and benches lined the area around the pool. In the corner were low stools with smaller pools for bathing.

Moira smiled at the shock and awe upon Sterling's face. "Do they not have bathing chambers in Duenin?" she asked Sterling.

Sterling shook her head as she continued to look around, "No, only copper tubs to sit in. They are cramped and uncomfortable."

"How unpleasant," Moira said. "The air and water are warmed by the fires from the kitchens and feed through a series of pipes into the bath." Moira pointed out the intricate pipe system that lined the far wall, "As more water is added it overflows into the drains and empties in the gardens."

Sterling couldn't believe what she was seeing. Never had she imagined a room such as this. She wanted to jump into the large pool of water and started toward the steaming liquid, but was stopped by a hand on her shoulder, "First, we must wash, and then we can relax in the pool." Moira laughed before hanging her gown on a hook, "You look like a little girl in that gown." Moira pointed to one of the low stools, "Come sit."

Sterling took a deep breath and pulled the gown from her bony frame and sat on the wood stool, "I'm not a little girl. I'm twenty-one."

Twenty-one? Moira smiled to hide her anger at the treatment Sterling had endured at the hands of the Severon. S*he looks much younger,* thought Moira, *her hip bones are protruding, and her skin is hanging loosely from her emaciated body.*

Moira cleared her throat. "We need to remove those bandages first," Moira said as she started to unwrap the gauze that encircled Sterling's arms, shoulders and waist. "These are mending nicely," Moira mumbled, examining Sterling's forearms. "They'll be healed in no time."

"Thank you," Sterling said, quietly.

"No mind," Moira said, "it was the least I could do."

"You've already done so much for me." Sterling felt some guilt at having Moira fuss over her. She imagined Mother Anwell would lecture her about being grateful and accepting of the care she was given.

Moira hefted a bucket of water over Sterling's head. "Hold your breath and close your eyes," Moira said before dumping the warm water over Sterling's head. The water sloughed off Sterling's shoulders revealing skin beneath the dirt and grime.

Moira sat the bucket down and withdrew a large vial from the pocket of her dress. She showed the glass container to Sterling, "My mother-in-law gave this to me, but I think it would best serve you." She uncorked the vial and sniffed, "Lavender," she said before holding the vial under Sterling's nose, "this will surely get that stench off you."

Moira poured a small amount of the liquid over the mass of matted hair and started scrubbing. The soap quickly lathered into soft white suds, but they soon turned a deep, reddish brown. She filled the bucket with water and poured it over Sterling's head, who just sat there unmoving as Moira scrubbed away the filth.

As the water washed away the suds Moira stood in shock at the dirt that remained in Sterling's mass of hair. Moira swept dampened hair out of her face in preparation for a long battle with the dirt. She filled another bucket and dumped it, preoccupied by the dirt, without warning.

Unprepared for the dousing, Sterling choked and coughed, "At least tell me when you're going to try to drown me." Sterling glared at Moira.

Moira poured more of the lavender scented soap over Sterling's dark tresses and dug in. She thought the color to be a dark brown, almost black but with the amount of dirt and filth there was no telling what Sterling's natural color may be. "This may hurt a bit," she warned Sterling.

"Wha – OW!" Sterling tried to duck away from Moira's fingers, but she held Sterling in place by the roots of her hair. Sterling wrapped her hands around Moira's wrist, trying desperately to get her to release her hold. "Let go!" Sterling yelled.

"Absolutely not," Moira returned as she worked up a lather. Her fingers dug into Sterling's scalp cleaning the dirt and filth. A distinctly metallic smell started to overpower the lavender scent. It was then that Moira realized Sterling's hair was matted with dried blood. What had this girl gone through? Moira poured more soap on Sterling's scalp and renewed her efforts to wash away blood, dirt, and filth.

"You're worse than Mother Anwell," Sterling mumbled.

"Who is Mother Anwell?" Moira asked, hoping to get some information about Sterling's past from her. She needed to sit down with the girl and figure out where she's been all this time.

"She was the Head Mother at the Orphanage," Sterling swallowed the lump in her throat. "She was like a mother to me, but the Severon, they killed her."

Moira didn't know what to say to Sterling to ease the grief she heard in her voice, so she said nothing and continued to scrub Sterling's scalp. In a more measured voice she said, "Close your eyes," before pouring the water over Sterling's head. As before, the soap slipped down Sterling's shoulders carrying away the remnants of the silver eyed girl's life as a prisoner of the Severon.

After some time, Moira stared down at Sterling's head and sighed, "I've done as much as I can." Moira left Sterling for a moment to pull a string that was attached to a bell in the kitchen. "At least until Gilda arrives," Moira whispered to herself. Moira returned to Sterling and handed her a soft cloth and the remainder of the lavender soap. Sterling used the cloth and started to wash her body. Slowly the dirt was scrubbed away to reveal warm olive toned skin. *A Devian with the skin of a Kai'Varian*, Moira thought it odd, *with those eyes she should have the fair skin and hair of the Devians.*

"You said you were an orphan," Moira started, "do you know anything about your parents?"

"Very little," Sterling responded. "My uncle told me before he died that my father was a Rin'Ovana, a Kai'Varian warrior named…"

A hard thump on the door interrupted Sterling. The door was pushed open and standing in the doorway was Gilda Dolman. "Ah Gilda, you're here." *I'll question Sterling more later about her parents*, Moira thought as she greeted Gilda.

Originally from Paard, Gilda was a fierce and frightening woman that had been a maid for both Moira and Brom since they were children in Sela'Char. She stood as tall as any man and had thick muscular arms and a head full of long gray hair that was neatly coiffed in a bun. She was the one person that Brom avoided at all costs when she was angered. Gilda stared down at Moira with a frown and her furrowed brows that told her she was not happy that Moira had called on her for help.

"What do you need milady?" Gilda asked, advancing into the room.

"Gilda," Moira smiled, "this is Sterling. She needs some…care."

Sterling looked over her shoulder at Gilda and stared at the older woman. She turned back around and continued to play with the ends of her wet hair. Gilda seemed somewhat more affected by Sterling's presence. Shock at seeing Sterling's silver eyes flashed across her face, but she was quick to compose herself, "Leave her to me, milady." Gilda reassured Moira. "Very…" A soft knock at the door interrupted Moira, "Yes?"

"My apologies milady?" The whisper came from one of the nursemaids charged with looking after her daughter.

"What is it Raane?" Although the young nursemaid stood a safe distance from Sterling, her eyes couldn't hide her fear of Sterling.

"It's the little miss, milady." Raane jumped when Sterling turned her gaze on the young girl, "S- She has come down with a fever. We've tried what we could, but we cannot get the fever to go down."

"Sterling," Moira said as she started to dry herself, "I must attend to my daughter, so I'll leave you in Gilda's capable hands." Moira finished drying herself before pulling her dress over her head and straightening the skirts.

"Gilda, please escort her to the room next to Brom's," Moira said.

"Yes milady," Gilda smiled with a curtsy.

Moira gave Sterling one last glance, and a reassuring smile, before hurrying from the room.

22

VESPERRIN

"Report," Orrven said as he entered the map room. He'd called his three Commanders along with Brom together to discuss the Severon. The object of their pursuit was with his wife. Apparently, Moira planned to give the little girl a bath this morning.

Brom stood in the dark corner and despite his large presence seemed to make himself as if he were not in the room.

"Their camp is just east of Flint, milord," Rory Dal'Rymple, his second in command, pointed at the large map spread across the center table.

"Their numbers?" Orrven asked looking to his three Commanders, Leonard, Spencer and Winston, who oversaw the Left, Center, and Right Arms of the Vesperrin.

"They arrived with just six, but after encountering Brom their numbers were reduced," Rory answered, "but, their numbers have tripled since then."

"Eighteen men is concerning?" Leonard Kin'Mont, Commander of the Left Arm said examining the map. "You could sneak that many men easily over enemy lines."

"Aye," Spencer Ar'Bethnot agreed, "they've tried many times to sneak past my men in the center, but we've pushed them back each time."

"How were they able to get past you in the first place," Orrven looked at Spencer for his response. "Weren't your men responsible for this area?" Orrven pointed to the section of the Sarno where the Severon had easily crossed onto Kai'Vari soil.

"I take full responsibility, milord," Though the youngest of the three Commanders, Spencer was a man of honor and responsibility, "I had my men guarding the village while Brom and the other Veillen hunted the graekull."

"Damn graekull," Winston Fan'Gorn growled. "That Streegar should have been here to protect the village."

"He'll return with reinforcements," Orrven said eyeing Winston. He disliked Winston's mistrust of the Veillen, but there was nothing he could do about it.

Orrven turned to his brother-in-law, "Brom has committed to staying here until Streegar returns," Orrven reassured his Commanders.

"With all due respect, Brom, but what can one Veillen do against a mass of graekull?" Winston scoffed at Orrven's words.

Brom stepped forward into the light and opened his mouth to respond, but the young Spencer beat him to it, "Have you never seen Brom fight? The man has more strength than ten of our warriors. He's fast, blindingly so, and his blade, Tryg, I think you call it Brom?"

"Aye," Brom looked at Orrven, amusement in his eyes.

"Tryg can cut through flesh and bone and muscle as if it were nothing. I'd trust Brom with a mass of graekull more than I would a hundred of Vesperrin."

Rory laughed at Spencer's overzealous lauds, "Those are quite the accolades you've piled on Brom's head."

"I'm sure most are true," Orrven chuckled, "but the matter at hand is the Severon camped just across our border."

"Yes, milord, apologies," Both Winston and Spencer said in unison.

"I wouldn't say double your guard," Orrven shook his head, "but be vigilant none-the-less. I don't want these bastards stepping one foot onto our soil. Your men have permission to engage and eliminate the threat if they cross the border."

The six of them turned when the door opened after a short rap on the wood, "Arl," a young man bent over breathing heavy, "Arl, excuse the interruption."

"What is it," Orrven asked.

"Horns." The boy looked at Brom, "Horns from the west."

"Damn graekull," Winston cursed the demons.

As Orrven followed Brom from the map room to the battle-ments, the three commanders were close on their heels. Brom took his horn from his belt and blew three short notes into the long curving horn. The horn bellowed a deep resonating tone that could be heard for miles. A long low moan from the west sounded in response to Brom's call followed by a one short note from the other horn. Horns that belonged to the Veillen occupied the watch towers that dotted the Kai'Vari landscape.

Brom returned with one long and then one short note. Orrven knew each note meant something to the Veillen, but he'd never bothered to ask Brom what they meant. "I know you're in the middle of a conversation, but do you mind telling us what you just said?"

Brom looked at Orrven and then to the Commanders that were staring at him with confusion. Brom sighed, "The three notes were asking them to repeat themselves. The long note they returned was to say they were starting over, which they followed with one short note, meaning there's only one graekull."

"And what did you say in return?" Spencer asked.

"I responded that one Veillen was responding to their call."

"It's all a bunch of noise if you ask me," Winston groused, "but nevertheless, if you need men to assist in the hunt, I'll lend what I can."

Brom replaced the horn on his belt and turned to Winston, "Though I appreciate the offer, it would be best to keep your men here to guard the borders. I'll meet up with the tower Veillen and take care of the problem."

"Brom!" Gavin, out of breath, came running up the stairs, "Can I go?"

"Absolutely not." Brom said in response as he left the rest to stare at his back.

"Don't be in such a rush." Orrven rustled Gavin's hair, and said to the others, "Go defend our borders from the Severon."

"Yes, milord," They all said in unison.

Brom rode Tor through the empty roads of Menarik. The villagers had found shelter in their homes. The wailing horns were a cue for any Kai'Varian to quickly find shelter.

Thankfully there was no traffic along the road as Brom turned Tor to the west. He'd rendezvous with the tower Veillen and they'd hunt the graekull as a team. Normally this would be Streegar's hunt, but the damn fool up and left Pan'Dale without any protection. Pan'Dale would be in trouble if a large hunting pack emerged from Abaddon.

Unfit for the likes of Empyrean, graekull were demons born from men who were corrupt, greedy, and had treacherous hearts. They were doomed to rot in Abaddon forever. However, with Moraug's death, the gates of Abaddon stood open and the graekull escaped their torment to hunt and kill the citizens of Kai'Vari.

The Veillen were tasked with keeping the graekull in check and to protect Kai'Vari from their random appearances. They hid in deep wells, ravines, and gorges. Any hole that was deep enough for them to find their way to the surface. The graekull would continue to use the passages until they were discovered and closed off.

Brom entered the western Sandori and unhooked his horn from his belt. He blew a long tone into the horn followed by a short tone letting the tower Veillen know he was close.

A response resonated through the forest that they had heard his call. Tor deftly navigated the large bareqs of the forest until they came to the clearing where the tall Veillen tower stood watch over the forest. Well above the trees, the tower was made of stone and housed two Veillen at a time. They lived in the tower for two months and then rotated with two other Veillen that would arrive from Var'Khundi. Every Veillen had their time in the towers. Brom was just coming back from his assignment in Sela'Char.

"Here!" Brom pulled up when the tower Veillen called Brom from the base of the tower. "Torre Ar'Bethnot," the Veillen introduced himself. Torre had the regal look of an Ar'Bethnot but most Veillen that came from the prestigious Tohm had lost their air of superiority in their six months of training.

"Brom Da'Gaihen." Brom reciprocated the introduction.

"Honored," Torre said, "The beastie is north of here," Torre said mounting his horse. "Vez is watching it from the treetops."

"Do you know where it emerged?" Brom asked following Torre.

"We first noticed it to the south, and it ambled its way to the north."

"Have any other come from the south,"

"Not on our watch, but the logs do show one from six months ago, but they found the well it used."

Troubling, Brom thought. If it was a new well that was dug or a possible sink hole they would need to find it and fill it in.

Brom smelt the graekull before it came into sight. The smell of rotting flesh was synonymous with the demons. Brom squeezed his legs into Tor's side and the horse came to a stop next to Torre's mount. Dismounting, Brom pulled Tryg from its scabbard and followed Torre. They each took up positions against the trees and waited.

"It's small for a graekull," The voice came from a limb above Brom. A nimble man jumped down, "Vez Dal'Rymple," he introduced himself.

"Brom Da'Gaihen," Brom said, then continued. "Let us take care of this beast," Brom had already fought a mess of graekull this week and did not want to spend more time than needed on this one. *Kerbodia for'velki*, all three men said the chant and faded into the Veil. All three of them stood together in the bluish hue of the Veil, "We'll surround it and then attack all at once."

"Aye," Torre and Vez agreed.

They advanced on the demon and moved into a triangle formation. Brom, the more senior of the group stood to the front and Torre and Vez with their sparse tanak took up the left and right rear of the demon.

With their weapons at the ready, Brom nodded and all three said the command to release their Velkuva. As they faded from the Veil into the mortal world they brought their swords down piercing the graekull. Unprepared for the attack, the graekull spun its long arms in a sweeping pattern and nearly knocked Brom on his rear, were it not for Brom deflecting the blow at the last moment.

"Watch it," Brom said, ready for the next blow from the demon. He shifted his stance so Tryg was vertical and at shoulder height, the blade poised over Brom's head. The graekull turned on Brom and charged. *It is fast*, Brom noted as he jumped out of the way, slicing Tryg through the graekull's arm. "Now!" Brom shouted when he had the graekull's full attention.

Torre took the opportunity and attacked, slicing through the graekull's thick skin and bone. Its head rolled off to stare sightlessly at Vez. "Damn graekull," Vez said, kicking the head away from himself. Vez smiled, "I never thought I'd get to fight alongside the great Brom Da'Gaihen."

Brom chuckled, "There are far better warriors than myself."

"I hear you have one of my Tohmsmen as a nor this season," Torre said wiping his blade clean.

"Tibal," Brom said, "he's part of the main family."

Torre shook his head, "That there is a smart lad, but he's spoiled as you'd expect. If you keep after him he'll prove his worth."

"Thanks for the help," Vez said, "its unsettling, the number of graekull that have been seen recently."

"They seem more organized," Torre rubbed his chin. "It's as if they are testing our defenses."

"Now you're just being paranoid," Vez laughed and smacked Torre on the back. "They're nothing but mindless beasts."

Brom could not deny that the number of sightings was troubling. He could only hope Streeger returned quickly with more men.

23

SHORN

"She's finally asleep," Moira whispered to Raane, pulling the door shut behind her.

"I'm sorry, milady, I blame myself for the little miss's fever. She insisted on going with me to hunt for truffles yesterday."

Moira smiled and patted Raane on the shoulder, "No matter, she's better now." Raane was such a sweet girl, but naïve. Everyone in the Pan'Dale Keep knew that Lirit had Raane wrapped around her little finger.

"You must be exhausted," Moira gave Raane a gentle push toward her room, "go rest while you can."

"Yes milady," Raane bowed and hurried down the hall.

Moira wished she could crawl into her own bed and take a relaxing nap. She was exhausted after caring for both Sterling and Lirit. Her back ached after hours of leaning over while tending to her daughter, but she found some relief knowing Lirit's fever had finally broken. Lirit wasn't a sickly child compared to some, but fevers seemed to shadow her more often these days.

The whole while Moira had tended to Lirit her mind kept wandering to Sterling. She hoped Gilda had not been too rough with her. Gilda was a strict woman, but she was also very caring. The maid had seen Moira and Brom through their most difficult times after their parent's deaths. Moira had been only six at the time and Brom eight. Gilda had taken care of them until Khort and Sylvie had taken them from their abusive uncle. Not wanting to be separated, Gilda had left Sela'Char and stayed with Khort at the Rin'Ovana Keep.

Moira wanted to check on Sterling, but her stomach ached from hunger. She made her way down the hidden stairs from the living quarters to the kitchens. She was certain that Sterling would be hungry as well after the grueling bath she had endured. Moira would have Vita fix a tray for them both.

The kitchen was bustling with activity. Moira had to dodge the housemaids as they moved about prepping for another great feast. Unlike most Tohms the warriors at Pan'Dale dined with their Arl. If left unchecked the dinners at Pan'Dale would turn into chaotic celebrations, especially if she was not there to keep the order. Moira found Vita standing over a huge pot, stirring a boiling concoction. Moira asked, "What are you preparing Vita?"

"Oy," Vita jumped in surprise, "this is not food, milady."

"Oh?" Moira looked in the pot.

"Gilda asked me to boil her skirts. She said something about removing a stench that no soap could clean." Moira thought Vita was joking at first, but her heart sank as the cook explained further. "She came in here with scratches all over her face and a bundle of towels filled with hair. She was grousing about having to bathe a wild animal. She asked that I boil her skirts to get the smell out of them."

"What a fool I am." Moira's heart fell to her stomach as she turned and ran from the kitchens. She rushed past the maids that were cleaning and right into her husband's solid chest. The impact nearly knocked her to the floor. Moira quickly steadied herself and brushed passed Orrven. She heard him call after her, but she had no time to linger.

What had Gilda done to Sterling? Moira lifted her skirts and took two steps at a time until she reached the living quarters.

"Oy," Orrven called out after her, following her up the stairs, "what is your hurry?" Orrven stopped behind her, grasping her shoulders.

Moira bent over briefly to catch her breath. Pushing away from the wall, she continued to Sterling's room. Her hand hovered over the handle. It was her fault for leaving Sterling with Gilda. She knew Gilda had a temper, but she never thought she would abuse a guest. She steeled her resolve and turned the knob, but Orrven stopped her, "What is going on Moira?"

"Sterling," Moira took a deep breath, "she's been through so much and I fear I may have made it worse."

Moira turned away from Orrven and gently opened the door, afraid of what she would find on the other side, her heart racing. The sun shone brilliantly through the open windows giving the room a cheery feel. "Sterling?" Moira called out but there was no answer. She pushed the door open and stepped fully into the room, Orrven following close behind. "You shouldn't be here," she said to her husband without turning.

"There is no way I'm leaving you alone with someone that could harm Gilda. That girl must be a monster."

"She's not a monster. I'm sure she is just frightened."

Orrven closed the door and leaned against the wall and waited while Moira searched for their guest. "Sterling?" Moira called out again. The bed had been made and there was no sign that it had been disturbed since this morning. "Sterling, where are you?"

Moira glanced at the open window when the curtains billowed in the gentle breeze. *No*, Moira whispered to herself, dread filling her heart as she rushed to the window. She leaned out the opening and looked down, knowing Sterling would not have survived a fall from this height. Relief swallowed the dread, Sterling was not below.

The fact that the room overlooked the barracks and training grounds deepened her relief. Sterling would have been noticed if she had leapt from the windows.

Approaching the bed, she got down on hand and knee and looked under the massive piece of furniture. "Where is she?" Moira asked aloud.

A thump followed by a muffled moan caused Moira's head to come up. She looked to Orrven to see if he had heard the noise. His eyes were trained on the large wardrobe that sat against the opposite wall from the windows. His hand was on the hilt of his sword, ready for any threat.

Moira stood, straightening her skirts as she walked slowly across the room afraid of what she would find. Her hands were shaking as she reached for the handles of the wardrobe. She frowned at the thick leather belt that was wrapped around the handles holding the doors tightly shut. She jumped when Orrven stopped her with his hands over hers, "Let me." He took Moira's place, removing the belt and pulling the double doors open.

He slowly opened the doors, and then knelt to put a hand out to Sterling. A swift, well placed kick came out of the darkness, knocking Orrven backward. Moira leaped forward, making sure her husband was unhurt. Seeing the sword still in his hand, and knowing her husband's need for order in his home, she quickly reminded Orrven, "She's only a girl." Helping him to his feet, she asked, "Are you hurt?"

"Don't mind," he said, rubbing his chest. He quickly stood, sheathing his sword, "See to your guest." *If Moira had not been here,* he thought, *I may have taken care of this problem forever.*

Moira turned back to the wardrobe. The sight before her sent her blood into a boil. How could Gilda have done such a thing? Sterling lay naked in the base of the wardrobe with her hands and feet bound with torn scraps of fabric. A gag had been stuffed cruelly into her mouth. Sterling's gaze zeroed in on Moira with distrust and anger swirling in their silver depths.

Moira's own anger spiked at Sterling's condition, but it wasn't only the sight of the gag or the bindings that fueled Moira's anger. No, it was Sterling's lack of hair that angered her the most. Sterling's long hair had been cut haphazardly with strands sticking out in all directions and at different lengths. Moira had wanted so much to see Sterling with her long hair hanging in waves around her shoulders, to see the girl whole again, but Gilda had hacked off the long tresses.

"Let me help you," Moira whispered as she gently removed the cloth from Sterling's mouth. "I promise I never meant for this to happen." Moira tried to explain as she helped Sterling into a sitting position. Moira took the small knife she wore at her waist and cut the bonds on Sterling's feet and then her hands. Angry marks marred Sterling's skin where the fabric had been tied tightly around her wrist. Her skin was bright pink and raw from Gilda's rough handling.

Bruises? thought Moira, *who could put bruises on this already wounded girl?*

Guilt caused tears to form at the back of Moira's throat, "I'm truly-"

Moira's apology was cut short when Sterling suddenly lunged for the knife. She threw Moira to her back, sitting on top of her with the pilfered knife held to Moira's throat. Moira had no time to react to Sterling's attack before she was pulled off Moira and thrust against the wall.

"Orrven!" Moira scrambled to her feet, her hand on her husband's arm.

Orrven held Sterling in place, his hand around her throat while she dangled inches from the floor. "Orrven, please, you're choking her," Moira pleaded.

"Do not think to harm my family," Orrven snarled at Sterling while ignoring Moira's pleas, squeezing his hand tighter around Sterling's slender throat. Being the leader of the Vesperrin, Orrven demanded his orders be followed without question. He demanded the same from Sterling. "If any harm comes to my family, or anyone within the Pan'Dale hold I'll run you through without a moment's hesitation."

Sterling desperately grasped on to Orrven's arm as he held her aloft. Her eyes were wide and full of fear. She tried kicking Orrven, but with her tiny stature her legs barely reached him. "Maybe this is why you were tied like a wild animal," Orrven said as he raised his sword slightly, "perhaps Gilda is smarter than us all."

"Orrven, please." Moira pulled on her husband's arm as Sterling's lips started to turn blue.

He finally released her, letting her fall to the floor in a disheveled heap, "Devian or no you will respect this Tohm and the care you've been given. If you ever lay a hand on anyone in this Tohm again, you will regret ever setting foot on Pan'Dale land." Orrven stepped back and looked down at Moira, "You are not to be alone with her again, is that clear?"

"Yes dear," Moira knew now was not the time to argue with her husband.

He was impossible to assuage when his temper was up. She would corner him when he was in a better mood. He gave Sterling one last glance before opening the door and bellowing for the guards. Drake and Culan, two his most reliable guards, quickly came to their Arl's call and Moira could hear him speaking to them about standing guard. Drake nodded and peered through the open door, his cheeks red with embarrassment. After Orrven left them, Drake stepped into the room, closing the door behind him.

"I'm to stay with you while you are alone with her." Drake's eyes were averted from Sterling, who sat huddled, naked, against the wall.

Moira sighed, "At least turn away while I tend to her."

"Yes milady," Drake jumped and turned facing the corner of the room.

Moira turned back to Sterling and stared down at her. She looked pitiful with her hair sticking up in all directions. Sterling ran her hand through the strands as if to make sure she still had hair on her head.

"Sterling." Moira crouched in front of Sterling, "I am so sorry this happened to you. I blame myself for Gilda's actions. It is my fault for leaving her with you. I knew she had a temper and had I not left, this wouldn't have happened."

Moira felt like she needed to connect with the girl about what had happened earlier. "I know that you've lost much," she said, looking deep into Sterling's silver eyes, "but if you trust my care at all, you must try not to hurt those who are trying to help you."

Sterling nodded slightly, in agreement. She considered Moira's apology for a moment. "It is only hair, it'll grow back," the emotionless response cut Moira to the bone. "I've had much worse done to me." Sterling looked at Moira, her eyes unwavering.

"Yes, I suppose you have." Moira stood and offered her hand to Sterling, "Come along, let me tend to your wounds."

Sterling stared at Moira's offered hand for a long moment as if trying to choose if she should trust Moira. Coming to a decision, she reached out and took Moira's hand. Moira was thankful she hadn't completely lost what little trust she had gained. Pulling Sterling to her feet, Moira wrapped a sheet around her shoulders and led her to the bed. "Come sit."

Sterling kept glancing at Drake, whose back was to them. "Don't mind him," Moira whispered, "he's as harmless as a fluffy kitten."

Drake coughed to indicate that he'd heard the remark.

Moira smiled at the surprise on Sterling's face and though she tried to subdue it, Sterling smiled behind her hand. "You have a beautiful smile," Moira said as she moved Sterling's hand away from her mouth, "it would be a shame to hide it."

Sterling's smile melted as the laughter fled from her eyes and she returned to the somber girl Brom had brought to Moira. *Little by little*, Moira said to herself, *I will break down the wall Sterling has erected around her heart.*

"My fool husband," Moira muttered, examining Sterling's neck. Orrven had left a large handprint around her neck. "He went and ruined all my hard work."

"He was protecting you," Sterling replied, adjusting the sheet tighter around her shoulders. "It's good that he does not trust me. If I were he, and given the chance, I would run anyone through that tried to harm my loved ones." Moira thought she heard a twinge of regret in Sterling's words.

"You've put on some weight since you arrived," Moira said, walking back to the wardrobe. She shuffled the dresses back and forth until she found what she was looking for, "You need some proper clothes to wear. We've burned the remains of the uniform you were wearing. This is an old gown I wore when I was much younger and no longer fits me." Moira pulled out a soft silvery blue dress that she thought would accent Sterling's eyes.

The look that Sterling gave Moira was one of pure disgust, "I'm not wearing a dress." Sterling shook her head and pointed at Drake, "Give me some boy clothes and I'll be fine."

"B- boy clothes?" Moira was both shocked and disappointed at Sterling's refusal to wear the lovely dress she had chosen for her.

"Yes, some trousers and a shirt." Sterling said it so matter-of-factly it was obvious that was her normal choice of clothing.

"Absolutely not." Moira shook her head

"Why not?" Sterling stood, the sheet wrapped tightly around her shoulders

"I'll not have a lady guest in my house wearing hand me down *boy* clothes."

"Well I'm not wearing that dress."

"Yes, you are."

"No, *I* am not."

Moira felt her temper flare. *Boy clothes.* She'd never heard the like, a girl wearing boy clothes. She'd be damned if she let a girl as beautiful as Sterling wear filthy boy clothes.

"After today," Sterling's eyebrow rose, "I think you at least owe me the clothes that I want to wear."

Moira's ire deflated at Sterling's comment. She knew Sterling was trying to use guilt to force her into giving her what she wanted, but still it disappointed her.

A soft cough from Drake drew both of their attention, "Milady, you could take her to see Master Bennet."

Moira thought for a moment, and agreed, "Yes, an excellent idea Drake." Moira held the dress up, "If you wear this dress for now, I'll have some proper clothes made for you. But I'll not have you wearing old hand-me-downs. Just for now of course until I take you to see Bennet, you'll have to wear this dress."

"Very well," Sterling conceded to the compromise, but the look she gave the dress was one of contempt.

Moira smiled. "It's a deal," she said as she approached Sterling with the dress. "We'll just see how this dress fits." With the experience of dealing with her daughter's penchant to wiggle and run away, Moira pulled the dress over Sterling's head and had both arms in the sleeves before Sterling could react.

"It's just as I thought," Moira smiled, "this shade of blue compliments your eyes perfectly. What do you think Drake?"

The poor man, he gave Sterling a quick look over his shoulder. His cheeks darkened as his eyes scanned Sterling's figure. He nodded his head without uttering a word. She knew he wished for nothing more than to sink in to the floor. "Ogan's breath, you can turn around now Drake," Moira said when he continued to face the corner. Moira laughed and whispered, "You'd never think he was married with six little ones running around."

"My wife will kill me if she finds out I'm in another woman's room," Drake groused under his breath.

Moira's smile faded as she watched Sterling run her hands through her hair again. It was obvious she missed her long tresses, but the short hair seemed to suit Sterling. She was tiny in stature, only coming to Moira's shoulder, but she had a graceful form with a slender neck.

"Before we do anything else, we need to do something about that hair." Moira pulled the stool away from the vanity, "Sit"

Sterling hesitated for just a moment before sitting. She examined herself in the mirror and then looked down as if unwilling to look at herself. Moira ran her hands through the strands, some were still to her shoulders, while the others stood up in spiky bunches. Moira pulled open a drawer in the vanity and rifled around until she found a tiny pair of scissors, "Don't worry, I cut Orrven's hair all the time."

They sat in silence for a while, the only sound was of the scissors snipping away at Sterling's hair. The brown tresses fell on the sheet that Moira had draped over Sterling's shoulders. After having been scrubbed half a dozen times, Sterling's hair was soft, and the thick strands seemed to accept the new style rather nicely.

The whole while, Sterling watched Moira closely in the mirror, her eyes following Moira's hands as she cut away the errant curls. Meanwhile, Drake continued to stand in the corner, though he'd finally turned around and was leaning against the wall.

"There, all better," Moira sighed once she finished with her task. She'd cut Sterling's thick hair down so that it didn't stick out in all directions. Sterling examined herself in the mirror, turning her head from left to right. The expression on her face told Moira she didn't dislike it, "What do you think Drake?"

"What?" Drake, who had been leaning against the wall suddenly stood at attention and said, "Oh, it's," he seemed to search for the right words, "it's practical."

Moira looked at Sterling in the mirror and their eyes connected and neither could help but laugh at Drake's embarrassment. "I think it's lovely," Moira said.

Sterling agreed with a slight smile and a nod of her head.

"Now, it has been a trying day and you need your rest." Moira felt guilty leaving Sterling in the room alone, but she knew Sterling was not yet well enough to wander the Keep. "When it is time, I'll bring you a tray for dinner." Moira stepped into the hall, with Drake following behind. He closed the door and turned the key to lock the door. "What are you doing?" Moira asked, both angered and surprised. "She's not a prisoner."

"The Arl's orders," Drake responded, tucking the key away in his pocket.

24

JUSTIFIED

Orrven found Brom in the stables. He was tending to Tor, the great beast of a horse that frightened most men away. It was the perfect mount for Brom, the horse matched Brom's ferocity perfectly. Though with Brom, the horse was more a lap dog than a well-trained war horse. He nuzzled Brom's shoulder while his master brushed his black hide until is shone.

Orrven cleared his throat to gain Brom's attention, "A word with you brother."

Brom led Tor into his stall and closed the door behind him. Tor turned around and nibbled at Brom's ear until his brother-in-law pushed away the affectionate horse. "How was your hunt?"

"Fortunately, an easy kill," Brom answered, but realized the graekull wasn't what was on Orrven's mind. "What is it you really wanted to discuss?"

"It's about that girl you found," Orrven could still feel the pain in his chest where she had kicked him. He was worried what would have happened to Moira if he had not been there.

"Sterling?" Brom's eyebrow went up. "What about her?'

"She attacked Moira," Orrven started, but was cut off by Brom's angry words.

"What do you mean she attacked Moira?" Brom's voice went icy cold at the mention of his sister being harmed, "Is Moira okay?"

"If I had not been there she could have seriously wounded your sister." Orrven said, rubbing his chest.

"Tell me what happened," Brom started toward the main building but stopped when he noticed Moira approaching them. Her look did not bode well for either man.

"Why did you order Drake and Culan to lock Sterling in her room? She is not a prisoner." Moira asked, her hands on her hips.

"She attacked you, what did you expect me to do?" Orrven responded, his voice icy.

Brom stepped forward pushing Orrven out of the way, "Orrven told me she attacked you. Tell me what happened."

"Relax, both of you," Moira waved her hands at them. Turning to Brom, "It was perfectly understandable. I had taken her down to the bath and had to leave her in Gilda's hands when Lirit came down with a fever. Gilda got a little," Moira pinched her fingers together, "out of control and cut off all of Sterling's hair. She then threw her in the wardrobe after tying her hands and feet together and shoved a gag in her mouth."

"That's no excuse…" Orrven started to interrupt Moira.

"Husband, you must have seen the scars that marred Sterling's back. She has been miserably tortured by the Severon, and I," Moira pressed her hand to her chest, "promised her that she would be well treated here at Pan'Dale. Not an hour later she is being thrown naked into a wardrobe," Moira took a deep breath, "And you Brom, I know you snuck into her room last night."

"I do not sneak," Brom rebutted her claim.

"Regardless, you sat with her through the night. You know full well the condition she is in, and do you know what she told me? She's twenty-one. *Twenty-one.*" Moira paused and took a deep breath. "We all thought she was just a child, but she's twenty-one. Tell me, how would you react in the same situation?"

"She has a point," Brom couldn't argue with Moira's reasoning.

"Point or no, I will not let that girl loose in my house." Orrven refused to relent, "I'll not let her threaten the safety of my family or those in my care."

"But-"

"There is no discussion," Orrven's voice rose as he stopped Moira's protest. "What would you do if she were to encounter Gilda again? You would have Gilda's blood on your hands? What if she attacked Lirit?"

"He has a point," Brom agreed with Orrven.

Moira glared at her brother, "You are not helping." She turned back to Orrven, "At least let me hold onto the key and rescind your order that Drake has to be in the room when I'm with Sterling."

Orrven heaved a heavy sigh, "Drake will keep the key, but I'll rescind the order."

Moira knew she should not press her husband. If pushed he may just order Sterling out of the Keep altogether. "Very well, I'll concede, but know I'm not happy about it." Moira started to walk away, but stopped and turned back to the two men, "I'll be taking her into the village to see Bennet in a few days." She left them before Orrven could protest.

"Well, there you have it." Orrven said frankly motioning at his wife's retreating back.

"She's your wife," Brom chuckled, "you should be able to handle her."

"I've tried," Orrven sighed, "but she has best me at every turn."

Twenty-one? A Devian and a Rin'Ovana... Brom's heart began to race in his chest. *No, she couldn't be Khort and Sylvie's.* He pushed the idea to the back of his mind. His hopes of ever finding their child had long since been put to rest. *But what if, what if she were their child?* Brom knew of only one way to confirm, but the consequences were far too severe if she were a Rin'Ovana.

"Vita, have you seen Gilda? I need to have a word with her." Moira asked as she stepped into the kitchen in search of the maid.

"Yes, milady. Gilda said she was takin' a tray up to the little miss," Vita said without turning.

Moira hurried up the stairs to the third level, where the nursery was located, just above the living quarters. On the third level was Lirit's room along with Raane and Gilda's rooms. Moira paused outside Lirit's door and caught her breath, breathing in deeply trying to calm herself. She pushed the door open, and found Gilda sitting with her back to the door. She was in a chair next to Lirit's bed while she quietly read from a book. Lirit sat wide eyed as she listened to Gilda's story. Moira remembered listening to Gilda's stories as a child as she too sat wide eyed. It was quite the contrast to what Sterling had witnessed from this woman.

"Gilda. A word with you."

Gilda's shoulders stiffened as she placed a ribbon in the book to hold her place. She tucked the blanket around Lirit and stood, "Yes milady."

Moira was shocked at Gilda's appearance. Vita had minimized the damage Sterling had done to the woman. The three gouges that had been carved into her right cheek stood out in contrast from Gilda's fair skin. Her gray hair framed her face and accentuated the red whelps that crisscrossed her neck.

Sterling must have tried desperately to get away from Gilda's powerful grasp to cause this amount of damage. Gilda's hands, clenched into tight fists and hanging by her sides, were also covered in scratches.

Moira stiffened her resolve. She could not let Gilda's state affect how she treated her old nurse. "Please explain to me why my guest was bound and gagged and thrown into the wardrobe?"

Gilda's jaw tightened as her teeth clenched. She looked at Moira with a mix of anger and confusion on her face, and asked, "What did you think would happen when I discovered she was a Devian?" Gilda threw the question at Moira.

The question caught her off guard. She stammered, "I-."

Gilda interrupted. "Did you forget my son was murdered by a Devian? *Murdered in cold blood, he was.*" Tears clogged her throat as she threw the last statement at Sterling. "I was justified."

Moira's breath caught in her throat. She had indeed forgotten that Gilda's son had been brutally murdered by a roving Devian some five years ago. Gilda's family had offered the Devian shelter in hopes he would bring them luck with their harvest, but the opposite happened. Instead, they'd found Baeron's body twisted and mangled and the Devian standing over him, Baeron's blood on his hands and clothes.

With more anger in her voice, Gilda exclaimed, "They're all wild beasts! Every one of them." Gilda took a deep breath, "They should all be sent back to Fin'Varrar."

"I apologize for bringing back such terrible memories," Moira said, "but you saw the condition she was in when she arrived. You saw the lashes on her back and the scars that cover her body. Did you not think that perhaps she's already been tortured enough?" Moira spread her arms wide, "I want her to trust me, but how can I do that when she is treated so poorly after arriving at our home?"

Gilda surprised her when she grabbed Moira's shoulders and started to squeeze. "Devians cannot be trusted and you're a fool for letting that... that *thing* stay here!"

"Sterling is not a thing, she is a person just like you and I." Moira's anger spiked at Gilda's statement. "Think about how Devians are treated, simply for the fact that their eyes are different than our own." Moira paused and calmed herself, "Again, I apologize for asking you to care for someone who brings back such bad memories. However, she is a guest in my house and I expect you to treat her as such. Is that clear?"

Gilda's skin blanched at Moira's words, causing the scratches to stand out even more. "Yes, milady," Gilda's contrite response caused a pang of regret to twist Moira's heart.

"Thank you, Gilda, and again I'm sorry if my actions have caused you distress."

Before Moira could dismiss Gilda, the woman grabbed hold of Moira's hands and with more thought and less anger, she warned, "She is fearsome milady. She fought with a strength I have not witnessed in one so tiny. She should be watched carefully."

Moira was taken aback by Gilda's insistence that Sterling was dangerous, "I'll be careful," Moira said, patting Gilda on the shoulder. "I'm sure everything will be just fine."

Gilda regained her composure, "I'll take my leave then." Gilda turned to Lirit and said, "We'll finish your story another time." She left the room giving Moira a pained smile, closing the door behind her with a soft click.

That had been more difficult than I thought it would be, Moira thought, breathing in a calming breath.

"Momma?"

Moira forced a smile on her lips and turned to her daughter. Lirit sat in the center of her giant bed looking more like a doll than a child. Her brown hair hung in ringlets, framing her round cherubic face. Like her father, she had bright blue eyes that could see through to one's heart. Because she was an only child Moira tended to dote on Lirit and was thankful she was a sweet girl, unlike the Ar'Bethnot's daughter. The youngest child, and only daughter, Bethany Ar'Bethnot was a spoiled brat who grated on Moira's nerves with her constant whining and demands.

She sat down next to Lirit and felt her forehead. Relieved the fever had not returned, she asked, "How do you feel?"

"Better." Lirit smiled for a moment, then her brow furrowed as if in deep thought, "Are all Devians dangerous?"

Moira forced a smile on her face, "Of course not, why do you ask?"

"Gilda said that I should avoid Devians and that they would hurt me."

"Well, I suppose that some Devians could be dangerous, but not all of them. Just like some of your papa's hunting dogs can snarl and snap, but not all of them are mean."

Lirit thought for a moment, "Can I see her?"

"Well, she's unwell right now, perhaps when she is better."

"Okay momma," Lirit sunk down in her bed.

"Go to sleep now," Moira kissed Lirit on her forehead, "Good night my sweet."

Moira heard Lirit whisper, "Good night momma," as she closed the door. Moira leaned against the door and took a deep breath hoping to calm her nerves.

It had been a long day. Sterling's bath, Lirit's fever, Gilda's reaction to Sterling and her argument with Orrven. Sterling's arrival had sent the Keep into a tizzy. Sterling claimed to be a Rin'Ovana, but Brom had cautioned Moira to keep the fact to herself. The Rin'Ovana's had suffered the King's wrath and it wouldn't bode well for Sterling if the news reached the wrong ears. *I'll keep it to myself for now*, Moira thought, yawning. But first she needed a well-deserved rest.

25

GUILT

Five Days Later
Dan'Idou, 14th Turcia

A heavy curtain of fog hung low over the valley giving the familiar terrain an otherworldly feel. Sterling stood on her small hillock surrounded by the dense fog. It was a place she was well accustomed to, this desolate valley with no other life but her own. The air was crisp, and the moisture carried by the fog caused the air to seep into Sterling's bones, her body trembling from the deep chill.

The feeling of isolation was overwhelming and made it hard to breathe. Every labored breath from her chilled lungs sounded like a rushing river in the absolute silence of the fog. With each exhale her breath hung in the air for a moment before disappearing.

The dense fog reflected the moons rays allowing Sterling to see her immediate surroundings. From her hillock she could see the charred tree that stood watch over the valley. She dared not leave this small patch of land or else she could wander forever in this impassible fog.

A soft thud in the distance brought Sterling's head up and her heart racing. She stood listening intently, but the fog muffled the noise. She held her breath and listened for anything in the fog. Just as she was about to exhale she heard it again. A soft thud in the damp earth, then another, this one closer. Each step seemed to come from a different direction. Sterling turned in a circle trying to pinpoint the location of whoever was lurking in the fog.

The hammering of her heart made it difficult to hear the slow, measured steps. With the fog surrounding her she could not tell from which direction they came. Sterling stood listening intently, but the sound of her rapid heartbeat was too loud.

"Who's there?" She yelled out. Her words fell flat as the fog absorbed them.

Sterling felt vulnerable standing with nothing at her back. Another soft thud sounded but it was closer this time, not muffled by the fog as before. She wanted to flee, but not knowing who or what was in the mist she stayed, her feet planted to the earth. The thuds started coming quicker now as if whoever was approaching had increased their pace. Sterling turned when she thought the sound came from behind her, but as soon as she turned the sound came from another direction.

"Show yourself!"

Sterling turned again when a louder thud, clearer than any of the others sounded just behind her. The fog swayed and swirled as if something had disturbed it. She kept her eyes trained on the mist looking for any other hint of movement. Just then a shadow darkened the moonlit fog. Sterling's heart stopped at the size of the shadow as it grew darker against the light of the fog. A smell like nothing she'd ever experienced before wafted from the thick mist followed by a deep growl that seemed to come from the depths of the earth. Sterling backed away from the shadow afraid of what would step through the mist. She was surprised, her eyes widening, when the sound of a child laughing emerged from the fog.

She knew that laugh. She'd heard it so many times the sound had been etched into her brain. Tears gathered as a child sized shadow emerged from the fog. "Brigit," Sterling whispered aloud to herself. A smile spread across her lips at the familiar sight.

Brigit stood just inside the clearing where the fog thinned. Her sweet round face was smiling back at Sterling, her eyes echoing Sterling's own joy. The little girl wore a white gown with a red bodice. Sterling's smile faded as she realized the red in the dress was stained with the blood.

"Oh Brigit."

Sterling wanted to run to the little girl and take her into her arms. She wanted to apologize for everything. The words were on the tip of her tongue when Brigit, still smiling, limped toward Sterling. She stooped so she could be at eye level with the little girl, and looked into Brigit's eyes and what she saw caused Sterling's smile to fade. There was something off about Brigit's eyes. There was what she could only call a *shining malevolence.*

"Why did you leave us?" Brigit asked. The question caught Sterling off guard. A sharp pain echoed in her chest.

"I'm sorry," Sterling whispered, hoping to see the light return to Brigit's blue eyes, "I'm so sorry."

"They burned them." Brigit's brow furrowed as she took a step forward. "Did you hear their screams as they burned?"

Sterling hadn't heard the screams. She'd been trapped in the cellar while the Severon had set the chapel ablaze.

"It is your fault," Brigit accused. Sterling's eyes widened as Brigit's voice bounced off the walls of the dense fog. "It's your fault," the little girl repeated the words again.

"I know –" Sterling tried to speak.

"It's your fault," Brigit interrupted again. The small girl's once childish voice had vanished to be replaced by one with a dark malevolent undertone.

"Brigit, I tried to get out." Sterling explained. She wanted the little girl to understand.

"*Die.*"

"What?" Sterling thought she'd heard wrong at first.

"*Die.*" Brigit's smile returned, but it was not one of happiness. There was hate behind the cherubic dimples, "*Die.*"

A dark shadow behind Brigit caught Sterling's eye. Her heart leapt into her throat as a monstrous beast stepped out of the grey mist.

It stood twice as tall as Sterling with long razor tipped arms. Its skin was a slick sickly gray with portions charred away allowing muscle and bone to be seen. The smell of rotting flesh permeated the clearing as it stepped closer. Its black beady eyes narrowed upon Sterling, its lip curled in a satisfied smirk revealing grotesque yellowish teeth.

Sterling stood, stepping away from Brigit and the monster that had closed in on her.

"It was because of you. You should never have existed."

"Brigit!" Sterling scolded the child unable to help herself.

Brigit giggled at Sterling's reprimand but there was no humor behind the childish laugh. She suddenly stopped and pointed at Sterling, "*Just die.*"

With Brigit's words the monstrous beast let out a fearsome growl and charged. Sterling stumbled backward into the soft earth. She scrambled to her feet and sprinted into the fog. Soaked through instantly in the damp air and blinded by the fog she was unable to see where she was going, but if she stopped the beast would be on her in an instant.

The sounds of heavy footsteps pounding into the earth seemed to come from every direction as she stopped to listen. Her heart sped up when she heard Brigit's giggle reverberating in the fog. She spun around to find Brigit standing just behind her. The ghostlike girl giggled again and pointed past Sterling, "*You're going to die.*"

A chill raced down Sterling's back as she glanced over her shoulder, the beast stood within arm's reach of Sterling. Drool clung to the fangs that protruded from its large mouth, it wheezed and its breath hung in the air like a noxious cloud. Sterling flinched when it roared a ferocious growl spraying her with spittle and drool.

She ran as fast as she could deeper into the fog. Another giggle followed by the demon's roar ushered her into the void. The ground changed from the soft floor of the valley to one filled with roots that ran like a spider's web across the moist earth.

She knew there was a forest right in front of her, but she dared not slow down. The root system became more pronounced now that she grew closer to the forest. She jumped and hurdled herself over the twisted roots stumbling once when her chemise caught on a knot growing from a fallen tree. She picked herself up ignoring the scrapes to her hands and knees.

The beast's growl seemed closer than before. Sterling glanced over her shoulder again and let out a surprised scream when again she found Brigit only steps behind her. The girl was standing alone in the fog, her cold blue eyes filled with menacing enjoyment at Sterling's attempts to flee. *She's toying with me.* Brigit's laughter followed Sterling as once again she renewed her efforts.

Running through the forest, Sterling was caught off guard when the ground suddenly gave way and her legs fell through a hole in the dirt. The crusty layer of earth gave way to Sterling's weight and she fell into a dark crevice. Dirt and debris rained down on Sterling from where the hole had opened. Roots jutted out of the earth, poking Sterling in the back where she landed. Sterling pushed herself upright into a sitting position. The crevice was dark, she was only able to see a few feet in either direction. She was thankful the fog had not permeated this far down otherwise she would be completely blind.

Sterling looked around and could see that there was just a crust of hardened earth where she fell through. She imagined the ground had hardened over many years where the roots of the trees had grown together. When the trees died all that remained was that thin layer of dirt held together by the remnants of the root system.

GUILT

There was no way she would easily climb out since the ground above was at least twice her height. She felt along the wall but found no handholds or footholds since the walls were soft and gave away easily when she tried to climb out.

"Damn it!" she cursed when she slid back down into the darkness of the crevice.

If only she could see, then she would be able to find a proper way out.

Sterling stopped to think. She flexed her aching hands and realized that she now could see her hands and the earth beneath her feet. Sterling glanced up and could not contain the smile that spread, "Finally some luck." The moon's light pushed away the fog and shone like an angelic beacon through the small hole she'd fallen through. Though the moon shed some light into the dark crevice it did not reach beyond where Sterling stood.

She needed a firm hand hold to climb her way out. She felt along the wall until her fingers felt something hard and round. A rock! She felt around and was pleased to find more of the moss-covered stones. She tested the first with her foot and was thrilled when it held her weight. She carefully and tentatively pulled herself up until she found the next foothold, her fingers digging into the soft earth searching for another stone that would hold her weight. She was nearly there, nearly to the surface. All she needed to do was knock the thin crust of earth away, so she could climb up and out of the dark hole.

Her fingers barely reached the ceiling of earth, but she was able to grab hold of the roots and pull, but the ground above held firm. She yanked again and nearly slipped but she pulled herself flush to the wall to keep from slipping to the bottom. Reaching for the roots again, she took a firm hold and pulled until the earth began to crumble. She closed her eyes as bits of debris fell into her face causing her to cough as she inhaled the dust. One more yank and she'd have it. She pulled, and a large piece fell away revealing the moonlit sky above the trees that shaded the forest.

"Finally," she huffed, out of breath from hanging on to the wall.

A giggle sounded above her, and Sterling's heart sank as Brigit appeared on the ledge. *"You're going to die,"* she whispered as she stomped down on Sterling's fingers. Sterling lost her grip and tumbled to the bottom of the crevice, landing hard on her bottom, knocking the breath out of her. She squinted in pain for a moment and then slowly opened her eyes.

Her eyes widened as a bevy of emotions shot through her mind: fear, guilt, sadness, and the last to take a firm grip was terror. "No," she muttered past parched lips. She recoiled as she realized that the faces of those killed by the Severon lined the wall of the crevice. Mother Anwell, Sister Treva...a sob shook her body. All the sisters and all the faces of the little girls burned to death by Engram. "Hemi," Sterling said when she saw the man who had raised her.

"It's your fault." Sterling screamed when she realized Brigit stood beside her in the dank hole. And then all at once the eyes of those she had loved opened in unison and looked at Sterling. *"You're going to die,"* they all said at once, in a chorus of death as the sky went black and the monstrous beast attacked.

Brom was woken from his sleep by a moan from Sterling's room. He yawned and sat up in the bed. This wasn't the first time her nightmares had woken him. Her nightmares had increased since the incident with Gilda and for the past five nights it had become a routine for him to visit her room to settle her down. The first night both Orrven and Moira had come charging in the room at Sterling's desperate cries, but after the third night his sister and brother-in-law had left her in his hands.

Out of habit he picked up Tryg on his way to Sterling's room. Opening the door, he walked over to the bed to find Sterling curled in a ball, tears streaming down her face and a deep furrow marring her smooth forehead. He leaned Tryg against the wall and sat on the side of the bed.

"Sterling," Brom whispered her name and ran his hand over her close-cropped hair, "wake up." She was a heavy sleeper and it was difficult to wake her from the dreams that seemed to consume her nights.

"No," another tear slipped passed her lashes, "Brigit, I'm so sorry." She mumbled in her sleep.

Brom wondered who this Brigit was. Sterling had mumbled the name on more than one occasion. That along with many other names, all girls. Brom suspected they were the orphans Engram accused her of murdering. If Brom had to guess, he'd say it was Engram that murdered them.

Her hand, as if on its own sought out Brom's touch. When he took her hand in his, her grasp tightened in his, too afraid, he thought, to let go. As Brom sat there watching her he noticed her breathing increase, as if she were running from some great beast. Sweet beaded her forehead, dampening the newly cut hair.

"No," Sterling mumbled again. The single word held such despair that Brom's heart felt a pang at Sterling's misery. *What is it that consumes your nightmares?* Brom thought, leaning against the headboard, he closed his eyes. "Hemi," Brom's eyes shot open at the name that escaped her lips.

Hemi? Brom knew of only one person with that name, but it had been so long ago.

Brom was deep in thought when a scream suddenly ripped through Sterling. Her fingers tightened around his hand in desperation. The ashes that had been smoldering in the fire place were suddenly engulfed, the flames licking at the hearth and the mantel, blackening the wood. Brom released Sterling's hand and threw a vase of water on the fire. Smoke filled the room and he threw open the windows.

Brom rushed back to Sterling's side, her silver eyes stared up at him in confusion, "You're safe," He said, sitting beside her. She immediately crawled into his lap and buried her face against his chest. Tears streaming down her cheeks as sobs shook her tiny body.

Devians. Brom shook his head. Their ability to control the elements was dangerous. He wondered if Sterling was even aware of her Devian abilities. She could have easily attacked Engram with fire while in Sionaad, but she'd been held for nearly six months. He would discuss it with her the next chance he had. Brom leaned against the head board again and held Sterling until she finally fell into a restful sleep.

26

PHAYO VENATO

Outskirts of Flint – Southern Duenin
Six Days Later
Dan'Ruok, 15th Turcia, 1021

It was just as he thought. The Orom was furious.

Engram stared at Orom Tydar's angry signature on the parchment. He read his orders again, then crumpled the paper, sending the wax seal fragmenting to the floor. His orders were to bring the girl or the Shard back or not to return at all. If it hadn't been for that damn Kai'Varian he would have had her, but that savage had intervened, and Engram had lost four of his men.

Their attempts to infiltrate the forest of Kai'Vari had been stymied at every turn. The Kai'Varians were persistent with their defense of the border, keeping them off their lands. Only one man, Phayo Venato, had been successful in his attempt to sneak past the hulking barbarians. Phayo had seized the opportunity when the Kai'Varians were distracted by a wailing of horns. He'd discovered the girl had been taken to one of the Kai'Varian Holds, Pan'Dale. It was unfortunate that the Pan'Dales were tasked with the protection of the border between Kai'Vari and Duenin.

"Where is Phayo?" Engram asked of the guard that stood just outside his tent. "Find him."

"Yes, Commander."

Phayo, a lad of only twenty-two summers, always came through for him. Phayo had found Sterling's trail after she disappeared from Shee and again after she escaped Sionaad. Engram knew that the Severon tracker was the only one he could count on.

The flap raised as Phayo stepped into the large tent. "You called for me, Commander?"

The low candlelight reflected in Phayo's blonde hair and highlighted the large scar on his exposed arm. He had received that wound from a wolf attack. Phayo had killed the wolf and would wear the animal's pelt while tracking. He generally kept to himself and was an enigma to the rest of the unit. He had become known as the White Wolf among the men.

Engram had recruited Phayo when he was just seventeen, after a Devian had murdered his parents, older brother, and little sister. Engram had cultivated the boy's talents and his anger toward the silver-eyed people of Fin'Varrar. Engram was thrilled that Phayo had made it his personal mission to hunt down every Devian they had a lead on.

"The Orom has demanded that we find the Shard, this fifth key," Engram said as he paced the tent. "It seems that backstabbing Beracian bounty hunter stole it when we captured the girl." Engram turned to Phayo. "I need for you to find him and bring me the key."

"And what of the bounty hunter?"

"I care not what you do to him, just bring me the key."

"Then I will take my leave." Phayo bowed and exited the tent.

Efficient and deadly, Engram thought. He was very pleased that Phayo was a Severon.

Engram rubbed the ache in his neck that had plagued him this past week. *Probably where the blade will hit*, he thought. If he didn't return with one or the other he was certain that the Orom would make sure that his head would be separated from his body. It angered him every time he thought how close he'd been to having both the girl and the key in Shee. Sterling had been right at his fingertips, but she managed to slip through his grasp repeatedly. His anger was at a burning point. If Phayo did not return with some news of Kellen Leiten's whereabouts, he feared it would boil over.

27

EYE FOR AN EYE

Pan'Dale Holdings
Dan'Kell, 17th Turcia, 1021

Brom paused just inside the Great Hall. Moira and Orrven sat with their heads together mulling over some papers. The sun was barely above the trees and Gavin was already dogging him about joining him on the next graekull hunt.

"Come on Brom, let me go with you."

"You are not ready," Brom was tired of repeating himself. "You've barely learned any of your chants, you can't draw the sendoa, and your sword experience is lacking. Do you actually believe I would let you go on a hunt with me?"

"We've been here for nearly two weeks, when will you start teaching me the chants?" Gavin's whining voice wore on Brom's nerves.

"I've already told you twice," Brom said, walking toward his sister and Orrven. "I'll train all three of you when Gregor arrives with the Ar'Bethnot and Fal'Barbner nor'Veillen."

"I can do it," Gavin pleaded again. "Just let me try."

"Absolutely not," Brom shook his head.

"But, how am I supposed to learn if you don't let me join you on a hunt?"

"What is this about?" Orrven asked.

Gavin threw his arms out, "Brom refuses to let me join him on a graekull hunt." Gavin pouted, "I'm ready."

"Can you not train Gavin before they get here?" Moira asked.

Brom shook his head, "Team work is essential when battling graekull. If the team is off it could lead to fatal mistakes."

"Surely it wouldn't hurt to-," Moira started.

"It's a Veillen matter, we should stay out of it." Orrven interrupted. Moira opened her mouth to protest, but Orrven interrupted her again, "Though, if you want to practice the sword, you can go see Rory. He is a master swordsman and always willing to train the young warriors."

"May I?" Gavin asked Brom, his eyes alight with excitement. Brom affirmed his permission with a dismissive grunt. *At least I won't have to listen to him for a bit*, Brom mused.

Gavin turned and ran from the room with a childlike exuberance.

Brom pinched his nose between his eyes. Moira felt for Brom, having to keep Gavin's energy under control could drain even the most stalwart of men.

"I don't know how or why you've become a Tarkain, your patience is non-existent," Orrven chuckled at Brom's exasperation.

Moira playfully punched Orrven in the shoulder, "Brom is known for his patience, but Gavin could wear on the patience of a rock."

Brom smiled at his sister's remark. "I can only hope he will settle down once Gregor arrives with the other two nor'Veillen."

"They were delayed in Sela'Char?" Moira asked.

"Aye," Brom sighed again, "the Ar'Bethnot was called to the Capital to meet with his father."

"Will the delay affect your travels to Var'Khundi?"

Brom shook his head, "No, we are not due in Var'Khundi until the first Dan'Yin of Perditio."

"You'll be here another month," Moira smiled, "and you'll be here for the new year." Moira turned to Orrven, "We should plan a celebration for your men. They've worked hard this year."

"Perhaps," Orrven said, examining a stack of papers in front of him. "We've taxes to pay to Sela'Char by the end of the year."

"Surely, we have some to spare for a feast," Moira looked over the papers. "What about your training fees?"

"We should have enough after the fees are paid," Orrven agreed.

"Yay," Moira clapped her hands, "we'll invite the whole village and give the servants the day off."

Orrven opened his mouth to reply, but stopped when Gilda stepped into the room, a heavy tray in her hands. Moira turned her attention to their old nurse, "Are you taking Lirit her breakfast?"

"Yes, milady," Gilda answered with a slight smile, "the little miss requested pancakes and apples this morning."

"Very good, thank you Gilda." Moira smiled.

Brom was happy to see the smile on his sister's face. She'd been down ever since the incident with Gilda and the girl. Brom didn't regret bringing Sterling to Moira, but he didn't like seeing Moira unhappy.

Gilda gave a small curtsey before leaving the room.

Moira's smiled faded as she stared after Gilda, "I worry about her. She has seemed disheartened and distracted since Brom brought Sterling to us."

"Her son was murdered by a Devian," Orrven reminded Moira. "I'm sure Sterling's presence continues to weigh heavily on Gilda."

Moira picked at a small dent in the large wood table, "I feel awful about what happened."

"It was not your fault," Brom said as he pulled a chair back from one of the long tables and sat down. "If it's anyone's, it is my own for bringing her here."

"What else were you to do?" Moira stood, her hands on her hips. "She'd be dead if I left her care up to you."

Brom glared at Orrven as he chuckled. "You would have done no better," Brom pointed at his brother-in-law.

"I would have at least washed the stench from her before dumping her in someone else's lap." Orrven stood and pointed back at Brom.

"Now, now," Moira stood and clapped, "you two boys mustn't fight."

"Who's fighting?" Orrven chuckled again.

"Pan'Dale!" They all turned when a deep booming voice came from the courtyard, "Get out here ya bloody bastard!"

"Fal'Traqer," Orrven stood, gathering his sword where it lay on the table in front of him, "what does that demon man want?" Orrven tied his belt and sword around his waist as he walked to the front doors. Moira followed behind curious as to why another Arl was shouting for her husband. Orrven threw open the doors to the Keep, "What are you yelling about old man?"

Curious, Brom came to stand beside his sister to see what the commotion was.

Antash, the Arl of Fal'Traqer stood at the base of the steps with his arms crossed over his chest, most of which was hidden behind a fiery red beard. At his feet a woman cowered in fear as she clung to a man who lay unconscious, his hands bound behind his back. "This man stole my daughter and then took her. He's one of yours Orrven, and I expect payment for his actions."

"Father!" The weeping girl shot unbelieving eyes at the man standing above her.

"The lass is useless to me now," Antash bellowed. "What man would want another's seconds?"

Moira's eyes darted to her husband. *He's furious*, she thought. He had no love for the Fal'Traqers who lived along the southern border of the Pan'Dale holdings. They were continuously raiding the villages and farms along the border, stealing goods and killing those that fought back. Orrven had put a stop to it years ago, but it seems the raids had started to increase again. The Fal'Traqer Tohm was known for its skilled warriors and had often been called on by King Norden to defend against Duenin invaders. They were no strangers to blood and battle. They were also no strangers to raiding their neighbors either and were often admonished by the realm for doing such. As recompense, Fal'Traqer's lands have shrunk over the years as payment to the other Tohms for their misdeeds.

"Father, please!" Antash's daughter pleaded, "I love him."

"Shut up whore," he pushed her away with his booted foot.

"Enough!" Moira jumped when the command erupted from Orrven. He walked down the steps, so he was on even ground with Antash, his hand moving to the pommel of his sword. "You have the gall to step one foot on to my lands and demand repayment?" Antash was a huge man and stood a good head over Orrven. "You, who have ordered your warriors to raid my lands and kill my people, demand retribution?" Orrven took another step forward, "I demand repayment for the lives you have taken and the goods you have stolen."

"You damn whelp," Antash took hold of his own sword and slid the steel blade from its sheath. "You were just a mere thought when I was fighting knee deep in blood. You dare threaten me?"

As the argument gained volume, so did it gain spectators. Orrven's men had started to gather around the two men. "I don't threaten," Orrven unsheathed his own blade after motioning to his men to move the unconscious boy out of the way. Antash's daughter followed them, weeping and clinging to his hand.

"These lands should belong to the Fal'Traqers, but you Pan'Dales stole them from under us."

"You think history that is over fifteen-hundred years old gives you the right to kill my Tohmsmen?" Orrven's voice was deathly calm, "*Think again Antash Fal'Traqer.* I'll have your head mounted on a pike if you dare raid another village."

"Orrven, you bastard!" Antash bellowed as he charged with his sword at the ready. Orrven took the full brunt of Antash's weight with his sword and pushed the larger man back.

Antash steadied himself and brought his heavy broadsword over his head, charging Orrven while swinging the blade with full force. Moira held in a scream as Antash forced Orrven back, his feet sliding in the dry earth. She looked around at all the warriors watching, cheering the combatants. Mixed in with the Pan'Dale warriors were those of the Fal'Traqer Tohm that had accompanied their leader. They were so focused on the battle that none appeared to be upset by the fact that Orrven was struggling against Antash's larger form.

"What's all the commotion?" Moira looked over her shoulder to find Drake and Culan running across the Great Hall.

"We were told to come help Orrven, that he was being attacked," Culan said, with his sword drawn.

Rory, Orrven's second in command came up beside her. "Don't worry," he said, "that Orrven is stronger and wilier than he looks."

Moira glanced at Rory then back at her husband just in time to see Antash's elbow connect with Orrven's jaw. "Orrven!" She quickly covered her mouth not wanting to distract her husband.

A great roar went up when Orrven launched himself at Antash. His shoulder connected squarely with the older man's chest, knocking him to the ground. Both men were breathing heavily as Orrven stood over Antash. Orrven's sword tip held steady just inches from Antash's neck. "I've had eno..."

Orrven was cut off when Antash twisted his body, catching Orrven off guard and throwing him off balance. Antash's sword sliced through the air razing across Orrven's chest. Blood spread across the front of his shirt as he put a hand to the wound. Moira turned to Brom, "Please stop this. You know you are the only one strong enough to stop them."

"I cannot interfere, you know that." Brom did not take his eyes from the two men facing off. His hand was raised, rubbing the back of his neck at the base of his skull. It was a gesture she'd seen hundreds of times. When there was trouble the Veillen would know about it before anyone else. She thought that it must be the battle taking place before them that was the cause of his discomfort. Moira turned at a loud grunt only to see her husband go flying into his men. They pushed him back into the fray with a loud cheer.

"Brom, *please*. You are the only one here that is strong enough to stop them. All you have to do is step in." *Why was he being so stubborn?*

"I cannot," Brom repeated himself, "Veillen cannot interfere with Tohm politics. It is forbidden." Brom gestured towards the men, "Besides, your husband does not need my help."

Moira turned to find Orrven sitting on top of Antash's chest his sword buried in the ground only a hair's breadth from the older man's right ear. Antash's sword had been kicked a way out of reach. "I warn you now Antash Fal'Traqer, if I find you or any of your Tohmsmen have entered my lands again I will bring the full force of my army down upon your head. Do not misinterpret my warning as a threat. *That is a promise.*"

Orrven stood and stepped back allowing the older man to stand. Without saying a word Antash sheathed his sword and skulked to his waiting horse. The men that had accompanied him mounted silently, their heads bowed at their leader's disgrace.

"Antash," Orrven called after him, "your daughter is now a Pan'Dale, do not attempt to see her again. But know she will be treated with the dignity that an Arl's daughter deserves."

Antash nodded and kicked his horse into a gallop, leading his men home. The remaining Pan'Dale warriors disbursed some grousing that there had not been more bloodshed.

Orrven waited until they had all left before sheathing his own sword. His hand went to his chest where the blood had spread even more. He mouthed something to himself, but she could not hear it over the pounding of her heart in her ears. "Orrven Pan'Dale." Her fear had been replaced with anger over her husband's recklessness.

"I'm all right, woman," he bellowed as she approached him. "'Tis just a scratch."

"Let me see," she ordered as she yanked the fabric of his shirt open. "Just a scratch, eh?" The wound was not that deep but if she left it, it would fester. "Come along then."

Moira cleaned the wound, which was deeper than she thought. "You're going to need sewing up, husband."

"Leave it," Orrven groused, "I hate that damn needle."

"You're such an *ima*," Brom laughed.

"I'm not a baby," Orrven glared at Brom.

Moira listened to them banter while she prepared the needle for sewing. She was happy they got along so well. When she'd fallen in love with Orrven she'd feared Brom would not approve of her husband. But the two seemed to understand and respect one another.

She quickly cleaned the wound, knowing that it would leave a scar. It would probably become one her husband would display with a great amount of pride. "Alright, husband, this may sting a little." Moira sat down in front of Orrven, the curved needle poised to stitch the long cut that ran across his chest.

"I am ready," Orrven said with a great sigh and leaned his head back, his eyes closed as if preparing for the worst. Moira couldn't help but chuckle. As strong as he was, Orrven was like a little boy when it came to needles.

"*Ima*," Brom said again.

Both Culan and Drake laughed at Orrven's childlike behavior. Brom continued to rub his neck when he looked at the two men, "Why are you not upstairs?"

Sterling heard the commotion from her window but could not see what had drawn the entire training field full of men to the other side of the Keep. They had been busy sparring, as they did every day, and then all at once they dropped their weapons and ran to the other side of the building. They were yelling something about a fight and then ran off.

"Like a bunch of kids," Sterling mumbled to herself. She put the book down that she was reading and stood to stretch. Sterling looked around the room. Although Moira had provided her with books and needlepoint, Sterling was bored out of her mind. "Needlepoint," Sterling glared at the distinctly feminine past time, "as if I'd ever do that."

Sterling never thought she'd miss the hard labor of working on a farm. She'd been in this room since Brom brought her to Pan'Dale ten days ago. The burns on her arms were healing along with the other wounds she'd gained from Sionaad. There were new cuts and bruises given to her by that monster of a woman, Gilda. Sterling wandered over to the mirror and examined her hair. Despite having endured Gilda hacking it off, Sterling was fond of the length after Moira had trimmed it for her. *It's easier to manage now that it doesn't hang in my face.*

Sterling stepped back from the mirror and turned, knocking the stool over with the skirts of the gown Moira had forced on her. They'd made a bargain that if Sterling wore the dress Moira would take her to a tailor for new clothes. Sterling picked up the skirts and wandered the room, pacing back and forth. *I'm bored*, she thought.

On a whim Sterling walked toward the door that separated her room from Brom's. She had a lot of questions about the man who had saved her from the Severon. His presence seemed to calm her nerves, whereas any other man sent shivers down her spine and made her nauseous. A couple of times she'd woken from a nightmare only to find him sitting next to her in the bed, her hand in his. She felt an odd comfort from that small gesture.

Sterling opened the door and stood in the entrance, examining his room. It was a mirror opposite of hers with the fireplace on the far wall from the door. His bed, like hers, was huge and the other decorations were distinctly masculine. The walls were a dark blue in contrast to the light blue of hers. Sterling nervously took a step into his room and looked around. It was a room that seemed to be rarely used. The furniture looked brand new and there were no personal items on display.

Sterling turned to leave, but the skirts of her dress caught on the wardrobe, "Damn dress," Sterling said as she tripped, falling against the piece of furniture. Something inside thumped hard against the door, pushing it open and falling to the floor with a loud clang. Sterling stooped to pick up whatever had fallen to the floor and nearly jumped out of her skin when a voice sounded behind her.

"What are you doing in master Brom's room?" Sterling looked over her shoulder to find Gilda standing over her. Before Sterling could react, the older woman grabbed hold of Sterling's arm and flung her back into her own room. She crashed into the chair and table knocking the vase to the floor, the glass shattering.

Sterling, tangled up in the dress, tripped while trying to stand, her hand coming down on the shards of glass. "*Devians*," Gilda spat the name at her, "you're all alike... manipulative, conniving, and deceitful." Gilda reached for Sterling, yanked her to her feet and back handed her across the face.

Sterling grabbed hold of Gilda's arm as she went flying backward taking the older woman with her. They toppled over in a tangle of skirts. Sterling was the first to her feet, but Gilda was fast and wrapped her hand around Sterling's ankle, tripping her. Sterling went down with a thud, knocking the wind from her lungs. Gilda, for someone of her age, was surprisingly nimble and scrambled to her feet. She stood over Sterling, pulling a long knife from a pocket in her skirts, "It's your kind that killed my Baeron, my son."

Sterling backed away from Gilda, pulling the skirts out of the way, she was able to stand and face the older woman. "I'm sorry about your son," Sterling said as she put her hand to her chest, "but I didn't kill him."

"The Devian that killed my son escaped, but I'll have my justice!" Gilda screeched, raised the knife and charged Sterling. Sterling dodged Gilda, pushing the woman away from her. Gilda fell against the bed, her gray hair falling out of its bun. "If you stay you'll bring nothing but bad luck to Moira and Brom. You'll kill them too."

Gilda pushed off the bed and charged Sterling again. Sterling backed away but tripped on the long skirts. The two went down again, with Gilda on top of Sterling. Sterling managed to dodge the knife, turning her head at the last moment, the knife tip sticking in the floor. Sterling pushed Gilda off her and rolled away. *These skirts will be the death of me*, Sterling thought as she lifted the heavy mass and ran to the door, "Help me!" She yelled, pounded on the door, and tried turning the knob, but it was locked.

"No one is going to help you," Gilda laughed before coming at Sterling again, the knife poised over her head.

Sterling backed away as Gilda stabbed the knife into the door. Sterling stumbled backward into Brom's room, landing on the floor next to the object that had fallen out of the wardrobe. Her fall disturbed the fabric revealing the tip of a black sword.

"Get out!" Gilda yelled, charging at Sterling again.

Sterling wrapped her hand around the fabric that covered the hilt and tried lifting the sword. It was heavy, but she managed to lift the sword just in time to deflect Gilda's blow. Off balance, Gilda fell backward giving Sterling time to run for the door. She prayed that it too was not locked. She dragged the heavy sword behind her and with her bloodied and cut hand she tried to turn the knob only to have it slip out of her grasp. Sterling looked over her shoulder as Gilda charged at her again with the knife. Sterling frantically turned the knob until it gave way and the door fell open and she stumbled to the floor. She kicked at Gilda's legs, throwing the older woman off balance.

Sterling lunged into the hallway, turning and lifting the sword as Gilda brought the long blade down, the knife slicing through the fabric wrapped around the sword. The covering on the sword ripped up to the hilt causing Sterling to lose her grip. The sword fell to the floor with a loud thud. Gilda screamed and lunged at Sterling, but the knife hit the wall and lodged in the paneling. Sterling rolled away grabbing the sword as she stood. "You're a mad woman!" she screamed at Gilda as she ran down the hall toward the stairs.

Blood was dripping from the wound on her left hand as she scurried down the stairs. She heard Gilda's footsteps close behind, but she dared not look for fear of tripping. At the bottom of the stairs, a door blocked her way, but with her momentum carrying her down the stairs she fell against the door with her shoulder. Gilda was on her before she could open the door. With both her and Gilda's weight, the door fell open spilling both into the Great Hall.

Sterling's skirts went up around her head as she tumbled into the room, knocking her head against one of the tables. She pushed her skirts back down and stood holding the sword in both hands, facing Gilda as she rose to her feet. Gilda's eyes were shining bright with insanity as she charged Sterling with the blade.

Somewhere in the back of her mind Sterling thought she heard a gasp and then loud shuffling of feet, but her attention was trained on the old woman running at her. Sterling prepared herself for the impact, but just as Gilda reached her, Sterling was suddenly plucked off her feet, the sword falling to the floor with a loud clang. Gilda screamed as she tried to free herself from Orrven's bear hug, "You killed my son!" Gilda sobbed, "You killed my Baeron."

28

FAREN

"You killed my son!" Gilda repeated, slumping in Orrven's arms, sobbing the words over and over, "My Baeron, my Baeron."

"Orrven, carry her to her room," Moira said softly, laying a hand on the older woman's arm. Orrven lifted Gilda and carried her up the stairs, her head buried in his shoulder as she continued to grieve for her son. Culan and Drake silently followed Orrven to the upper floors leaving Brom and Sterling alone in the Great Hall.

Sterling waited for Brom to release her, but he continued to hold her with his arms around her waist, "You can let me go now," she said pushing at his arms.

Is he angry? Sterling could not judge his mood.

After a long moment Brom released Sterling and stepped away. He pulled a tablecloth from one of the long tables and wrapped it around the sword, placing it on the nearest table. "You're shaking," Brom said, pointing to the table where he'd placed the sword. "Go ahead and sit down."

She felt weak, the adrenaline that had fueled her fight with Gilda melted away. She sat down in front of the sword, Brom standing over her, silent. "You're bleeding," He said, sitting across from her. He ripped a strip of fabric from the tablecloth, "Give me your hand."

Sterling put her hand in his.

"Who is Hemi?" he asked while he wrapped the fabric around her hand.

The question caught Sterling off guard, "Hemi?"

"Yes," Brom tied the fabric in a knot and released her hand. He stood before continuing, "During one of your..." he waved his hand, "nightmares you called out to someone named Hemi."

Sterling could feel the blood drain from her face. Her nightmares had escalated over the past week. It seemed they followed her during her waking moments. "Hemi," Sterling licked her lips, "was the man who raised me, he was my uncle."

"Your uncle?" Brom leaned forward, hands on the table. His eyes stared deeply into hers.

"For most of my life I thought he was a blood relation," Sterling shifted in the seat, "but I learned too late that it was in name only."

"Too late? What do you mean?" Brom asked.

Sterling thought back to the time that seemed so long ago. A time when her life was normal, and she was surrounded by love and warmth. "It was my birthday, my twenty-first," Sterling swallowed past a lump that had suddenly formed in her throat, "Hemi called me into the study." Sterling could distinctly remember the look on Hemi's face when he revealed the truth. Sterling smiled at the memory, "He was so nervous when he told me that he was not my uncle. I was so confused, he had always told me that my parents had died in a fire when I was a baby."

"What else did he say?" Brom stood as still as a statue as he listened to Sterling.

"He told me that my father was a Kai'Varian warrior and that he was his slave," Sterling laughed, but there was no humor. "I thought

227

he was joking. I remember his face was so serious, he was always so stoic and matter of fact." Sterling took a deep breath, "But he wasn't joking, he'd never been more serious. He said that on the day I was born, there was a battle of some sort and my parents were killed."

Sterling looked down at her hands, "Hemi always told me I looked like my mother, but he never talked about her."

"You said you were a Rin'Ovana, did Hemi say any more?" Brom encouraged her to continue.

"Yeah," Sterling said looking up at Brom, "my father, he said, was a Veillen warrior and that his name was Khort Rin'Ovana."

Brom turned away from her, but she could tell by the way the muscles in his back trembled that he was on the verge of losing his composure. Sterling imagined it was a rare occurrence for Brom to show even the slightest bit of emotion.

"Rin'Ovana?" Sterling jumped from the shock of hearing Orrven's voice behind her, "What's going on Brom?" Orrven closed the door to the upper floors as he stepped fully into the room. He glanced at Sterling, his brow furrowed before turning his piercing gaze to Brom, "Explain."

Brom took a deep breath as if to clear his head, "I've suspected this for a while now," Brom said, looking at Sterling, "but I wasn't certain until today." Brom turned his gaze to Orrven, "Sterling is the heir to the Rin'Ovana Tohm."

"You cannot be serious Brom," Orrven laughed, but there was no humor, "the heir to the Rin'Ovana's? Everyone knows that Khort's child died in the graekull attack that nearly destroyed Sela'Char. Just because she *claims* to be a Rin'Ovana does not make it true. I swear," Orrven turned his gaze to Sterling, "if you cause any more troubles I'll throw out of Pan'Dale."

Sterling could tell Brom was barely holding his anger at bay. His jaw was clenched, and he held his hands in tight fists, "The body was never found, it disappeared along with Khort's slave." Brom pointed at Sterling, "The man who raised her, his name was Hemi Rhesida, the same name as the man who was Khort's slave."

"That is your proof?" Orrven scoffed at Brom's reasoning. "You just want her to be Khort's child. Hemi is a common name in Duenin, you know that. Why are you so desperate to find the Rin'Ovana heir?"

"Because I made a vow to Khort that I would protect his child," Brom confessed, taking a deep breath. "A vow that I have been unable to fulfill," Brom looked at Sterling, "until now."

"Brom, listen to what you are saying," Orrven tried to reason with Brom, "she has no proof of who she says she is."

"You want proof," Brom glared at Orrven, "the proof is right in front of you!" Brom pointed at the sword on the table in front of Sterling.

"It's just sword," Orrven sighed. "You claim she is the Rin'Ovana heir and the only proof you have is a name and this sword."

"This sword," Brom's voice remained calm, but Sterling could tell he was barely holding in his anger. "is a Veillen bloodsword. This sword is the most important tool a Veillen has in fighting the graekull," he explained to Orrven. "When it is forged, the Veillen's blood is mixed in with the steel."

"Yes, I know," Orrven dismissed Brom's explanation, "I know all about your bloodswords. I find the whole process creepy and weird."

"The process ensures that only the Veillen can wield that weapon," Brom explained, reaching for the hilt of the black sword. Sterling gasped when red spikes suddenly appeared preventing Brom from picking up the sword. "This was Khort Rin'Ovana's sword, he named it Faren. It saw him through many battles and protected him from graekull up until he died." Brom pointed at Sterling, "If she has Khort's blood running through her veins then the sword will accept her." Brom stared at Orrven for a long moment, "and that, brother, is your proof she is the heir of the Rin'Ovana Tohm."

My father's sword. Sterling stared at the weapon that lay before her, examining it in a new light. *My father wielded this sword, his hands touched it.* The blade's presence was overwhelming as it lay against the stark white of the tablecloth. The longer she stared at it the greater her desire to run her fingers along the edge of the blade. She could hear her heart beat as it pounded in her ears, the blood coursing through her veins seemed to culminate into her finger tips. The sword called to her, demanding that she reach out her hand and take it. Sterling could not deny the blade and with trembling fingers she took hold of the hilt, her blood rushed to the palm of her hand and pushed, excruciatingly, against her skin as if trying to escape her body and meld with the sword.

As her fingers wrapped around the hilt she could feel heat emanate from the weapon. The heat began to throb and vibrate in time with her own heartbeat. The heat pulsated up her arm, over her shoulders, and down her spine until her entire body drummed in time with the sword. As the rush of heat consumed her, an over-whelming force of happiness and joy washed over Sterling. She could feel the tears as they gathered along her lashes and fall down her cheeks to drop on to her hand.

The feelings were so overwhelming she found it hard to breathe past the emotion. She closed her eyes, and memories that were not her own filled her vision. Visions of a woman laughing, her hand resting on her round belly large with a baby.

Sterling gasped when the woman opened her eyes and stared back at Sterling with silver eyes that mirrored Sterling's. Sylvie, her mother, was beautiful, with long brown hair that hung in waves around her shoulders. Her round cheeks were bright with a flush as she smiled at Sterling. Sylvie raised her hand from her belly and reached for Sterling. She could feel the soft touch of her mother's fingers as she ran them along Sterling's cheek. She raised her own hand to her mothers, but the hand was not her own. It was Khort's hand, rough and worn with calluses from many years of battle.

The emotions of love and happiness flooded Sterling until she could no longer bear it. She released her hold on the sword and the vision vanished from her sight. Her heart ached from the emotions she hadn't felt in a long time. Sterling turned her eyes to Brom who stood above her with a stunned look upon his face. His usually olive skin had gone pale and a sheen of sweat dotted his brow. He wiped his face, turned and walked away to the far corner of the room with his head down, his hands on his hips.

The mood in the room turned somber, with Brom deep in thought and Orrven staring down at her as if she were some oddity on display. *What am I supposed to do now?* Sterling thought. She wanted to reach for the sword again, but she was unsure she could handle the overwhelming emotions she felt while touching the weapon.

The door to the upper chambers opened and all eyes turned to Moira as she stepped into the room. She looked from Sterling, to Orrven, and then to Brom. She must have realized something was wrong, "What's happened?" When no one answered she walked over to Sterling and wrapped a blanket around her shoulders, "Are you all right?"

Sterling couldn't speak but nodded and turned her gaze back to the sword.

"Orrven?" Moira questioned her husband. "Tell me what happened."

Orrven glanced at Brom, "Your brother claims that she is the heir to the Rin'Ovana Tohm, that she is Khort and Sylvie's daughter."

Brom turned around and approached Orrven, his face was hard with anger, "You witnessed her touching the sword, there is no *claiming*, there is proof right before your eyes."

"I've never seen that sword before," Orrven countered, "that could be any Veillen sword for all I know."

Moira stepped in between her brother and husband, "Will you two stop arguing?" Moira glanced at the sword on the table. Although she was young at the time she would never forget the love she received from Khort and Sylvie, they had taken her and Brom in when Moira was just four, and Brom seven. She would also never forget the weapon that was never far from Khort's side. "That is Faren, Khort's Bloodsword."

Orrven sighed, "What now, Brom?" Orrven conceded and stepped away, "What are your plans now that we know she is a Rin'Ovana? You can't just march her into Sela'Char."

"The Ar'Bethnots would eat her alive," Moira said, "but the Dal'Rymples may be more open to receiving her as the heir. They've always been kind to the Rin'Ovanas."

Sterling was lost in the conversation and opened her mouth to speak but could not get a word in when Orrven talked over her, "You'd have to convince not only Karroll as the Arl of Da'Gaihen, but Norden as well. You'd have an easier time with Karroll, but the King," Orrven shook his head, "King Norden is as stubborn as any mule."

"Um…" Sterling started but was interrupted again by Moira.

"Norden may be stubborn, but he's not unreasonable."

"Excu…" This time it was Brom that interrupted.

"We'll start with Karroll, he has a great influence over my uncle." Brom rubbed his bearded chin, "The Dal'Rymples will follow what the Da'Gaihen's do and that just leaves the Ar'Bethnots."

Tired of being ignored, Sterling stood up and slapped her hand on the table, "Excuse me, but what are you talking about? What does my being a Rin'Ovana have anything to do with what you are talking about?"

"A Rin'Ovana?" A new voice entered the conversation from the front doors of the Keep.

Moira, Brom, and Orrven all sighed in unison at the boy that stood in the entrance way. He was slim, with lean muscle and had the same olive skin as everyone else in Kai'Vari, but it was smooth and well-kept unlike those who spent their days in the sun. His hair was blonde and hung in tiny curls around his head. His green eyes held an air of superiority as he sneered down at Sterling. Next to him stood another boy, but he was the exact opposite. This boy was darker and well-built with a broad chest and arms that had seen hard labor. He had the same green eyes as his companion, but they seemed much softer.

Behind them was an older man that bore the same tattoos as Brom, "Brom! There you are." He bellowed the greeting and marched his two captives across the hall and released them at Brom's feet. The two fell on their hands and knees grousing about their treatment.

"Gregor." Brom greeted the man.

"I give to you Oramek Fal'Barbner and Tibal Ar'Bethnot – your nor'Veillen." He hit both boys in the back of their heads, "Bow to the Tarkain, you will be at his mercy for the next six months. I would not gain his ire if I were you."

"Tarkain!" Both Oramek and Tibal yelled out the strange greeting and bowed to Brom.

"Brom trains the nor'Veillen to master their Velkuva," Moira whispered to Sterling while Brom greeted the two, "*Tarkain* is an ancient honorific given to a trainer while the *nor* in nor'Veillen means new or young. The Veillen guard must learn to speak the ancient tongue because many of the chants were written over five hundred years ago."

"Rin'Ovana?" Tibal stood and stepped forward and his tone was one of disbelief, "*Impossible*. You very well know the Rin'Ovana clan was disbanded some twenty years ago."

Sterling's heart stopped in her chest. She could feel the blood drain from her face. He directed his question to her, "What? You didn't know?" Tibal laughed, "This is grand. The Rin'Ovana clan was dissolved after the death of that prig Khort. After he went and got himself killed."

"That's enough Tibal." Brom growled. His hazel eyes had gone dark with anger.

"But she should know that those idiot elders couldn't decide who the Arl should be. The King dissolved the clan and divided their lands among the three neighboring Tohms when an heir could not be produced."

She could tell by the look in Moira and Brom's eyes that Tibal was telling the truth. Sterling could feel her anger heighten as the realization took hold. *I have no family? It was all a lie? What was the point of coming here?* Her one desire to have a place to call home and family to surround her was gone? What was the point of traveling to this homeland, this foreign place, to only find herself in the same situation she'd left? "It was all a lie!" She yelled, striking her hand against the hard table. All at once the fires in the Great Hall flared. The torches and the fire that was a constant in the fireplace were set ablaze.

Brom had seen this before, the night of her dream when she yelled out. The fire had ignited and scorched the hearth and mantel. *She truly is a Devian with unknown powers.* Before her anger could get out of hand Brom approached her, "Sterling," he said standing in front of her, blocking the other's view of her. He leaned over and very calmly spoke to her, "it wasn't a lie, you still have a family, they just need to know you are alive and they will come to you." Brom prayed to Orla that no one else noticed the fist-sized imprint on the thick oaken table. *Her strength is something to be wary of.*

Moira thankfully stepped in, "Let us get you upstairs, you must be exhausted from your ordeal."

Sterling nodded, her anger sloughing off her shoulders and leaving her weak. She stood on wobbly legs, her vision started to dim, and she suddenly found herself lifted off the ground and in Brom's arms. His gentle concern despite his hard exterior caused tears to gather in the back of Sterling's eyes. She refused to let a single tear fall and buried her face in his neck. She was exhausted. First Gilda, then the ordeal with Orrven and Brom, seeing her parents, and then that awful Tibal. She clung to Brom, his warmth soothing and the pull of exhaustion was too much for her to push away.

"She's asleep," Brom whispered to Moira as he followed her to the upper floors.

"She must be exhausted," Moira stopped outside Brom's door and said, "I don't think we should put her back in that room for now."

Brom understood her hesitance and nodded his agreement. Moira pulled the covers over Sterling after Brom laid her in the middle of his bed. "I can't imagine what she has been through and to find out she has no family." Moira took a deep breath to clear her mind, "We'll be her family."

"Aye," Brom agreed as they left Sterling to her dreams.

29

LESSONS LEARNED

Dan'Kell, 17th Turcia, 1021
Evening

Sterling jolted awake, a scream on her lips. Her heart raced as she clutched her chest where the beast's claws had pierced her heart. The night shirt she wore was soaked in sweat, as was the bed cover she lay upon. It was the same nightmare that had plagued her recently, of being chased by a monster.

She glanced around the room as she forced herself to relax. The sun had fallen beneath the horizon, the sky a fiery orange as the sun's rays were pushed aside by the oncoming night. *I'm in Brom's room*, she thought, throwing the covers off. Just like the man, the room was simple and served a purpose.

She was glad they had not put her back into her own room, as she had no desire to be back in that gilded cage with the possibility of Gilda attacking her again. Sterling felt bad for the old woman having lost her son. She imagined it felt much like the loss of Brigit and Hemi. Sterling could understand Gilda's desire to get revenge, after all the same feelings swirled around in the pit of Sterling's stomach every time she thought of Engram and what he did to her loved ones.

Sterling gingerly put her feet on the floor. "I'll kill him," Sterling mumbled as she stood. The sounds of metal on metal drew her attention to the windows and the field below. She wobbled her way across the room to the windows.

Like her room, there were two windows on either side of the fire place, each with a padded seat where one could sit and look out over the grounds. The twilight air was cool, and the thin dress offered little protection against the chill. Sterling pulled the warm blanket off the bed and sat on one of the padded benches.

Sitting in the window she watched the comings and goings of the many warriors that still sparred in the courtyard despite the waning light. The warriors here were much larger than Duenin's soldiers. They were built like oxen and carried swords that Sterling knew most men of Duenin would not be able to lift.

She spotted Brom as he crossed the courtyard, the man Gregor beside him. Brom was an enigma to Sterling. He seemed at times very caring but at other times his demeanor was hard and unforgiving. She was fascinated by the markings that covered his upper body. The design was intricate, starting on his shoulder and working its way down to his wrist, then again on his upper chest and much of the right side of his back. The design seemed to be random swirls with images of demons depicted. She watched him as he said something to Gregor, then turned toward one of the buildings that stood against the wall surrounding Pan'Dale. The building had several windows that were nearly floor to ceiling, allowing spectators to see the many beds that lined the room.

Brom stepped into the building but stood at one end observing the occupants. At the other end of the long row of beds

Sterling could see the two boys she'd encountered in the great hall. Between them was Gavin, the boy she'd taken hostage on her first day in Kai'Vari. Tibal Ar'Bethnot was the blonde's name. He was the one that thought it funny to tell her that she no longer had a family. He seemed to gain a great amount of pleasure in telling her such horrible news. She made a mental note to avoid him. The dark headed one was Oramek. He was built like an ox, but from what she could tell he had a much nicer demeanor than Tibal. Gavin had a completely different look about him than the other two. His clothes were filthy, and his brown hair was disheveled as if he'd taken a roll in the dirt with a pig.

The three boys were completely unaware of Brom's presence. She wondered how anyone could miss Brom. To Sterling his very presence overwhelmed her. She could barely breathe when he was near.

A yawn suddenly ripped through Sterling. Despite having slept most of the day she was still exhausted from the nightmares. She leaned her head back against the stone wall and closed her eyes. She prayed for a dreamless sleep.

Brom stood in the entry way of the barracks watching the three he would be training. Gregor had stopped him on his way here. He'd warned Brom of Tibal, saying he'd have his hands full with the Ar'Bethnot heir. But Brom was already familiar with the Ar'Bethnot heir's cocky behavior.

The three had yet to notice his presence. That would be at the top of the list in their training. *Always be aware of your surroundings.*

Tibal laughed. "Did you see the expression on her face when I told her about her family?"

"You're an ass, Tibal," Oramek mumbled under his breath glaring at Tibal.

"And she is a Devian, with eyes that shine like my mother's finest silver. She is a fine specimen," Brom could hear the lecherous tone in Tibal's comment, "and a Rin at that. What I wouldn't give to have her in my bed."

Gavin was the first to notice Brom standing there listening to their conversation. He quickly stood and bowed in the formal fashion, bent slightly at the waist with his hands clasped behind his back. The other two realized quickly what Gavin was about and in turn bowed at the waist as well.

"Tarkain." Gavin said using the honorific.

Brom walked slowly down the center aisle of the barracks. The three would stay bowed until he acknowledged them. He too had gone through the same training when he was a nor'Veillen. It would teach them discipline and endurance. At first it would not bother them but after a while the angle of the bow would cause their backs to burn and their legs to ache.

Brom walked around the three not saying a word. Gavin was the smallest of the three, but Brom knew he had plenty of strength when he spent time with the boy in Sela'Char. Brom paused next to the largest of the three, Oramek. At only fifteen he was large. His muscular body told of his peasant's existence. His hair was sun-bleached to a light sandy brown and his skin tanned. He had several calluses lining his hands. Brom had no worries about Oramek being a hard worker.

Tibal on the other hand was Oramek's opposite in every aspect. He was his father's son, blonde hair and skin that rarely felt the burn of the sun. Quemby Ar'Bethnot was a conniving council member whose only goal was to become the lead council to the king, and he would do anything to get to that position. *I wouldn't put it past him to have eyes on the throne*, Brom thought. His son was no doubt just like him. From what Gregor had said, the boy showed signs of promise, but Brom knew he'd have to keep an eye on Quemby's son.

Brom took one last look at the three, never saying a word. He definitely had his work cut out for him, but the outcome was worth the pain if they had just one more Veillen to fight off the never ending graekulls.

Brom turned to leave when the sudden grumbling of Oramek's stomach stopped him. The boy's face turned a bright red from embarrassment. It wasn't bad enough that it found such an inopportune time to express itself, but that it was punctuated by the silence. Oramek's stomach reminded him that he had missed the evening meal. He left them in their bowed position wondering who would give up first.

Gavin's back was already starting to burn, but he dared not leave his position. He'd heard of this test of endurance and Brom would surely know if he did not stay the course. Sweat beaded on his forehead and his hamstrings trembled, but he maintained the bow. Gavin glanced to his right at Oramek whose face was still red from the embarrassment of having his stomach growl in front of Brom. Though Oramek's eyes were closed in concentration his brow was also beaded with sweat.

Gavin glanced to his left to find Tibal with a smirk creasing the corner of his mouth. Gavin was surprised when Tibal stood. "This is ridiculous," Tibal said, stretching his back.

"What are you doing?" Gavin whispered.

"I do not need to prove myself to anyone," Tibal replied.

"Brom – err the Tarkain," Gavin quickly corrected himself, "will know if you come out of position."

"And what?" Tibal waved his hand in dismissal, "What will he do?"

Gavin could not believe Tibal's audacity, "You obviously don't know Brom then."

Tibal flopped down on one of the beds and put his hands behind his head and crossed his booted feet on the bed. "So, you're Norden's youngest. My father tells me King Norden is losing his edge and that your older brother, Karroll, is nowhere near ready to take his place."

Gavin looked at Tibal, "Your father talks too much."

"And what of you Oramek, what of your family?"

Oramek took a deep breath before answering, "We live on a small farm in the Fal'Barbner hold. Our cattle are the best in all Kai'Vari."

"Ha! A peasant. It seems the Veillen are lessening their standards."

"Shut up Tibal." Gavin growled.

"So, the Tarkain is your cousin?"

"Yes." Gavin wished Tibal would shut up. He was already having a difficult time maintaining the position and Tibal's nonsense wasn't making it easier.

"I've heard of Brom Da'Gaihen." Oramek said, "His tanak are impressive."

"Ah yes, his tanak, they are quite impressive, but I've seen Veillen with more tanak than the Tarkain."

"Yes, but they are twice his age." Gavin argued.

"Either way your cousin does not scare me," Tibal boasted.

Tibal's bold words irritated Gavin. *He has no idea what Brom is capable of.* If he'd seen him deal with the Severon that had tried to take Sterling, he'd realize very quickly that Brom was not a man to take lightly.

"Then you are a fool." Oramek's words mirrored Gavin's thoughts.

For a while they fell into silence. Tibal dozed while Gavin and Oramek stood in their bowed positions. Gavin's legs were shaking while his back burned from having to remain in the same inclined state. His arms felt like heavy logs, his fingers struggling to maintain their grip.

Brom had always protected him from harm and from his father's rage when Gavin made careless mistakes. His cousin treated him with the reverence a crown prince deserved. He would not be angry if Gavin relaxed. But then he didn't want to disappoint Brom.

"Surely, you do not think your own cousin will punish you if you do not maintain the bow," Tibal said. His eyes closed while his head was propped on his folded arms.

Gavin tried to ignore Tibal, but the thought had entered his mind. He was Brom's cousin and of the royal family, Brom would not punish him.

"Don't do it," Oramek groaned.

"Don't listen to him, he is but a peasant. He is used to the rigors of physical labor, we are nobility."

Gavin looked at Oramek and then at Tibal. He slowly stood, his back screaming in pain.

"See, you were not stricken down by some unseen force."

Gavin was relieved to be out of the painful position and after stretching out his back he sat on the bed opposite of Tibal while Oramek remained in the bow. Gavin immediately felt guilty for leaving Oramek alone. "I'll keep a look out." Gavin couldn't sit by and watch Oramek.

An hour passed without a word from Brom. Gavin glanced at Oramek. His body was shaking with the effort of holding the position, his eyes closed, and jaw clenched. How much longer would Brom leave them? It was too cruel of his cousin.

"Oramek, please do not do this to yourself." Gavin pleaded, "Brom will not punish you."

"No," Oramek said behind his clenched teeth, "this is the task we've been given."

"Stubborn."

"More like a fool." Tibal sneered at Oramek.

"Shut up Tibal." Gavin was tired of Tibal's attitude.

Tibal laughed, "You're both fools. The Tarkain is all hot air. Yes, he is good with a sword, but do you honestly think he would do anything to nobility?"

Gavin's heart jumped when the light of a door opening shone across the courtyard and a long shadow appeared in the light. "He's coming," he half whispered before jumping up and returning to his position beside Oramek. He glanced at Oramek's shoulder and could feel his entire body shaking. "Come on Tibal."

"I'm coming," Tibal said lazily as he stood, yawned and found his place beside Gavin.

Gavin clasped his hands behind his back and returned to the inclined bow. The minute he found the proper angle his back started to ache again. *How could Oramek endure this for so long?* Gavin wondered.

Brom's booted footsteps grew closer and with each step Gavin's heart rate increased. Would Brom know that he had not stayed in position? Would he really punish them for not remaining? Surely Brom would not lay a hand on him. Would he?

"Relax," Tibal whispered

"Yeah, yeah." Gavin responded. He flinched when Brom's footsteps finally reached the wooden stairs to the barracks and he opened the tall door. For the first time in his life he did not want to see his cousin's face. He respected Brom and because of that he did not want to see the disappointment in Brom's eyes.

"You may stand."

Both he and Tibal stood, but Oramek remained in a bowed position. "He said you can stand Oramek." Gavin said.

"I bloody well know that," Oramek groaned in pain as he tried to stand.

"Come with me," Brom said, turning away from his students.

Oramek tried to take a step, but stumbled to his knees when his legs gave out.

"Help him." He ordered pointing at Oramek.

Tibal ignored Brom's order and left Gavin to help Oramek to his feet. Gavin put one of Oramek's arms over his shoulders. He eased Oramek into a standing position. Oramek groaned in pain but found the strength to stand. They slowly followed Brom out of the barracks and across the courtyard. The night air was cool, and he was sure it offered some relief to Oramek. The boy's clothes were soaked through with sweat. "You did good," Gavin whispered to Oramek.

Brom led them around the side of the keep to the door that led to the bathing chamber and unlocked the door with a set of keys. He glanced at the three of them before entering, still not a word leaving his lips. They followed him down the dark stairwell that was lit only by dim candles that flickered precariously in the draft that followed them. Gavin could hear the water as it dripped, echoing off the damp stone. The further down they went the more humid the air became until they emerged from the stairwell into the Pan'Dale bathing chamber. Three maids stood waiting along the side of the pool of steaming water.

Tibal chuckled under his breath, "See I told you." He whispered looking back at Oramek and Gavin.

The relief that filled Gavin's chest nearly took his breath away. He could barely contain the smile that wanted to escape. "So, you did," he whispered back.

Brom waved with an impatient hand and Gavin carried Oramek to the waiting maids. He eased him down onto one of the stone benches that circled the pool. One of the maid servants immediately began working to remove Oramek's boots while the other two gently pulled his sweat soaked shirt over his head. Every now and again Oramek would grimace in pain.

Tibal could no longer contain his happiness. He laughed and sat down on another of the benches and started to work on the laces of his high boots.

"What do you think you are doing?" Brom's irritation was evident in his words.

"I'm removing my clothes, what does it look like?" Tibal's tone was one of a spoiled noble.

"You are mistaken." Brom's words were cold, "the two of you are to come with me." He glanced from Tibal to Gavin and in that instant Gavin knew that Brom was aware that neither of them had endured the hardship of his test.

Guilt turned his cheeks red as he walked over to stand beside Brom. "Did you not think I could tell you hadn't remained?" Brom asked quietly. "Look at Oramek's condition. If you had remained you would be in the same shape."

Tibal ignored Brom and continued to unlace his leather boots. Gavin heard the impatient sigh as Brom walked around the pool to stand behind Tibal. Completely unaware of Brom's presence Tibal pulled his boot from his foot, a proud smile showing off his white teeth.

Brom reached down and grabbed Tibal by the scruff of his shirt, plucking him off the bench to stand before him. "You will not disobey me again." Gavin had never heard Brom utter words with such an icy unflinching tone before. When Tibal took a breath to protest, the look in Brom's eyes caused Gavin to cringe. Tibal was not stupid and realized very quickly that he would be in even mroe-trouble if a single breath passed his lips.

"Yes Tarkain," Tibal's sullen words were said behind a pouting lip.

"Follow me," Brom ordered, taking one of the torches that hung in the sconces along the perimeter of the chamber.

"But, my boot," Tibal moaned, but Brom ignored his pleas.

He ascended the stairs and once in the courtyard he led them down the long winding road that led to Menarik. The moon was high in the night sky and highlighted the sleeping houses that lined the streets. Brom walked past the main thoroughfare and continued past the outlying homes until he reached a farm house that sat out alone by itself, surrounded by fields of unplowed soil.

Gavin saw a grizzled farmer standing along the side of the road as if waiting for their arrival. His toothless grin did not bode well for he or Tibal. Gavin started to get the sinking feeling that he and Tibal were about to find out what happens when Brom's orders were not followed.

"Are these the nors?" The old man's voice was as gravelly as the road they stood upon.

Brom turned to face them, "Do you know what this is?"

"Our punishment." Gavin responded, his heart sinking to his stomach.

"You disobeyed an order and for that your punishment is what you see before you."

"A field of dirt?" Tibal scoffed, "You must be joking."

"Not just a field of dirt, a field of farmland that must be plowed by morning. Veillen who cannot follow orders are nothing more than mules fit only for plowing a field." Brom pointed to a plow that sat waiting at the far end of the field. The old farmer was climbing into the seat, but the places where the mules would have been harnessed were empty. Brom walked between him and Tibal. "Go, Berk is waiting for his mules," he said, before pushing them both forward toward the waiting plow.

"You cannot be serious," Tibal protested

"I am very serious and because you continued to disobey me, once you are finished plowing the field the stone wall needs repair. You will move the stones from the farm house to the wall."

"I will…" Tibal started again

"Shut up," Gavin growled at Tibal. "If you keep on he'll have us doing even more work. Just keep your mouth shut and follow orders." Gavin was angry at Tibal for talking him out of staying with Oramek, but even angrier at himself. He pulled Tibal by the shoulder and walked across the hard-packed earth.

They both paused once they reached the plow. It was an old piece of equipment with rust covering the iron fittings and two wood yokes covered in worn leather. Gavin ducked under the arm and put his head through the yoke, so it rested on his shoulders. He looked at Tibal who had a piteous look on his face, "Let us get this over with."

"I only have one boot," Tibal sighed as he lifted the yoke mimicking Gavin's position.

"Get ready boys, you're in for a long night," Berk laughed as a whip cracked between his and Tibal's heads. Gavin jumped and pushed with all his might into the yoke. He could feel the leather digging into his shoulders as he pushed as hard as he could, but the plow refused to budge. He glanced over at Tibal who was barely putting any effort into the task. He was about to tell his him to help when the whip suddenly cracked again. Tibal yelped in pain as a spot of blood stained his right shoulder. "Get a move on," the farmer yelled. Tibal looked over his shoulder to see the jovial old man gone, and replaced with an unrelenting task master.

Tibal grimaced at the pain and dug into the dirt with his one booted foot, his face red with exertion. Gavin joined him, and he felt some relief when the plow started to move. They continued to push forward with all their strength, the plow slowly moving forward. He gripped the yoke with both hands and pushed forward leaning into the task.

"Come on mules! Dig in!" Berk yelled, cracking the whip so close to Gavin's ear that all he could hear for several minutes was a loud ringing.

Gavin's legs and calves burned with the exertion. His shoulders screamed from the constant pressure from the yoke. His eyes stung where sweat dripped into them and blurred his vision. They pulled for what seemed like an hour until they finally reached the end of the first row.

"At this pace you'll still be plowing for another three days. Get this thing turned around." Gavin took the yoke from his shoulders and with Tibal helping turned the plow around. Gavin's spirits sunk when he looked out on the field before them. His body was already screaming for relief, but he knew there would be none. This was their punishment for not obeying an order. He glanced at Brom who stood motionless, his eyes never leaving them.

"This is ridiculous," Tibal groused. "How dare he force me, an Ar'Bethnot, to do manual labor?"

Gavin's temper exploded at Tibal's words. He threw the yoke down and pulled Tibal out into the open field, "Ridiculous you say? This is your fault! You and your spoiled views of the world have put us in this predicament! You think you are so much better than everyone else, yet it was a peasant farmer who has bested the both of us! Oramek is the one sitting in luxury because he followed orders! We are the fools." Gavin's temper had finally run out, "We, a prince and noble, are the fools that must plow this field because we could not follow simple orders. So please shut up and get to work."

Gavin could feel Tibal's eyes on him as he pulled the yoke back over his head and waited. After a moment Tibal followed suit and together they pressed forward. At the third row, Gavin's legs nearly gave out, "May we have a break?" He asked Berk.

Brom waved his approval and Gavin took the opportunity to find a secluded spot to take care of his needs. Upon his return he said nothing to Tibal as he lifted the yoke and they continued. Six rows went by and then another three as exhaustion set in. He could barely lift his legs to take the next step. His shoulders were burning from the pressure of the yoke, the skin beneath rubbed raw. He glanced at Tibal and wondered if he had the same agonized look that furrowed Tibal's brow.

The moon was setting, and the sun's first rays started to light the morning sky by the time they reached the last row. Gavin was covered in dirt and mud, his skin was rubbed raw, both knees bleeding where he had slipped and fallen numerous times during their trek across the field. Every muscle ached as he pushed forward, struggling to reach the end of the last row.

Half way across the field Tibal collapsed. His breathing was more labored than Gavin's and his eyes were squeezed shut in exhaustion and pain. "No more, I can do no more." He heaved the words between breaths.

"Come on Tibal, we are almost there." Gavin pointed to the end of the row, "Look, we are half way to the end."

"I," he lifted the yoke off his shoulders, blood stained his once white shirt and fell to his back, "can do no more."

"But we've come so far, do not give up now." Gavin's heart stopped when he looked over at Brom and found him heading towards them, "Get up. The Tarkain is coming," Gavin half whispered.

"I do not care." Tibal wheezed, "Let him come."

Brom stopped in front of the plow and looked down at Tibal. Without having to say a word Gavin knew that Brom was disgusted by Tibal's behavior.

"I will finish the row," Gavin said, thinking to appease Brom's anger.

"Very well, you may finish alone if you wish, but know this, if Tibal is not beside you when you finish you will both be sent home disgraced, stripped of your honor."

"What?" Gavin was shocked by Brom's words. "But..." he stopped himself from protesting for he knew it would fall on deaf ears and lead to more punishment.

"You need us too much to do something so rash," Tibal said, his forearm covering his eyes as he spoke. "It is well known the Veillen Guard has a shortage of nor'Veillen. You are too desperate to throw the two of us away."

"You are mistaken," Brom said very simply. "I do not need two pathetic weaklings who cannot obey orders and do not understand the concept of team work. So, if you cannot continue, then leave. Go home to your mother's tit like the *ima* you are. I have no use for babies."

Tibal heaved a sigh as he turned over and pulled himself onto his hands and knees before standing. He took up the yoke and placed it over his shoulders. A grimace of pain creased his face when the yoke pressed against his raw skin. Gavin joined him when he started pressing forward. Tibal half laughed, before muttering, "I hate the Tarkain."

"Yeah, I know," Gavin said, "but he's right. Let us finish this task."

"Yeah," Tibal groaned as he leaned into the plow.

Together he and Tibal put all their might into pulling the plow the last few arduous feet. It felt as if it would never come but as his feet stepped upon the road, a sense of relief, mingled with accomplishment, shuddered his body. They both collapsed to the ground, breathing heavy and with aching bodies.

"Finally. We are finished," Gavin said through labored breathing.

"Think again," Berk cackled.

Confused, Gavin opened his eyes and looked at the old man. He was pointing toward the farm house in the distance. Gavin glanced in the direction he was pointing and saw a pile of stones. He'd forgotten the wall that Brom had mentioned earlier. Gavin groaned and pulled himself onto shaky legs. He offered a hand to Tibal, "Let us do this quickly so we can at last rest."

Tibal took his offered hand and pulled himself up as well. Together they walked across another unplowed field.

Brom watched as Gavin and Tibal stumbled their way to the farmhouse. He knew they were in agony, but it was a lesson they had to learn. He'd seen too many men die because they did not follow an order. It was essential that everyone knew what their role was in the battle to successfully fend off the demons. Tibal wasn't wrong though. Over the past several years the number of babes born with the mark of Orla had diminished leaving the Veillen order in a bind. Every nor'Veillen was a commodity that could not be squandered.

The boys were no good to him exhausted, so once they finished this task he'd let them wash and sleep for the rest of the day. "Berk," Brom called to the wrinkled old farmer, "make sure they finish the job and send them back to the barracks."

"Aye." Berk waved his hand.

"Tell them to clean up before sleeping. Moira will have my hide if there is mud and filth everywhere."

30

THEY WILL LOVE YOU

Fifteen Days Later
Dan'Idou, 2nd Alba, 1021

Sterling was exhausted. It was only mid-morning and she felt as though she had not slept at all. It had been the same for the past two weeks. Her nights were filled with visions of Brigit and that monstrous demon chasing her. Always it was Brigit's sweet innocent voice telling Sterling that it was her fault everyone at the orphanage was dead. Every night Sterling would wake up screaming. Consoled by Brom's presence beside her, she would fall back to sleep when he took her hand in his.

She'd protested at first, having to stay in his room, but Brom ensured her nothing would happen. Keeping his promise, he would sleep in the chair on the far side of the room, only venturing to the bed when the nightmares gripped her.

I must be losing my mind, Sterling thought. *I even hear Brigit's laughter during the day.* Sterling would hear childish laughter that faded up and down the hall outside her room. On one occasion she had seen Brigit running across the field below her window, her brown hair trailing behind her. Brigit's ghostly torment was unrelenting and only added to Sterling's feelings of guilt. She felt the hole in her heart grow a little more each time she heard that childish laugh.

Moira would visit her every day, but despite the woman's efforts, Sterling resisted letting anyone get close. Sterling feared she would wind up losing them again. If she just pushed everyone away she would have nothing to fear.

Moira was stubborn, and insisted she give Sterling updates on the goings-on of the Keep. She'd informed Sterling that Gilda had left the Keep for Sela'Char. Her mind was still not whole, and Moira thought time away from the Pan'Dale would heal the woman's soul. Despite Gilda's departure, Orrven had forbidden Sterling from leaving her room.

It had been two weeks since then and Moira had promised Sterling to take her to Menarik today for new clothes. Sterling, although apprehensive, was excited to leave this room and rid herself of the awful blue dress. Waiting for Moira's arrival, Sterling sat on the bench and observed the men of Pan'Dale and their never-ending need to spar.

The training was difficult and brutal. Unlike the Dueninians, who used wooden swords, the Pan'Dale warriors sparred with real weapons and she'd seen several of the mighty warriors wounded just from the practices. It was always Moira that tended to their wounds. She was skilled with a needle and thread and would sew up a warrior's wound quickly, so he could continue his training.

Sterling thought nothing could faze these men. They were strong and larger than any men she'd ever seen, even taller and broad-chested than Hemi, who, for a Dueninian, was very tall. They were all shirtless with their leather armor as their only covering. *What was with the Kai'Varian men and their lack of clothing?* Sterling wondered.

A knock at the door drew Sterling's attention. She stood when Moira's head poked into the room, "Are you ready?" A smile lit up her face as stepped into the room.

"More than you can imagine." Sterling lifted the cumbersome blue folds of the cursed dress, so as not to trip and fall, and jumped to her feet. She'd learned very quickly to lift the fabric out of the way. She'd tripped and fallen numerous times from her feet getting tangled in the skirts.

"Come then." Moira grabbed hold of Sterling's hand and pulled her quickly down the hall and the stairwell, then out the door into the bright warm sun.

Sterling stopped for a moment to feel the sun's rays on her face. The rays soaked into her body like a healing warmth after being inside for so long. Her eyes watered from the brightness of the sun.

"Come on," Moira laughed, "the day is half over," A stable boy helped Moira into the driver's seat of a waiting wagon.

Sterling lifted her skirts to her knees but paused when the maids gasped. Sterling glared at them as she lifted the fabric even higher and climbed into the wagon to sit beside Moira. "Prudes," Sterling whispered under her breath.

"You're shameless," Moira laughed. The wagon jerked forward as Moira slapped the reigns. "You'll love Menarik. The villagers are wonderful and kind. They welcomed me with open arms when I married Orrven and they simply worship Brom. I know they will love you."

Sterling's anxiety increased as they neared the village. Menarik lay nestled below Pan'Dale against the sheer cliff face and was protected by a wall that surrounded the main village with a heavy wood and iron gate. The cobblestone roads were bustling with activity as villagers went about their daily lives. Shops like the bakery and seamstress lined the main thoroughfare, while a pub and the blacksmith sat on the outskirts of the village. To Sterling, it was as perfect a village as she could imagine. Unlike the chaos of Shee's busy market, Menarik was peaceful and well organized.

Moira pulled up on the reins and brought the wagon to a stop in front of a seamstress. She lifted her skirts and climbed gently to the ground, "Well, come on," She laughed.

Sterling lifted her skirts and then jumped to the ground, her dress billowing up around her legs so that passersby got an unexpected peak at Sterling's bloomers.

"Sterling, do you have any sense of decorum?" Moira scolded, but their seriousness was diminished by the laugh that followed.

Sterling apologized as she followed Moira down the street toward the seamstress, but instead of going inside Moira bypassed the shop window filled with fabric. "Aren't we…" Sterling started to ask.

"What you want is not made in that type of store." Moira rounded the corner to a side street that was less traveled. The buildings here were not quite as bright as those that lined the main thoroughfare. Moira went down another street that narrowed even further until she came to an alley that did not invite one to enter without caution.

"Are you sure we're in the right place?" Sterling glanced over her shoulder for any suspicious characters. An alley like this in Shee would surely have any number of thieves waiting to rob travelers *or worse.*

"I'm certain." A bell chimed as Moira pushed open a door. The little hovel was dimly lit and had the overwhelming scent of leather. A large and tidy worktable, covered in clothes in varying shapes and colors, stood at attention with candles lighting the work area. The walls were filled with shelves that held stacks of more fabric and clothes folded neatly ready for their wearers. "Master Bennet?" Moira called out to the empty room.

"I'm coming." A hoarse voice full of impatience came from a back room. Upon seeing Moira, he bowed, "Afternoon, milady."

"Master Bennet, I was hoping to persuade you to make something for…" She paused as she stepped aside and let the man get a good look at Sterling.

His weathered face could not hide the surprise in his blue eyes. "You want me to make clothes for a girl? Pssh, I clothe warriors, not little misses," he scoffed at Moira's request.

Moira glanced at Sterling then back at Bennet, "I promise you your talents will not go wasted. Sterling, after all, is a Rin'Ovana." Moira winked at Sterling, hiding a giggle behind her hand.

"Rin'Ovana you say?" Bennet stepped around the table and lifted Sterling's arm. Feeling her bicep and shoulder for a moment and then running his rough thumb down one of the scars inflicted by Helios. "Who was your father, girl?" he asked.

Sterling looked at Moira and when she nodded Sterling said, "Kh-" her voice cracked on the name, "Khort Rin'Ovana."

Bennet circled her again pulling at her arms and feeling her muscles in her shoulders. "The dress will have to come off."

"Master Bennet, I don't think it is appropriate to…" Moira started to protest but stopped when the blue dress Sterling had been wearing landed on Moira's head. "Very well then." Moira pulled the dress from her head and folded the garment.

Sterling stood in front of Bennet in her bloomers and chemise. She waited for Bennet to react to the patchwork of scars covering her body, but he seemed to pay them no mind. Moira on the other hand turned her back on Sterling, but Sterling did not miss the tear she wiped away.

"Turn around," Bennet directed Sterling. He stretched a tape measure across her shoulders and then the length of her back. Sterling jumped when he put the tape measure to the inside of her thigh and measured to her foot. "Turn." Sterling turned again to face Bennet. He measured the length of her arms and around her neck and waist. She felt her cheeks blush when he wrapped the tape around her chest and brought the ends together between her breasts. After writing down the measurements he said, "I'll have it done today." He disappeared into the back room.

"Very good." Moira handed the dress to Sterling. "We have shopping to do."

Sterling looked at the dress and took a step away, "Can't I just stay here while you go shopping?"

Moira's disappointment was written across her face, "I suppose," she said after a moment. "Make sure to behave yourself, Bennet has a short temper." Moira left Sterling alone while Bennet rummaged around in the back room.

"You're still here?" Bennet did not seem pleased that she had not accompanied Moira on her errands.

"I'd rather die than put that dress back on." Sterling answered, sitting on a stool that stood in the corner of the room. She sat quietly, not wanting to disturb Bennet's work.

Sterling watched as he pulled a large piece of leather from the pile he brought with him from the back room. He ran his hand over the leather and then glanced at Sterling for a moment, his eyes examining her closely. Sterling fidgeted a moment but did not feel the revulsion she expected to feel under a man's gaze.

Bennet shook his head and mumbled something before putting the leather back only to pull another piece from the pile. "Come." He motioned for Sterling to feel the material. Sterling hesitated for a moment and then joined Bennet at his work table. "Feel the texture of this leather."

Sterling ran her hand across the dark brown material, surprised at how soft and supple the leather felt. It felt like water in her hands but was thick and durable. "What animal is this from?" she asked, unable to imagine this quality of leather came from any normal bovine.

"This is the leather from a manuk," he explained.

"What's a manuk?" Sterling asked, as she'd never heard of such an animal.

"They are frightening creatures that live in the canopy of the Midori." Bennet ran his hand along the soft leather, "Manuk leather is the best quality leather that can be found in all Taaneri, but it is difficult to get since the manuk are so dangerous. The skin is tougher than any other animal and that is why it is usually reserved for the Veillen."

"What do you mean?" Sterling asked, not understanding.

"Manuk leather is only used in armor for Veillen warriors. They need the protection from the claws and teeth of the graekull they hunt."

"If only the Veillen warriors wear this leather, why then do you use it for me?" Sterling's curiosity forced the question past her lips.

A half smile creased the old man's cheeks as he chuckled to himself. "You are such a tiny thing, you'll need all the protection you can get."

"I can take care of myself," Sterling mumbled as she returned to the stool in the corner. She watched Bennet as his calloused hands quickly cut the fabric into various shapes. He sat the pieces aside and pulled a lever on his table. Sterling was surprised by the odd mechanism that flipped up from underneath the table. "What is that? She asked jumping up to examine the contraption.

"This is for peddle sewing," he responded as he started to push the peddle with both feet. A long rod extended from the peddle to a wheel, which when turned, caused a needle to go up and down. Across the top were spools of thread that were gathered into a single thread that was fed through the needle. As he peddled, the needle moved up and down in quick succession. Bennet put two pieces of the leather together and pushed it through the contraption. The needle went up and down quickly through the fabric and in no time at all Bennet had completed a pair of trousers.

Bennet sat it aside and started working on a second piece. Sterling grew quiet again as she watched Bennet sew several more trousers. In only an hour he had sewn six pairs in what would have taken Sister Treva days to make. Sterling rubbed her chest when she felt a pang in her heart. Memories of watching Sister Treva mend all the girls' dresses at the orphanage had immediately brought feelings of sadness. Sterling fondly remembered times when she would help when the pile became too large for just Sister Treva.

Occasionally Bennet would glance at Sterling and then back at the piece, making sure his measurements were correct. Sterling grew sleepy listening to the staccato sounds of the needle as it went up and down. She closed her eyes for only a moment and was startled when Bennet spoke.

"You have too many scars for a child of your age."

"I am no child," she returned. "I will be twenty-two next spring season."

Bennet continued to push the leather through the machine, "At my age you are still an infant." He glanced at her without lifting his head, "Do not evade the question."

Sterling avoided looking at Bennet and examined her fingernails. "They were a gift from the Severon," she muttered still not looking up from the ragged nails.

He mumbled something under his breath. Sterling knew it could not have been good, for his brows furrowed causing a deep chasm to appear in the old flesh. She was thankful that he dropped the topic and did not bring it up again.

Sterling put her chin on her hand and waited, and her eyelids grew heavy as the time passed.

"You are a Devian, like your mother," Bennet said, not looking up.

Sterling nodded, "Though I do not know much about her."

"Some say that the Devians brought bad luck with them from Fin'Varrar."

Sterling sat up. She wanted to hear more of her mother's people, "Why do they say that?"

"Kell Wrenkin nearly wiped out the entire Devian race when he attacked Fin'Varrar. Those that were able to escape were followed by Wrenkin's army to Kai'Vari. Any Kai'Varians found harboring the refugees were murdered. Some Kai'Varians, fearing Wrenkin's soldiers, gave up the Devians they were harboring. Because of this betrayal the remaining Devians became suspicious of almost everyone and many turned against the Kai'Varians that tried to help them."

Sterling fell silent as she thought on Bennet's words. She wondered if that was what happened to Gilda's son. Had he helped a Devian only to betray him to the Severon? Were there still Kai'Varians that would sell her out for the coins the Severon offered?

"Would it be too much trouble to add a hood to what you have already sewn?" Sterling asked.

Bennet paused in his task and stared at Sterling, "Why would you need a hood?"

Sterling shrugged. "In case it rains," she lied. She knew he was doubtful, but he agreed to the request.

"There," Bennet stretched, "All done," He placed the last piece in a stack that had steadily grown. He looked down at Sterling's feet. "You'll need a pair of boots as well, and stockings." He walked out from behind his table with a thick piece of leather in his hand and placed it on a raised dais, "Come, stand here."

Sterling slid off the stool and stood where he pointed. Bennet traced around her foot with a piece of charcoal and then repeated the process with her left foot. "Why are you so tiny?" He grumbled as he stood from where he had been sitting on the floor. "This will take a few minutes," Bennet said, returning to his work table. When Sterling hesitated he looked up, eyebrow raised, "Well? Get dressed."

Sterling blushed at Bennet's words, but she was happy that she could finally put something on other than the dress. Bennet handed her a pair of the trousers and a leather top. "You'll need these as well," he said, handing her a thin cotton undergarment that fit snug against her skin. Sterling's cheeks burned with embarrassment. "Stop being such a girl and go change," he groused, pointing at a screen that sat hidden in the dark corner of the room.

Sterling took her pile of new clothes and stepped behind the screen. She pulled the bulky bloomers off and pulled the fitted underpants up her legs. They were so different from what she was used to, but she liked how they felt much better than the bloomers Moira had forced upon her. Next, she stepped into the leather trousers, bent, and pulled them up her legs reveling in the feel of the soft leather. They melded to her form allowing a wide range of movement, but they were durable and the seams were well stitched.

Sterling put on the fitted leather vest Bennet had fashioned for her. The leather was lined with a soft breathable cotton fabric that felt like silk next to her skin. The outside was the same supple leather as her trousers. It was fitted around her stomach and waist and cupped her breasts. The two pieces in the front overlapped so the front was doubled. She tightened the laces that were offset down the left side. Her arms were bare which gave her more freedom to move. The hood she had requested from Bennet was attached perfectly to the vest and when she pulled it over her head it hung at just the right angle to conceal her eyes from onlookers.

Sterling was thrilled with Bennet's work and could not contain the smile that spread as she stepped out from behind the screen. Sterling admired his work in a mirror that stood against the opposite wall. The leather felt like water against her skin when she moved.

"It's perfect," Sterling declared as Bennet stepped from around his table.

"Try these on." He handed her a pair of stockings and the boots he'd fashioned for her.

Sterling could not control the giggle that escaped as she plopped down on the floor and pulled the stockings over her feet. She pulled the boots over the thin stockings and up her leather clad leg. The fit of the boot was perfect for her smaller foot. She'd always had to stuff her boots with extra socks because they had been made for a man's larger foot. She was thrilled to have boots especially made for her. She tightened the buckle along the top of the boots that came just below her knees. The black leather of the boots contrasted with the soft brown of the trousers.

"They are perfect." Sterling stood, and without thinking gave Bennet a quick kiss on the cheek before he could pull away.

The bell on the door rang and Moira walked in just as Sterling was kissing Bennet. "I see I made it back just in time to stop Sterling from ravaging you Bennet." Moira closed the door behind her as she stepped fully into the room, "All done?" Sterling nodded, examining herself again in the mirror. "You look happy now that you are out of that dress."

"I am," Sterling responded.

Moira couldn't help but notice how the trousers and vest molded to Sterling's form. *I can't wait to see Brom's expression when he sees Sterling.*

Bennet packaged the rest of Sterling's new clothes, "You have five extra trousers and four other vests, including a jacket and a long sleeve shirt for when the harvest season passes." He set the package on the ground and then went back to his work table. "These are yours as well." He returned with two forearm guards. He held one out for Sterling to put her arm in and he laced it up. Like the vest, it was lined with a soft cotton that was to keep the moisture away from her skin. He laced the second one before handing her a belt.

"It is too much," Sterling said as he wrapped the belt around her waist and buckled it so it sat askew on her waist. Pouches were sewn onto the belt, so they sat in the small of her back and there was a small scabbard for a dagger that hung along her left leg.

"For a fellow Rin'Ovana, it is never too much."

"Fellow..." Bennet's revelation shocked Sterling. "You are a Rin'Ovana?"

"Aye, but I go by Pan'Dale now. It was a shame what happened to your parents." Bennet picked up the package and handed it to Sterling before returning to his work table. "Perhaps one day the Rin'Ovana's will be written back into the Book of Tohms and its honor restored."

"Are you ready then?" Moira asked, smiling tenderly.

"Yes," Sterling said, happier than she had been in a very long time. She felt a pang in her heart, but this time it was one of happiness and not guilt or fear or dread. "Thank you," Sterling said to Bennet before stepping through the door and into the bright sun.

"They really suit you." Moira headed towards the main road, "Much more so than that awful dress." Moira glanced over her shoulder, her smile gone, "You really don't need that hood. The people here will love you."

Sterling hesitated. She had seen their stares when she first arrived, but perhaps it had simply been out of curiosity and not malice. Sterling pushed the hood off her head deciding that now was the time to start trusting. Hopefully this one small gesture will open her heart just a little. She followed Moira back out to the main street and stopped for a moment to truly take in Menarik.

Menarik was a wild array of shops and homes. The shops were on the bottom, while the homes were on the second floor. Signs hung outside each of the buildings advertising their wares. Candle makers, butchers, a bakery and the blacksmith all lined the same side of the street as Bennet's shop. Across the street Sterling saw a fletcher and what looked like a sweet shop. *Strange neighbors*, Sterling thought.

The streets were clean, unlike the dirty streets of Shee where trash lined the small narrow streets. The market sat at the far end of the road and Sterling could see stalls with various vegetables and other homemade goods. She could hear the squeal of pigs echoing off the white and brown walls of the shops.

"I want you to try something." Moira said as she crossed the street and Sterling followed. At first the villagers greeted them with pleasantries, but as more noticed Sterling, the pleasantries turned to wary glares. Sterling looked over her shoulder to see the villagers pause to watch them pass. Their behavior went completely unnoticed by Moira. She was busy chatting with an old woman and did not notice the gathering crowd. Moira said her goodbyes and pulled Sterling into a shop.

The smell hit Sterling full on as they stepped into the sweet shop. The most wondrous aroma swirled around Sterling and invited her to step further into the store. Sterling's stomach growled at the enticing aroma.

Moira laughed, "It is wonderful isn't it? Here, try this." She plucked a piece of chocolate off a tray and handed it to Sterling. Sterling placed the dark brown chocolate on her tongue and it melted into the most glorious thing she had ever tasted.

"This is chocolate?" Sterling asked. She'd heard of the sweet that many of the shops in Shee sold, but she'd never tasted it. The price for a piece was far outside what she or Hemi could have ever afforded.

Entranced by the sweet morsel, Sterling stepped up to the counter to look at all the different shapes of the wondrous chocolate. The lady behind the counter was smiling at Sterling's reaction until Sterling looked up. Her smile disappeared from her round face and was replaced by an angry stare that creased her brow. "Devian," she hissed, "You don't belong here. Get out of my shop," she said angrily before throwing a handful of flour at Sterling.

Sterling coughed as she inhaled the flour. She felt the blood rush from her face at the woman's anger. Moira was surprised by the woman's reaction, "Robena! What are you about? She is a guest and should be treated with the same respect you show both Orrven and myself."

"I'm sorry Milady, but I'll not have her kind in my shop. It was her kind that murdered Gilda's son and caused Gilda so much pain. Nothing but misfortune follows her kind."

"I'll speak to Orrven about this." Moira was livid with Robena. "Come along Sterling." Moira grabbed her by the arm and pushed the door open. Sterling said nothing as an enraged Moira pulled her towards the wagon. Villagers lined the streets parting to form a path as Moira shoved her way through.

"Get on," Moira said behind gritted teeth.

Just as Sterling was about to climb into the wagon she was hit in the back of the head by something soft and wet. She turned and was hit again by a tomato in the shoulder and again on the side of the head. A man yelled, "Go away Devian!" as he hurled an egg at Sterling, hitting her in the center of her chest.

"Sterling! Get on the wagon, now." Moira's tone was one of pure rage. Sterling did not hesitate again and climbed up beside the furious woman.

Sterling quickly pulled the hood over her head to hide herself from onlookers. Her heart sank in her chest. This place was no different than Duenin; they were no different than the people of Shee that had scorned her because of her eyes. Her misery would follow her for the rest of her life. There was nowhere for her to go where she would be accepted as anything other than a monster. Would it have been better if she'd just died at the hands of the Severon? The thought wiggled its way into her brain as she looked at Moira. She softly said, "You lied," and then turned away. Distrust, anger, and self-loathing swirled in her vision as they jolted forward.

31

WAKING NIGHTMARE

"*You lied to me!*" Those were the words that met Brom as he rounded the corner of the Keep. A crowd had gathered around Moira and Sterling as they faced one another in the courtyard. Moira's face was white as she held her hands up trying to calm a very upset Sterling.

"Is that Sterling?" Orrven asked as he stopped beside Brom, "Who would have thought that small frame had that many curves?"

Brom couldn't help but noticed the form-fitting trousers and vest that Sterling wore. He also noticed the way the men surrounding them looked at Sterling.

"You lied to me!" Sterling repeated the words when Moira tried to speak.

"Did she just call my wife a liar?" Orrven started forward, but Brom stopped him.

"You promised me they would be different. You promised me they would love me!" Brom could hear the desperation in her voice as she yelled at Moira, "This place is no different than Duenin!"

"Sterling, they don't understand yet that you are a good person. Give them time."

"No, they don't and neither do you! You live up on this hill with your perfect life and with your perfect family. You know *nothing* of suffering, you know nothing!"

"Sterling, please," Moira said again trying to calm her.

"I should have just given up and died in that Severon prison." Sterling's anger seemed to deflate at her words.

"Don't say that!" Moira pleaded, trying to console Sterling.

"Why not? It's the truth isn't it? Everyone would have been better off if I never existed!" Sterling threw her arms in the air out of frustration and turned to leave.

"Sterling!" Moira called after her.

"Well that was unexpected," Orrven mumbled as they both started toward a visibly upset Moira.

Brom did not take his eyes off Sterling as she stomped toward the front doors of the Keep. Her thoughts about not existing coupled with the nightmares she had that ripped screams from her worried Brom greatly. Her screaming would continue until he sat beside her on the bed. It was only then that she would sleep peacefully. He wondered what it was that caused such terror.

The men in the courtyard began to disperse as the drama ceased. Moira wiped a tear away and leaned into Orrven, "It was just awful," she mumbled into Orrven's chest.

"What happened?" Brom asked, keeping an eye on Sterling.

"The villagers," Moira glanced at Sterling, "they threw food at her and called her the most horrible of names."

Brom decided to follow Sterling and started in her direction. She had just reached the steps and was half way up when the doors suddenly opened. Sterling stopped in her tracks when she spotted Lirit standing in the dark opening. Brom's niece stood at the top of the steps in a white gown with a red stain running down the front. Brom thought he heard a gasp as Sterling backed down the stairs away from Lirit. Her head was shaking, and she held out her hands in front of herself as if to ward off Lirit. "Please leave me be," Sterling pleaded as she backed down the stairs.

Brom was nearly to her when she tripped on the bottom step and landed with a thud in the dust. "Please," Sterling pleaded again as she stumbled to her feet, "please, do not torment me any longer."

Lirit started down the stairs when Sterling fell. Lirit was a compassionate child, who Brom was sure only wanted to help, but

Sterling back peddled away from the child, "Please." Sterling begged as she gained her feet. Tripping and skidding across the loose dirt she ran towards the woods.

"Sterling!" Brom called after her, but she was in a panic. He'd seen her face as she raced past and it had been as white as a sheet as if she'd seen a ghost.

Lirit called out to Moira, "Momma, I spilled paint on my dress." Lirit looked back at where Sterling had run past, "Did I do something wrong?"

"No dear, she is just upset. Now, let us get you cleaned up."

Brom left Moira and Orrven behind to tend to Lirit and went after Sterling. Her tracks were not difficult to follow. She'd left broken tree limbs and bent grasses in her wake in her hurry to flee. He could see where she'd fallen to her knees on the soft ground and then hurried away. *How far was she planning on running?* Brom asked himself. He continued to follow her trail until he came to a small clearing with a shallow pond. She was on her knees leaning over the water, peering at herself in the stillness, her body trembling. Brom slowly walked toward her, clearing his throat so not to startle her. He had no desire to go chasing after her deeper into the forest.

Surprised, her head came up and she turned in his direction as she scrambled backwards for a second as if expecting someone else to be there. She looked at him with vacant glassy eyes that glistened with unshed tears. Her face was white and devoid of color.

"Sterling," he said calmly, "what was that all about? What happened in the village?"

She ignored his question and turned back to the mirror-like water, "It's my fault." She peered at him for a second, "It's my fault they are all dead."

Saying nothing, he knelt beside her.

"It's my fault." She repeated, "Hemi, Mother Anwell, Sister Treva," she paused, "Brigit." Her voice cracked on the name. Sterling buried her face in her hands, "Brigit," she sobbed, "why did they have to kill Brigit? She was such a sweet little girl."

Sterling looked up at Brom. Tears rolled down her cheeks and her eyes had turned a dull gray as if her life had seeped out of them. She wiped the tear away that clung stubbornly to her lashes.

"You cannot blame yourself for the brutality of others." Brom tried to keep his voice calm, but inside he was seething at what the Severon had done to Sterling.

"I saw him earlier that day... I saw Engram on the road. He tried to stop me, but I managed to sneak away into the forest. I found Brigit and two of the other girls collecting flowers in a field." Sterling laughed, "Brigit was collecting flowers for my birthday. We had a party. All the girls sang to me and Sister Treva prepared all my favorite dishes. It was wonderful until Engram came."

Brom listened to her story, his heart beating faster as she continued.

"Hemi had just told me of my father. After twenty-one summers he tells me that my father is from a land I know nothing of and that he is not my uncle. But before he could tell me more the Severon arrived. Hemi hid me in the cellar under the dining room. Engram, he..." Sterling breathed in a heavy sigh. It was obvious the retelling of the story was difficult, "he had Mother Anwell gather all the girls into the dining room. They were all right there above me while I hid. He questioned Brigit about me and when he knew she was lying he..." Sterling hiccupped, a sob shook her shoulder as she paused, "he killed her. Engram, that bastard stabbed Brigit when she wouldn't tell him were I was hiding. She was seven, she was still a baby."

Brom could feel his anger rising at Sterling's retelling of what happened. He regretted not killing Engram in the forest when he had the chance.

"I can still hear her screams. I was right there hiding like a coward, but I couldn't move. I couldn't help her and now she haunts my dreams, my nightmares. Is it not enough that I must suffer at night? Is it not enough punishment that the little girl I helped raise wants me to die? Is it not enough that I see the faces of those that died wishing death upon me? Now Brigit appears before me when I am awake. I can endure *no more* of this torture."

She thought Lirit was Brigit, Brom surmised. He understood now why Sterling reacted as she did upon seeing his niece. He understood now why she screamed during the night. "Sterling," Brom eased closer to her, "Sterling, that was not your Brigit you saw just now. That little girl is Lirit, Moira and Orrven's daughter."

"No, it was Brigit." Sterling shook her head. Her hands covered her eyes as if trying to rip out the memory of the little girl, "She had the blood stain from where Engram stabbed her."

"Listen to me." Brom grabbed her shoulders shaking her, "That was not Brigit." Do you hear me? That was *not* Brigit."

She stared into his eyes for a moment until his words finally seemed to sink in. The tension in her body seemed to melt away. Along with the tension, so too did the wall she erected collapse. He saw the moment when her world seemed to fall to pieces around her.

Tears gathered in her eyes as she confessed her true feelings. "It should have been me. It should have been me that died, not them." Her words were thick with tears as she continued to claw at her eyes, "All because of these damn eyes!" She looked at herself in the pond before smashing her hand into the water to break up the image. "I hate these eyes! I *hate* them. I'd rather be blind that have my mother's accursed eyes."

Her words angered him. "You dishonor your mother by denying your Devian heritage." No matter how upset she was, Brom would not let her malign Sylvie, the woman who had been a mother to him.

Sterling looked at Brom, anger replacing the sorrow and despair, "Dishonor my heritage? These eyes have brought me nothing but misery. Because of *these* eyes I have endured what no person should have to endure. Because of these eyes everyone I have ever loved is dead. It should have been me that died. It should have been me." Her shoulders started shaking as the sobs took hold. "It should hav–"

"Sterling..."

"Why didn't you leave me for dead?" She lashed out shrugging his hand off her shoulder.

"What?" Brom was taken aback by her words.

"Why did you have to save me?" The question was thrown at him from behind clenched teeth. Though tears streamed down her cheeks, there was unadulterated anger in the silver depths. She flew at Brom attacking him with fist and claw and teeth. Brom held her off easily enough, but she kept repeating the question over and over again, "Why? Why? Why did you save me? You should have let me die."

"Sterling," Brom tried consoling her again, his hands on her shoulders.

Sterling growled and pushed Brom away and pulled the dagger that was sheathed in his boot. "It should have been me," she growled the words behind clenched teeth as she raised the dagger to her own throat. "It should have been me.'

Brom's heart ached at the sorrow in her words, but he had made a promise to Khort to protect Sterling. He would let no harm to come to her. He reacted in an instant and knocked the blade from her hand, "No!" she yelled as she dove for the knife that landed in the shallow water of the pond. When her plan failed she glared at Brom and launched herself at him again.

She fought until she was too exhausted to move. Sterling collapsed in his arms with heaving sobs shaking her body. Brom knew then that this was the first time she'd been able to grieve for those she'd lost at the hands of the Severon. *The Severon*. Brom's hatred of the Severon grew when he thought of what they had done to her. Sterling had been in their prison being tortured and had no one to comfort her. She had no one to hold her while she mourned for Brigit, Hemi, and the others that were taken from her. Brom did the only thing he could think of and just held her until her body gave out. Tears still clung to her lashes that lay against her high cheek bones. Brom wiped the tears away and gathered Sterling in his arms. Her head nestled his shoulder as he stood and made his way to the Keep.

What had happened all those years ago? Brom wondered. He wondered what her life and the rest of Kai'Vari would have been like if Hemi had not left with Sterling. He still didn't understand why Hemi would take Sterling so far away from her homeland and into the nest of their enemies. He of all people should know how dangerous that was.

When Khort announced the pending birth of their first child Brom's emotions wavered between elation and jealousy. Khort must have known of Brom's torn emotions and had asked a favor of Brom. He'd asked that Brom protect his and Sylvie's child if anything were to happen to them. He'd only been ten at the time, but he promised without hesitation that he would never let anything happen to their child. Brom looked down at Sterling and wondered if it was too late for him to make good on that promise. As it was, he was doing a poor job.

Brom entered the great hall after leaving Sterling to rest in his room, only to be attacked by a tiny ball of glee.

"Uncle Brom!" Lirit squealed as she charged toward his legs grabbing hold and sitting down on his foot. Brom pretended to ignore her and continued toward her mother. Lirit giggled and squealed with laughter as Brom lifted his leg and carried her.

He looked down, "What is this? I've a bug on my foot."

"No, Uncle Brom it's me!" Lirit giggled again.

"Oh! So it is." Brom adored his niece and despite her sickly nature she was a ball of joy that seemed to have no end. Brom lifted Lirit and placed her on the table, "My, you have gotten big." It had been over six months since he'd last seen his niece.

"Off the table!" Moira picked Lirit up and placed her on the floor, "Honestly Brom, you teach her such bad manners." Moira was quiet for a moment before asking about Sterling.

Brom could tell she was upset by what had happened in the village and the words Sterling had thrown at her. Brom motioned that Moira should have Lirit leave the room.

"Lirit, run upstairs now, your uncle Brom and I have something to discuss."

"Aw, but he just got here." Lirit protested.

"I'll still be here when we're done, run along now."

"Yay!" Lirit bounced around for a moment before running for the stairs.

"I wish she'd behave for me like that." Moira sat across from Brom. "Tell me."

"She's been having nightmares of a child she was close to that was about the same age as Lirit. The Severon killed the little girl and Sterling blames herself. She mistook Lirit for this child."

"Oh, how horrible." Moira put her hands over her mouth, "It makes sense, her reaction to Lirit."

"Yes. She… she begged me to kill her." Brom's jaw clenched at the memory of Sterling's pain.

"Oh." Tears gathered in Moira's eyes.

"I promised Khort I would protect his child. I intend to keep that promise."

"Brom…" Moira was interrupted as Orrven walked into the room.

"Good, you are here. Where is that Sterling?" Brom could tell Orrven was upset by Sterling's behavior. "I warned you that if she caused any more problems I'd not be happy."

"Orrven, really it wasn't her fault."

"It never is, is it?"

"Orrven, they threw food at her and called her horrible names. These are your people! Are you truly going to allow them to treat a guest of your house this way, and a *Devian* at that? To think that a descendent of the gods would be treated so horribly. I couldn't believe what I heard when Robena told her to leave. The whole of the village was standing there waiting with such malevolence towards her. The hatred they felt was palpable."

Orrven heaved a sigh, "Can you not blame them? A Devian murdered one of their own and now Gilda is gone because of another. The name Devian has lost quite a bit of its weight over these many centuries. The bloodline has been weakened," Orrven sighed, "It seems these days a Devian is just someone with pretty eyes."

"Do not," Brom banged his fist against the table. "Do not speak so lightly about things you do not know, brother. To you the story of the Devians is just that – a fairy tale to tell your children at bed time. In Devi flowed the blood of the Elementals as well as Orla and Moraug. Do you even realize what that means? Devi, with a flick of his finger, could topple even Mount Izanami if he desired. Having even a drop of Devi's blood would make even a babe more powerful than the Nine Perikuva. They would not stand a chance against that kind of power."

"Brom." He knew Moira hated it when he and Orrven argued.

Brom stood, unable to sit any longer, "Have you even noticed the purity of Sterling's eyes?" He threw the question at Orrven.

"What do you mean?"

"A Devian's eyes are more silver, the higher the concentration of Devi's blood that flows through their veins. The Devian that killed Gilda's son had eyes that were just a faded gray that could barely be called silver."

"That would mean that Sterling has…"

"Pardon me." Cinri interrupted and whispered in Orrven's ear. The news must not have been good by the look Orrven threw towards the front doors.

"Brom." Brom followed his brother-in-law outside to find a gathering of villagers yelling at the Pan'Dale warriors guarding the entrance to the Keep. When the villagers noticed Orrven they turned their attention to him.

"Milord! How could you give sanctuary to a Devian after what happened to Gilda's son?" The crowd's noise rose as others threw more questions at Orrven. The yelling continued with their desires that the cursed Devian leave Pan'Dale.

"She'll bring bad luck to us, just you wait and see. Just look what happened to the Rin'Ovanas."

Brom was stopped by Orrven when he made to say something. "No." He whispered to Brom, "This is a Pan'Dale matter."

Brom stepped back and let his brother-in-law do his job as Arl. Orrven had been the Pan'Dale Arl for as long as Brom had known him. His people counted on him and knew if they were in a bind he would protect them and lend a hand when needed. He was a fair and just leader, but when pushed he was known for his temper. It was these times when he was at his most quiet that Brom knew his top was about to blow.

"The Devian should hang! They bring nothing but bad luck!"

"*Silence!*" The crowd instantly quieted at Orrven's command. "Brom," Orrven glanced over his shoulder, "has reminded me what an honor it is to have a Devian in our presence. He has reminded me what horrors these once great people have and still are enduring at the hands of the not only the Severon, but it seems Kai'Vari as well. *You should all be ashamed of yourselves.* Treating a guest of your Arl like common rabble, but I too am ashamed for I also misjudged Sterling. She has done nothing to incur your hatred, or mine. She is a guest of the Pan'Dale family and she is welcome to stay for as long as she likes, and I expect everyone in Menarik to treat her as a Pan'Dale."

A wave of unease went through the crowd at Orrven's words.

"If," Orrven continued, "any one of you does not like this you are free to leave. Go, find another village and hope they will take you in. If I hear of any mistreatment of my guest, the wrath of the gods will be the least of your worries. Now, go back to your homes and your lives and leave the worrying to me. I am your Arl, it is my job to look over these lands and protect you all. Do not think I would let someone so untrustworthy into my home."

The anger in the crowd deflated as they realized the wrong they had committed against Sterling. Robena, the baker, wiped a tear from her eye as she turned away.

"I will convey all of your apologies to Sterling when she wakes." Orrven yelled after the retreating mob. He turned to Brom, "Promise me I won't regret my words."

Brom chuckled, "I will try my best."

"No, you will *do your best*." Orrven commanded before returning to the hall.

Sterling's head felt as if she'd pounded it against a rock. The dull throbbing was unending and all she could do was lie on her bed with her eyes closed. Her eyes felt swollen and Sterling knew if she opened them it would feel as if they were filled with sand. She groaned at the memory of Brom carrying her back to the Keep after she'd wept on his shoulder. *What a fool I am to show such useless emotions.* But she had to admit, telling Brom everything seemed to lift a weight off her shoulders. She no longer had to keep the memories to herself. She wasn't the only one who knew of the horrors that were jumbled up in her mind.

From today on, she would try her best to live her life, not in the past, but in the here and now. Though she loved Brigit with all her heart, the little girl was gone and there was nothing Sterling could do about it now. She would keep her fond memories close to her heart and when she felt down, Sterling would recall the happy times with Brigit. She would recall her memories of Hemi and Mother Anwell and their strict but overwhelming love. *Memories of times much happier than now.*

She would start her life anew. Find what was left of her father's family and start over. She would speak with Moira about how to go about reinstating the Rin'Ovanas. It had been Bennet's wish that the Tohm be reformed. With her new resolve, Sterling eased into a sitting position and opened her eyes. She gasped when she was met with a smiling little girl sitting on the end of her bed.

"I'm Lirit," the little girl introduced herself, "you have pretty eyes."

Sterling's heart ached just a little, "I'm Sterling."

ABOUT THE AUTHOR

Fantasy author Shanna Bosarge is the creator of a popular web series set in the world of Taaneri. Inspired by her love of gaming as well as the fantastic worlds of Marco, Hennig, Miura, Ohba and Obata, she began the decade long task of designing her own universe – one that holds magic, hope, and the ever-present battle of good versus evil. In that universe, Ms. Bosarge presents characters who, each in their own way, encounter the true essence of The Elemental Union – showing that conflict can and does lead to growth.

Ms. Bosarge holds a Bachelor degree in Computer Science, and she has used her education as well as her experiences in programming to help craft detailed and compelling characters who could just as easily appear in a multiplayer game as they could the pages of a book.

A successful business consultant and single mother, Ms. Bosarge carves time out of her schedule to visit Taaneri as much as she can, often without having to leave her home state of Georgia.

Visit www.shamibopublishing.com to learn more about the history and lore of the Elemental Union.